Catch the Earth

Catch the Earth

Juliet Rose

Above the Rain Collective
2023

Above the Rain Collective
abovetheraincollective@gmail.com
North Georgia, USA

Contributing Editor: J.A. Sexton

Publisher's note:

ISBN: 978-1-7377970-6-7

julietrose.author@gmail.com
authorjulietrose.com

Cover graphics and interior/exterior formatting by J.A. Sexton
Original cover photograph by Joshua Woroniecki
Above the Rain logo artwork by Bee Freitag

For Lenora, who taught me about my Irish ancestry and family. Thank you for keeping the history alive!

Prologue

I t certainly hadn't been the first time he'd transported contraband with passengers on the plane. It was how he made his bread and butter. He didn't want to spend the rest of his life schlepping assholes back and forth. Use them as a cover, load the plane with high-paying illegal cargo, and retire a lot sooner. It'd worked well so far. He'd invested in a small passenger plane after his father died and left him a nice nest egg. Not too much, but enough to put a down payment on the used plane. He'd loved being in the air since he was a kid. He did a stint in the air force but ultimately wanted to be his own boss. The first couple of years he did alright, providing passenger flights. However, the first time he was approached by a gentleman offering a hefty sum to move some secret cargo, he was intrigued. After that, not a flight went by where he wasn't moving something. The people, well, they were just to keep eyes off him.

This flight, though, was different.

He hadn't wanted to transport such a volatile substance. The money was more than fair, but the risk kept getting higher. It wasn't like he'd been given a choice, anyway. The cargo arrived and was loaded on the plane. He worried the weight was too much, they told him to let them worry about it. Which pretty much meant, "Sit down and shut the fuck up." It maxed out the weight the plane could handle with passengers, but he had a feeling if he challenged them, he'd be found with a bullet in his head. The gun in his hand with some type of niche porn mag in his lap. They'd make sure to fuck him up good.

He sighed and pulled his slacks over his bulging belly. Flying people and cargo was like being a glorified truck driver. Move shit from here to there. No exercise, no glory. Not like it was in the movies. No fancy pilot hat and wheeled luggage. Just get out of bed and drive one vehicle to the next. Turn the engines on, check the equipment. Ignore the nervous passengers loading and get it over with. Now, he fucking hated it. But the money was decent. Not from the passengers, of course, they were just there for visibility. It was all mainly chartered, but he filled in with extra flights for people who were willing to shell out a little more. To not be stuck next to the guy going to an insurance convention, looking to get lucky.

That was today, a fill-in flight. Heading to Idaho with this load of shitheads. Really, to get the cargo to Boise. He didn't know what his clients needed with so much of the substance and he didn't ask. It wasn't his problem. His job was from point A to point B. That was it. He watched the ragtag group of passengers cross the tarmac. A middle-aged couple, a single businessman, and two guys who appeared like they were in some sport... well, except one guy was missing his left arm

from the elbow down. They put their bags on a cart to be loaded into cargo before ascending the stairs. He'd handle that, he didn't want anyone fucking around in there.

Following behind the pair of sports guys, was a young woman, maybe thirty or so. She was pretty with straight, dark brown hair which was cut at her chin, all one length, and fell over her large, hazel eyes. She kept her head down, peering around while she clutched a carry-on bag under her arm. Wherever she was going, she clearly didn't want someone to know. Bringing up the rear, was a young couple. Maybe honeymooners or perhaps off on a tryst away from their actual partners. Either way, they made him want to vomit, fawning all over each other like that.

After loading the cargo, he put on his best customer service smile and greeted them as they climbed the stairs onto the plane. He followed them up and closed the door. The group made their way to the seats and sat down, staring at him for assurance he gave a fuck less about giving. He waved his hand in the air.

"Welcome to flight 282 from Spokane to Boise. Please have your seatbelt buckles fastened at all times. I'm David, your captain. Please make yourselves comfortable and I'll do my best to get us there safely," he said with an aura of humor, making everyone laugh nervously. Well, except for the one-armed guy, who was watching him with an air of distrust.

"Dick," he muttered to himself as he made his way to the pilot's seat.

He didn't give a shit about any of them and just wanted to get the damn cargo to its recipient. Maybe after this flight, he'd take a leave of absence. Fly somewhere *he* wanted to go. He'd had about enough of everyone's demands. He taxied down the runway and took a breath of relief as the wings caught the sky.

"This is the last time I'm doing this shit," he grumbled as the ground below faded under the clouds.

No truer words had been spoken.

Chapter One

She wasn't sure why she'd stayed so long. Maybe it was the fear of him chasing her down and beating her to death. Maybe it was because when he bared his soul and told her he was sorry, she believed him. She knew she felt sorry for him, it was in her empathetic nature to feel what she thought others were feeling. Even if it wasn't true. Even if she was filling in the blanks with way more compassion and understanding than was deserved. It was played out in every Hollywood movie about domestic abuse ever. She was smarter than that but couldn't break the cycle. Until now.

After he left for work, she called her friend Bren in Boise and asked if she could come to stay. Her voice was shaking, but she couldn't take no for an answer. Her life depended on it.

"Of course, Audra!" Bren exclaimed, knowing some of the history. "I don't want him coming here, though, so you need to swear you won't tell him anything."

Bren knew her well. Audra was a buckler. They'd all worked together in their early twenties at a themed restaurant. Bren eyed him first but Audra was the looker. Long, shiny brown hair she'd highlighted with auburn and golden streaks. She was petite and thin with big amber eyes and a wide smile. She was used to the attention, but he approached her differently.

"I'm James. You think you're hot stuff, don't you?" he said in a teasing, yet cutting manner.

This threw her off her guard, however, she was enamored by his ice-blue eyes and confident air. She'd blushed and fumbled as he took control of the conversation. By the end, she'd agreed to a date. He seemed so put together and intelligent, rattling off facts about history and technology. She wasn't stupid by any means, but he spoke with such surety, she often doubted things she believed. She always felt slightly off her game. It was growth, she convinced herself, he was worldly and expanding her mind. The sex was good and she just knew he was the one. She could picture the children they'd have, the vacations they'd take.

They dated for a year, then married shortly after. Things took a turn about a year later. After a night of drinking with friends, he turned on her in the bedroom, throwing her against a wall over a small argument. The next morning, he swore he didn't even remember and was going to cut down on drinking. Which he did, so she was sure they'd moved on. Time passed with no incidents and she put it behind her.

Audra worked at a daycare and took classes in early childhood education, hoping one day for children of their own. James didn't seem too keen on it when she brought it up but didn't try to prevent it either. He worked as an assistant manager of a big box, chain store and came home unhappy and bitter. He bitched constantly and talked about dreams of owning his own business. If Audra offered suggestions, he'd flip out on her, calling her names and telling her she was clueless. It hurt, however, she knew work was taking its toll. It wouldn't always be like this.

One day, while taking out the trash, she noticed a tied-up bag in the can. When she lifted it, bottles clanked together. She opened the bag and saw countless empty liquor bottles. He was drinking heavily again, which would explain his vacillating temper. That night at dinner, she tried to gently bring it up and he flipped a switch, screaming as he threw his glass at her. It hit her in the face. She ran and locked herself in the bathroom. He left and didn't come back for hours. She cried herself to sleep and when he slipped into bed in the early morning hours, she hoped he'd reach out for her and beg her forgiveness. He didn't and reeked of booze.

It went on like this for years. He'd come and apologize later and talk about his fears; how he felt shut out and pressured as a child. This pulled at her heartstrings and she knew if she stood by him, she could help him out of the dark hole he was in. After all, he was her husband and she'd sworn for better or for worse.

Nine years later, tired of patching walls and hiding bruises, Audra knew she'd had enough. She was jumping at every little thing, relieved they'd never had children. She wanted to wake up and feel like she had something to live for. Now, she knew she was in a prison and he was never going to change.

The last night was it. James came home and they had plans for a nice dinner and to watch a movie. She'd cooked the meal, put on music, and changed into a slinky, purple dress. Over the years, he'd pointed out how much he liked blonds, so she'd continued to lighten her hair until it was honey-golden and down to the middle of her back. He'd come in complaining about so-and-so at work as she tried to distract him, smiling seductively. He hardly noticed and when he did glance at her, he eyed her up and down.

"You may want to cut back on the sweets, Audra. Looks like you've put on a few pounds."

She sighed and brought the food to the table. He always had little digs to offer. She questioned herself, conflicted because men at the grocery store still stopped and stared when she passed. James really messed with her head. They ate dinner in silence. When she suggested a movie for them to watch, he smiled and nodded, setting his fork down as he shifted gears.

"Yeah, I guess. It's been a long day at work. Sorry, my brain is elsewhere. Your dress is pretty."

They were back on track. They finished dinner and Audra put the dishes in the sink for later, so they could spend some time together. James went to the kitchen for a soda and sighed heavily.

"I guess I have to do everything." He started washing dishes by slamming them around and muttering to himself.

"Hey, I'll do those later. I thought we could watch a movie first?" Audra said quietly behind him.

"You know I can't relax if there is work to be done, Audra. Being lazy isn't attractive."

"I wasn't being lazy. I cooked the dinner."

"Oh, so it's my job to clean up after you?"

"I wasn't saying that." Audra felt her face get hot and regretted the words as soon as they came out of her mouth. "I mean, I did cook the whole meal, already."

He spun around, his pupils large, staring at her. "No one asked you to. You're such a little bitch."

"James. That's not fair. Can we just try to spend some time together?" She reached out to touch his arm and he yanked it away.

"Don't fucking touch me," he seethed.

She dropped her hand and walked out of the kitchen. Better to drop it, than for it to spiral out of control. He followed her, trying to pick a fight about nothing. How she forgot to do the laundry, how she never considered him, how he worked so hard and she was dirty and messy. It went on and on. She thought it was better to let him wear himself out, but rage bubbled up in her and she couldn't let it slide.

"I work, as well, James, and you hardly lift a finger around here. I pay the bills, I do the shopping, I cook and clean. I run myself ragged taking care of things. I don't know why you can't see that."

His eyes shifted and he took a step at her. He grabbed her by the arm and leaned in close. "Don't fucking speak to me like that."

She felt her heart palpitating and drew in her breath. "Calm down. I know you work hard, too. I was just saying-"

He slapped her across the face, cutting off her words. She jerked back, quickly looking for an escape plan. He was much larger than her and she knew she needed to get somewhere safe. She went to move toward the bathroom, but he blocked her and shoved her down to the floor. He bent over her, breathing heavily.

"You always think you're so much better than everyone else, you cunt. You're nothing. You're disgusting and ugly and no one wants you."

The words hurt, but she was used to them. She tried to scoot back and he punched her in the face. She couldn't see as flashes of light filled her brain. She leaned over onto the floor to try and stop the room from spinning when he kicked her in the gut. She heard him grab his keys and slammed his fist into the wall by the front door. He paused and she prayed he wouldn't come back at her.

"I fucking hope you die," he whispered, then left. She heard his car start up and screech out of the driveway.

No one in her life hated her as much as he did. At times. Tomorrow, he'd come back and apologize and say he didn't mean it, that she was the most beautiful woman, and he didn't deserve her. He cried sometimes and called himself names. It wasn't that she believed him anymore. It was that she felt trapped. Trapped by responsibilities. Trapped by fear. He said if she ever left, he'd commit suicide. She felt burdened by that. She knew for sure if she left, he'd come after her. He would kill her.

Now, though, she'd rather die than stay. If she stayed, he'd eventually murder her, anyway. She imagined killing him sometimes. Taking a knife and stabbing him over and over. Buying a gun and shooting him. Pushing him over the banister.

She knew she'd never go through with it because if she failed, he'd kill her. Bren knew some of it. Audra tried to leave before but lost her nerve. This time was different. She felt dead inside. Numb enough to leave.

Bren agreed to pay for the plane ticket, so he couldn't track her. Audra had been stashing money and packed that in a carry-on bag with some essentials. Just enough stuff to get her to Bren's, then she could start over. James didn't know she still was in contact with Bren or where she lived, so it gave Audra some time to figure out what to do. He came in stinking drunk and passed out on the couch. She heard him get up and shower for work. Pausing by the bed, he stared down at her but she pretended to be asleep. He wouldn't be late for work, that much she knew. He was the stellar nice guy at work. Friendly and helpful. He sighed, then left for the day.

As soon as she knew he would've clocked in at work, Audra grabbed her things, called out sick from work, and left. The flight was out of a small municipal airport, so she wouldn't be on any passenger lists. She mapped the address, deciding to ditch her car downtown and take a taxi the rest of the way. Paying in cash, she gave a fake name to the driver. She was Audra Banner, then married as Audra Letsky. Now, she didn't know who she was. She was Audra, that much she knew.

She had three hours before the flight took off. Rather than waiting around the airport, she ducked into a salon and asked if they could squeeze her in. The lady behind the counter eyed her.

"Whatcha wanting to have done?"

"Can you dye my hair back to its natural color?" Audra requested.

"Well it looks pretty processed, but I think we can. You want a cut, too?"

Audra considered this and peered around at the pictures in the salon. There was one of a blond girl in a tennis outfit, her hair cut to her under her jawline with bangs. Audra pointed to the picture. "Like that, but no bangs."

The lady turned around to look at the picture and nodded. "Chin-length bob? Yeah, that'll be cute on you."

They moved to the back and the lady pulled a cape around her. She hummed to herself, turning Audra to the mirror. Her makeup wasn't hiding enough. The lady leaned in and whispered.

"I know those injuries well. I hope you're running because otherwise, you'll end up dead. I've been there, honey. There is no way out, other than to run and hide. I can style the hair to cover that eye with just a tiny bit of layer near the front, creating a swoop."

Audra nodded and started to sob softly. The lady handed her a box of tissues and let her compose herself. Audra looked in the mirror, knowing she needed to fight for the girl staring back at her. The black eye was seeping through the makeup and her eyes gazed back at her empty.

The lady patted her on the shoulder, then began the process of chopping off her hair.

Chapter Two

T he passengers were buckled in their seats and Audra
listened to the pilot drone on. She just wanted the plane
to take off, so she was out of James's reach. She glanced
in her compact mirror and almost didn't recognize herself. At
least fourteen inches of hair had been cut off and what
remained was dyed back to her natural, deep brown she hadn't
seen since her parents permitted her to have highlights in her
teens. The stylist added light layers to the ends, allowing a few
wisps to fall naturally over her eye to better hide the bruising.

She'd given Audra the name of a really good concealer
as well, which she was able to find at the pharmacy before
leaving for the airport. It had done a decent job of hiding the
black eye, though her eye was still swollen and partially closed.
She made sure to let the hair fall over it, not making eye
contact while she was waiting to board. The pilot was
watching her intently from the plane, so she stared down at the
ground.

The plane was way smaller than she expected, seating under thirty passengers. It was nice, but the size of it sent a panic through her. Bren had secured the ticket and said the guy assured private passage. She needed to suck it up. At least it was a short enough flight. A few of the passengers seemed familiar with riding in this type of plane and weren't acting concerned. They took their seats and chatted or read the paper.

There was no co-pilot and no stewardess. Just the pilot, her, and seven other passengers. The couple in the back were practically mauling each other, so she took a seat near the window, in the middle by the wing. She put her bag in the seat next to her to deter anyone from joining her. A couple of guys were in the row across from her and were chatting about rock climbing. The guy in the aisle seat had an accent she figured to be Scottish or Irish. His arm closest to her was gone from the elbow down. Other than that, he was lean and muscular. She tried not to stare and glanced out the window as they moved down the runway. Her nerves shot up and she clasped her hands together as they took flight. At least now, James couldn't reach her.

She peered around the plane and wondered about the lives of those around her. The couple going at it in the back were young, maybe mid-twenties. The guy in the suit looked to be in his forties and well off, not fazed at all about the size of the plane.

The other couple was close to her parents' age and talked kindly to each other, laughing and looking at a travel book. Audra watched them, wondering what it was like to be happy like that. The guys next to her were probably about her age, obviously pursuing rock climbing pretty seriously as they were mapping out where they were going to climb as soon as they landed.

At thirty-one, she'd barely lived, getting by day to day. Living in fear will do that. Now, she was heading to a new town and hopefully freedom. She wanted to be excited but was still jumping at every turn, expecting James to find her and drag her back. She glanced at the one-armed guy next to her and he caught her eye. He smiled politely, then looked away. She stared at her hands and coughed, her throat tightening from any human interaction. She just needed to get to Boise and go from there. Far away from James and his utter hatred of her.

A quick check of the time let her know James would think she was still at work. She got home before he did, so as soon as he got home, he'd know something was up. That was in two hours. She'd called and changed her cell number while she was waiting for the flight and texted the new number to her parents and Bren. New phone, was all she told her parents. She wouldn't let her parents know what was going on until she was there. James had successfully created a distance between her and them by demanding her attention, so they wouldn't even know anything was off. Now, it was just her, one bag, and a few hundred dollars she'd been able to skim off the top, so he wouldn't notice. Not enough to start a new life, but enough to flee.

She glanced at the guy with the accent from the corner of her eye. She generally distrusted all men now, but he had a nice look. Curly, golden-brown hair which fell to about to his shoulders. When he smiled at her, she noticed he had greenish-brown eyes and a kind smile. He was pointing out the window and talking to his friend in hushed tones. Audra stared back out her window, then sighed. Nine years wasted. Nine years with no friends and nothing to show for it. James robbed her of her youth and she'd let him. She'd made him more important than herself. If it meant being alone for the rest of her life, it was better than waking up, wondering what misery the day would bring.

As she was gazing out the window a bit later, she could see mountains below but they seemed too close. Maybe it was her eyes playing tricks on her, but it appeared like they were banking toward the mountains and not rising above them. She squinted her eyes and looked again. No, she was wrong, it was just the way the wing was tilted. It felt like something shifted underneath the plane and it started to turn toward that wing. She'd never been in a small plane and wasn't sure if this was supposed to happen or not, however, the guys next to her glanced at each other with a look of concern. The plane seemed to straighten back out and their demeanor relaxed a little, but the guy with one arm chewed his lip pensively.

All of a sudden, it felt like the plane lost altitude and Audra gripped her seat arms. A collective gasp went through the group. The plane leveled out again but something was wrong. The pilot banked, searching for a place to put the plane down. This caused another shift in the cargo and the plane veered too far off and down. The descension was immediate and the pull toward the ground apparent.

Audra could see the tops of the trees zooming toward them and felt the bottom of the plane start to hit them. The pilot was shooting for an opening when a tree, or trees, ripped the left wing off the plane, sending it spinning. Audra gripped her seat, trying to get her bearings when she saw the side of the mountain appear in the window next to the one-armed guy's friend, smashing into that side of the plane and everything went black.

. . . .

White-hot pain brought Audra back to consciousness and she leaned over, vomiting violently. She was no longer in her seat and when she opened her eyes, she came to the realization she was no longer even in the plane. She sat up and gasped, the pain she was feeling coming from a huge gash down her leg, revealing muscle and what she hoped wasn't a glint of bone. Pieces of the plane hung in the trees above her; she needed to move before they toppled onto her.

She tugged off her button-down shirt and ripped the sleeves off it with her teeth and hands. The pain was so excruciating in her leg, she paused to vomit again, then dry heave. She tied the sleeves around her leg as tight as she could to pull the flesh back together. She got herself upright enough to drag her leg behind her out of the trees. She slipped back on the remaining pieces of her shirt and stared around. Her leg was more or less useless, barely able to bear any weight, but she needed to find somewhere safe to get to avoid falling debris. She spied a spot with no trees and a rock she'd be able to lean against or sit on. Hopping toward the rock used every bit of energy in her, and she collapsed against it.

Once there, Audra peered around. Where was the rest of the plane? Where was everybody else? A glimmer caught her eye. Through the trees, she could see the crumpled hull of the plane, minus the back, wings, and cockpit. Just the middle and it was crushed on one side. She didn't know if she could make it over there, but she needed to see where the other passengers were. She found a branch and broke it down until it was a decent size for a crutch and began the slow and painful trek to the body of the plane.

She was drenched in sweat by the time she made it to the plane. To her horror, she quickly discovered other passengers dead inside. The middle-aged couple and friend of the one-armed guy had been crushed when they hit the mountain. The back end with the younger couple and businessman was just gone. The cockpit was further down and she could see the pilot half out of it with his body twisted in a way no one could survive.

The side she'd been sitting on had developed a huge hole in it when the wing was ripped off. She must've been sucked out, as the pair of seats on her side were missing. She wondered if her seatbelt had been defective or if she'd not buckled in correctly, because she was most definitely not in her seat when she came to. The seat was nowhere to be seen. It was simply gone.

Audra sat down and surveyed the area. Where the hell were they? Somewhere in the mountains, however, nothing was around. Her phone was missing and she doubted anything on the plane still worked. She needed to get down to the cockpit to see if she could radio for help. Fear froze her in place and she didn't move. Somebody must have seen them go down and would be on the way to rescue them. Or her. Since it seemed like she was the sole survivor. She remembered noticing a first aid kit in the plane cabin and hobbled toward it.

Seeing the dead bodies scared the hell out of her and she couldn't make herself go in. Finally, knowing she risked infection, she climbed through the opening left by the absent wing. The row of seats across from hers had shifted over, leaving only a narrow walkway to shimmy through to get to the first aid kit attached to the wall near where the cockpit had been. The guy sitting with the one-armed guy lay lifeless, the side of his head caved in. She paused, feeling a pang of sadness. He'd been young and she remembered hearing him laugh as the flight took off. Now, he was an empty shell.

Audra yanked the first aid kit free and squeezed back out, finding a rock to sit on. Opening the kit, she found some antiseptic and bandages. She lifted the sleeve material enough to squirt the antiseptic into her wound and held her breath in pain. She lay back against the rock and cried as it radiated through her body. In escaping one trauma, she ended up in another. The universe was cruel like that. Once the pain settled to a constant hum, she sat up and tried to make a plan. No one had come and she wondered partly if the same thing that made her able to fly incognito, also might have prevented anyone from knowing they'd crashed? But this was the US, someone somewhere had to know they were down there. The other passengers were sure to be expected and would be reported missing. That thought gave her hope.

Night crept on and she shivered. It was late summer and it was going to get cold. She had a sweater in her carry-on bag but looking around, it was nowhere to be seen. Maybe if she could get into the cargo hold, she could find something to put on or blankets. Question was, where was the cargo hold, now? She got up and moved back over to the main part of the plane, careful to not look in. She searched for the door to the cargo section.

When Audra found the door, she wasn't able to pry it open. She tried with sticks and her fingers, but it wouldn't budge. Frustrated, she stepped away and screamed at the top of her lungs.

"Fuuuuuuuuuuuuuck!"

Birds above her took flight, startled by her voice, then landed back in the trees. She wiped snot away from her nose and gray fabric in the trees caught her eye. It was from chairs ripped out of the plane. She wandered over to them and set them upright, collapsing on the seat in defeat. She had no food, no way to contact anyone, her leg was throbbing, and she was alone. Maybe she should've stayed and let James beat her to death. The delirium at the thought made her laugh. Instead, she'd slowly die out there.

Those birds are probably waiting to pick my bones clean, she thought and giggled. She was losing it for sure.

"What in God's name are you laughin' at?" a soft, accented voice said from behind her.

Audra turned around, stunned, convinced her cracking brain made it up. A figure approached and came around in front of her.

"Are you alright, there? I thought I was the only survivor, like," he said quietly, almost as if he was trying to avoid spooking her. He knelt and met her eyes.

Audra reached out and touched his face to convince herself it wasn't a figment of her imagination. She jerked her hand back and stared. It was the guy with one arm. He was bleeding from his head, but he was there.

"Hey, it's alright, yeah?" he whispered. "We made it out. I checked and found the back of the plane. We're the only survivors. The radio in the cockpit isn't workin', either. Do you have a phone?"

Audra shook her head. She had nothing.

He stood up and glanced around. "I found a cave a little ways off, do you think you could make it? We may want to get there for the night. I can build a fire that should keep animals away. I found a bag with some clothes in it. Looks like men's clothes but there were sweaters and such. Should keep us warm enough tonight. We can come back in the mornin' to try and get into the cargo area. Maybe by then, someone will be searchin' for us, so."

He put his hand out to Audra and helped her up. She nodded, rising painfully beside him. "Thank you," she said. "I thought I was alone."

"I thought I was, too, until I heard you yell the word *fuck*. Best soundin' *fuck* I've ever heard," he replied.

"I'm Audra."

"Well, Audra, aren't we the pair? Me without me arm and you with that leg. What'll they think if they find our bodies out here? You think they'll waste time lookin' for me missin' arm?"

Audra snickered, surprised at his humor. "Probably not. After all, we'd be dead and I think that would be the least of their concerns."

He smiled at her and nodded. "Fair enough. I'm Lucas by the way. Luke."

Chapter Three

They made it to the cave before nightfall. It wasn't deep but was a shelter from the weather. Luke set to building a fire while Audra rested her leg, which was screaming in pain. They brought the bag he found and the first aid kit. She dug through the bag and pulled out a sweatshirt; more like a dress on her. She'd only been wearing shorts and a blouse, so anything was a welcome relief. She drew out the remaining items; a shaving kit, more clothes, and multiple single packs of spicy peanuts. Like, a weird amount. They were either a favorite or a gift for someone. Inside the shaving kit were a toothbrush, toothpaste, razors, trial-size shampoo, and a shaving cream bar with a brush and mug to lather it up in. It wasn't much but Audra was glad for the peanuts. She hadn't eaten all day and it didn't look like they'd eat tonight except for the peanuts.

Luke grabbed the mug from the shaving kit and headed out to find water. Audra rinsed her wound again, knowing if she got gangrene out there, it'd kill her. The fire was warm and she fed it from a stack Luke left while he was gone to make sure it didn't go out. A little bit later, he came back with the mug filled to the brim. He handed it to her but she was afraid to drink it all.

"No worries, I drank some at the stream. Looks pretty clear, so we should be good. Drink it," he said in his soft, lilting accent.

Audra guzzled the water, wishing there was more. "Thank you. If you don't mind my asking, where are you from?"

"Ireland. I've been on this continent for the last five, or so, years competin' but grew up there. You?"

"Originally Cheyenne, Wyoming but moved to Spokane when I was a kid. Not too exciting, I know. The world I've seen is pretty much just there."

"So far. Obviously, you were flyin' somewhere, yeah?" he asked, stoking the fire.

Audra blushed and clammed up. Had she not left, she'd be sitting at home with James as he did his cycle of trying to make things right. She would've eaten it up just to avoid conflict. Instead, he'd now know she was gone and be texting her, maybe calling her work. Would he be worried? She doubted it. It was more about control and keeping secrets secret. He'd be working out his story to cover his ass.

She didn't answer and stared into the fire. Luke didn't press and handed her a pack of peanuts. They ate them, realizing they should've saved water to drink after, the spice and salt from the peanuts drying their throats. Luke laughed and grabbed the mug to get more water. He left again as Audra leaned back, closing her eyes. They were in a plane crash today and that wasn't the thing she was most stressed about. How fucked up was that? She was still worried about James tracking her down. Here she was in the middle of nowhere, one of the only two survivors of a plane that went down it seemed no one knew about, and she still expected James to come walking up, ready to make her pay.

A little while later, she heard footsteps and panic set in. She bolted upright and looked for something to grab when Luke came in, appearing confused.

"Were you expectin' someone else? I promise we're the only ones out here for miles, if not more."

Audra let out her breath and rested back carefully, her leg reminding her it existed. She shook her head. "Sorry, I just... it's nothing."

Luke watched her, handing over the mug. "It's not nothin', like. People don't react like that over nothin'." He pronounced the "th"s in words like a soft "t", which sounded endearing to Audra.

She smiled wearily and took a sip from the mug. "I'm just putting something behind me I should've done a long time ago. Well, I was... but a plane crash wasn't part of the plan."

"No. No, it wasn't. We were on our way to a competition and needed to get to Boise for a connectin' flight. Our original flight was canceled and we booked this last minute to get there in time, so," Luke replied, deep in thought with his brows furrowed.

"I'm sorry about your friend."

Luke shook his head and walked outside. She regretted saying anything but could see they were close. When he came back, he went to the bag and found a jacket to put on over his tank top. It was getting colder, so they inched closer to the fire. Luke poked at it with a stick and glanced over at her, the flames dancing in his eyes.

"His name was Adam. We rock climbed together since I moved to the States. He was me spotter, too, since, well..." He lifted his shoulder to his missing arm and shrugged. "Right now, I'm not tryin' to think about it. Just tryin' to survive."

Survive. Audra knew it well. Tunnel vision to get through. She'd been doing it for years. She watched him, wondering if he'd be offended if she asked about his arm. They were stuck in a cave waiting for rescue, so she took the chance.

"How did you lose your arm?"

He grinned, then cocked his head. "Most people don't ask, yeah? There's no excitin' tale, no war story, like. I was born and for some reason, the bottom half of me left arm below the elbow just didn't grow after birth. Me parents decided to have it amputated then, so I could adapt and never know anythin' different. Sometimes, I think about makin' up a lavish story because people always seem disappointed by the truth."

Audra listened and while she found his story fascinating, it seemed shallow to say so. He adapted and now was a competing rock climber. She tried to imagine it, however, she couldn't.

As if reading her thoughts, he continued. "I got into rock climbin' when I was a young lad. First, I went to indoor climbin' walls to practice on. Eventually, I began climbing outside. It was hard at first, I had no strength. Over time, the rest of me body got stronger and I could climb farther and faster. I had somethin' to prove, you know?"

He laughed softly and watched Audra. She glanced at him, then away. She didn't feel unsafe with him but hadn't been around anyone else alone in nine years. The sleeves from her blouse tied around her leg were soaked in blood and fluid she couldn't identify, so she shifted over to the bag of clothes. Everything in there was clean and she pulled out a dress shirt, attempting to rip the seams. Realizing what she needed, Luke came over and unscrewed the razor to pull out the blade. He deftly cut the seams and knelt beside Audra.

"Can I help?"

She nodded and started to untie the sleeves holding the wound together. As soon she did, the wound opened and sent shock waves of pain through her. She glanced down and was relieved to see she couldn't see bone, but nausea overcame her as she realized the pulp she was looking at was her insides. She turned away and swallowed back the vomit that had risen in her throat. Luke quickly rinsed the wound and re-tied it with the new sleeves, using his teeth to hold one end while he cinched the other firmly closed with his hand.

"Thank you," Audra muttered, disgusted, partly from the gruesome image and partly with herself.

"If we can get into the cargo hold, I have some minor medical supplies in me bag. Adam and I used to have to stitch up some cuts durin' competitions to keep goin'. I don't know how deep that is, however, I might be able to pull it together some."

Audra didn't want to think about it and lay back, so she wouldn't have to look at the wound anymore. She didn't think she'd sleep from the pain, however, exhaustion won out and she dozed off. When she woke up, she was shivering and peered around the cave. Luke was sleeping sitting up with his back propped against the cave wall. The fire was getting low, so she threw a couple of branches in to feed it. Luke opened his eyes and yawned.

"Cheers. I was tryin' to keep it goin' but must've fallen asleep. Are you alright?"

Audra bobbed her head but tears started falling. She wasn't. She hadn't been for a long time and now to add insult to injury, she'd added more injury. Why had no one come, yet? They couldn't stay there forever and she could hardly move. Luke came around the fire and sat next to her, putting his arm over her shoulders in a friendly way.

"Sorry, daft question. Of course, you aren't. Neither am I. We'll figure this out tomorrow, yeah? I'll try the radio again and we'll see if we can find anythin' to help us get out of here. Someone had to have a phone on them, like. I can search the bodies and find one."

Search the bodies. That's where they were at. Everyone boarded that plane with plans for the future. Only the two of them made it out alive. Luke was right, someone had to have a phone on them. They just needed to make it back to daylight to take the next steps. Luke pulled out a pair of slacks from the bag and handed them to her. She slipped them carefully over her wound and hips, then fastened them. They were too big but were warm. She rested on a sweater next to the fire and watched the flames dance. At least she wasn't by herself. Had Luke not survived, she would've been out here all alone, attempting to fend for herself.

Luke lay down near her, being mindful of her space. She wanted to move closer for body heat but stopped herself

out of embarrassment. What would he think about her doing that? They didn't know each other, yet right now, were the only two people who could. She sighed and spoke quietly.

"I'm running from an abusive marriage. For nine years, I let him hit me, demean me, and control me. I thought I could help him get through it and become the person I believed he was. Last night he punched and kicked me, then went out and got drunk. I finally got up the courage and left this morning. I was on my way to my friend's house in Boise."

Luke was silent and Audra felt shame creep over her. The next thing she knew, he was lying next to her and put his hand out. She put her hand in his and glanced over.

"Well, you're a survivor, so. In a lot of ways. We walked away from a plane crash after you walked away from nine years of abuse. You sound like a fighter... stop hidin' who you are," he said, staring at her. "That where you got the black eye from, then?"

Audra swallowed and shifted her eyes down, nodding. She didn't feel like a fighter, but his saying it made her feel a small ounce of determination. When she was a teenager, she'd been the outspoken one. The girl who'd walk right up to boys and talk to them. She'd been an excellent student and ran track. Nothing seemed out of her grasp, she was going to take on the world. Everything changed when she met James and he began to systematically break her down. First with his words, then with his fists.

Had someone told her when she was twenty, two years later she'd meet someone who'd take everything from her, she would've laughed in their face. She was fearless. Then. Now, she was shattered and trying to put the pieces of her life back together. She'd think it was impossible, but Luke pointing out she'd survived a plane crash and a marriage to James for nine years, reminded her of the girl she used to be. It was going to be slow going, however, she felt two of the pieces come back together and squeezed Luke's hand.

"Thanks, Luke."

"Anytime, Audra."

They lay by the fire, warmer from each other, and held hands. It wasn't romantic or more than it was. It was two people who'd fallen out of the sky to the ground and got back up. Plain and simple. It was not being alone stranded in the wilderness. It was having another person to guide each other out of the darkness. As the saying went, *two heads are better than one.*

They needed each other to survive.

Chapter Four

The next morning, they knew they needed to head back to the crash site. If anyone was searching for them, they'd start there. They needed to find something to eat or some way to get food. It was a smaller plane meant for short trips, so any kind of stored food was unlikely. Audra's knowledge of the wild was at zero and she wasn't about to start eating things growing around. She hoped Luke had more insight into what was and wasn't edible. Even then she wasn't sure she trusted plucking plants out of the ground and consuming them. With her luck, rescuers would arrive minutes after she succumbed to poisoning herself by eating a flower.

Luke offered to go alone, but Audra didn't want to stay in the cave by herself and knew he could use the help if they did find things they could use. They cleaned and secured her leg wound and she checked the gash on his scalp. In a perfect world, it needed stitches but was crusting over either way. She rinsed and dabbed it with gauze from the first aid kit.

She admired the way the curls grew out from his head and touched them lightly. They sprung back under her fingers. Luke didn't notice, thinking she was only dealing with the wound.

Luke helped her down from the cave and they made their way at her speed toward the site. Audra figured she'd been sucked out of the plane from the hole the wing made, but wondered how Luke survived.

"Do you remember anything from the crash?" she asked as she followed behind him.

"Yeah, actually. I remember the wing bein' ripped off and seein' the hole form near you. We began spinnin' and I noticed your seat belt wasn't clipped. Right about the time we hit the mountain, you were pulled out through the hole. I'd unbuckled me seat belt to try and grab you but got sucked out, as well. Because the plane was still turnin', I guess I was tossed away from you. I got knocked out and when I came to, I thought it was just me, like."

"Wait, you unbuckled your seat belt to try and grab me? Why?"

Luke paused and turned back to her. "What do you mean *why*?"

"You didn't even know me."

"So, that's the barometer for tryin' to save a life? You have to know the person?" He chuckled and started moving again.

Audra was at a loss for words. They hadn't so much as spoken a word at the time, yet his instinct was to risk his life for hers? Who did that? Would she have done the same? She was ashamed to think she probably wouldn't have. Not so much from selfishness, rather it wouldn't have even dawned on her as an option. She was so caught up in what was happening to her, she hadn't even thought about the other people on the plane. Not until she saw them dead.

When they neared the site, panic set in and Audra didn't want to see the bodies again. She didn't know how long it took for a body to decompose and she wasn't keen on seeing the process. Luke saw her hesitate, then stopped.

"It won't be bad yet, it was cold last night. Likely, animals will get to the bodies before they get a chance to decompose too much. If we get what we need today, I can come back alone for anythin' else. I'll check the bodies for phones, alright?"

"Should we bury them?" Audra asked, more out of ethical obligation than truly wanting to.

"With what? Our hands?" he responded sardonically.

Audra hadn't thought about it. They had nothing. The bodies would need to stay where they were until Rescue came. *If* Rescue came. She shook her head and they continued to the plane. Luke tried the radio again but it wasn't responding. He left it turned on in case it managed to get any kind of signal out. He checked the pilot's pockets for a phone but there wasn't one. There were a couple of candy bars stashed under the seat and a two-liter of soda. He poured out the soda onto the ground.

"Why did you pour that out?"

"That stuff is shite, yeah? The bottle can hold water, though."

He wasn't wrong. Water would serve them better. The candy bars at least were the kind with nuts, so offered some, albeit very little, nutrition. They'd serve more to shut up the rumblings. He shoved them into the bag they'd emptied of the clothes to bring with them. They moved to the body of the plane and Luke climbed in to check for phones. He threw out other items from the hole he thought they might be able to use. Seat pillows, a couple of blankets from a storage closet, and a few of rolls of toilet paper from a small bathroom, Audra hadn't even noticed. She gathered everything into a pile. Luke climbed out with an armful of jackets and bags. He found two phones from checking pockets and they dug through the bags and jackets for any others.

They found two more phones, a packet of mints, some feminine products, and a bunch of other useless stuff. The score was a folding knife Adam had been carrying on him. Luke used it to pry open the cargo door and began pulling stuff out. This was where the luggage was stored and they found a lot more usable items. The older couple had gifts they'd purchased stashed in their bags, which included baskets of niche food items, coffee, and tea. Luke found his rock climbing equipment, including matches and a couple of foldable camp dishes and pans. He found another first aid kit with needles and thread for stitches. He had energy bars and some other type of compressed sealed food, Audra didn't recognize. She guessed if they were out rock climbing for the day, they'd want to carry light items to eat to keep going. He grabbed a couple of canteens as well, which would allow them to stock up on water and save trips.

Once they'd sorted through what they needed to take back to the cave, it was a decent pile and there was no way they could carry it all. Audra felt bad, knowing she wasn't much help. With Luke working with just one arm, it would take multiple trips. He chewed his lip, staring at the pile and his eyes lit up.

"What?" Audra asked, confused.

"There is a tarp coverin' some kind of large cargo in there, like. If I can get it loose, we can put everythin' on there and drag it back to the cave," he explained.

"Do we want to check the phones first, so we don't drag everything there, then Rescue comes and gets us?"

"Fair play. Smart girl."

They sat down and opened the phones. One was dead. One was completely shattered and the screen was nothing but blotches and spider webs. The other two were password protected but they should still have been able to send emergency calls. At the top of both, it said no service. They must be in a dead zone, Audra thought ironically.

"What I don't understand is, wouldn't air traffic control have tracked the plane?" she asked, frustrated.

"It all depends, yeah? He would've had to submit his flight. However, it's a small, privately chartered plane, so probably just as a log to be on record. Not like a large commercial jet. Unless someone reported it missin', I'm not sure they'd be lookin'," Luke said thoughtfully.

"What about the other people on the plane? Someone must be looking for them, right?"

"You'd think so. Let's see. You were on the run, but your friend was expectin' you? We didn't show up to a competition, however, that just probably made other competitors happy. There was that guy in the suit. Maybe he lives alone. The older couple were together and obviously

40

traveled a lot, so maybe not missin' to anyone yet, and the younger couple kind of seemed like they were travelin' on the down-low, so."

Audra nodded. "My friend probably thought I just chickened out. Stayed with James."

Luke considered this. "Ultimately, maybe no one is missin' just yet, are they?"

"But still. How does a plane go down and no one notices?"

Luke rubbed his chin. He got up and ran down to the cockpit. He came back with a topographical map and spread it out.

"When I went to get water, I noticed we're on this side of the mountains," he said, pointing at the map. "The river I got the water from is here. I believe the cave is in this area."

Audra peered at the map, not understanding. "Okay, what are you saying?"

"Well, if the flight was from Spokane to Boise and we crashed about a half an hour in, we should've been somewhere around here." He moved his finger over the map, away from where he said they were.

Audra shook her head even more confused. "I don't understand."

Luke met her eyes. "For some reason, the pilot was way off course, like. We're nowhere near where they'd be searchin' for us, if or when we're reported missin'."

He tapped the map with his finger where they were supposed to be and dragged his finger back to where he thought they were located. Audra's mouth dropped open as she stared at him.

"Pretty much what you're saying is, we're fucked?"

"Basically, yeah? Once you can climb, we can try hikin' out. We could follow the river, but it looks like it goes for a hundred miles at least before hittin' a town. Or we can climb and get to this area here." He pointed at a small dot on the map. A town. "If we get high enough the phones may work, but that's if they're still charged."

"What if you left me and went alone? You'd move faster without me."

Luke sighed. "I thought about that, but when I was in the cockpit, I noticed bite marks on the pilot's arms and he was missin' some fingers, like. Mountain lions, I think. It's best if we stay together. Also, I found this."

He pulled out a pistol and Audra instinctively drew back. The pilot had a gun? She'd never handled one and it made her uncomfortable.

"What are we going to do with that?" she asked.

"Hopefully, nothin', but it may be able to scare off predators, won't it?"

Audra nodded. This wasn't a camping trip. They were nowhere near civilization and to the animals out there, they were nothing more than prey. Especially with the smell of blood on them. They needed to stick together.

"Do you think anyone would hear us if we fired off the gun?"

Luke shook his head. "Doubt it. Even if they did, they'd just think it was hunters."

Back to square one.

They needed to get back to the cave and keep the fire going. Once she was able to climb, they had to get up as high as they could to try and get a cell signal. They turned the phones off to preserve the batteries. If they couldn't get a signal, they'd continue until they reached some semblance of society. They stared back at the pile. First things first, get back to the cave. Luke got up and went to the cargo hold to try and free the tarp. Audra began to organize everything into the most compact pile to fit on the tarp. Luke came back out to grab the knife and watched Audra for a moment.

She glanced at him and cocked her head. "What?"

"I'm glad you survived," he replied.

Audra laughed. "That's an odd thing to say. I am, too. I mean, both of us. I wish everyone did."

Luke put his hand around a necklace he was wearing, which she hadn't noticed before. A Star of David. He glanced at it, then sighed. "It was Adam's. I grabbed it while I was in there earlier. I saw him die when we hit the mountain right before I was sucked out. He was there, then just wasn't. Like flippin' off a light. Anyway, I thought I was alone. When I heard you yell, then saw you, I knew there was a reason we made it out."

"A reason? Like what?"

"No idea. Maybe it will come to us, yeah?" Luke replied, his voice sounding distant.

Audra watched him as he headed back to the cargo hold with the knife. He was in there cussing and yanking on the tarp. Finally, the tarp came flying out of the cargo hold and landed on the ground. Audra went to pick it up to start loading their supplies. At that moment, she heard Luke's voice in the thickest Irish accent she'd heard yet.

"What in the actual fuck of all that is holy?"

Chapter Five

udra moved over to the cargo hold to see what Luke was exclaiming about. He stepped back and was staring in the door at a large amount of plastic-wrapped packages. Audra stepped forward, but he put his hand out to stop her. She glanced at him, then back at the packages, confused. Were they drugs? It was so packed in tight, she was surprised the luggage had fit at all. Granted, she only had a carry-on and there were eight passengers total, so they didn't have much. The packages had codes on them and a hazard warning.

On closer inspection, they had the letters PU and *airborne contaminant* written in bold letters underneath. Airborne contaminant? So, if they were opened, they'd be dangerous to breathe in? She didn't understand and looked to Luke for clarity.

"What is it?"

Luke leaned in and read the words again. "Rememberin' chemistry class... PU stands for plutonium."

Now, Audra was thoroughly lost. Why would a plane be carrying plutonium? "What's plutonium used for?"

"I'm no scientist, but I think it's a substance used for energy and fuel-type things. Also to make bombs," Luke explained.

"Why is it here?" Audra asked and took a step back.

"I don't have a fuckin' clue, so."

"Is it dangerous to us?"

"Not currently because it's sealed, but had it come open in the crash and we breathed it in, it would've been."

"Oh." Audra took another step away from it on the off chance there were tears they didn't see. "Do you think the pilot knew it was here?"

"He had to, yeah? He loaded the luggage. He was clearly transportin' it for someone. Maybe for money."

Audra nodded and felt sick to her stomach. He'd risked all of their lives, anyway, before the plane crashed. "Is this why we went down?"

Luke rubbed his head to think. "I supposed it could've been a factor. It's a fair amount of weight for the plane and it slid to one side, crushin' other luggage, which likely threw the weight off."

Audra remembered feeling a shift when she thought the mountains looked closer than they should and they were flying at a slight angle. After that, the wing dipped down and caught the trees. That probably was the plutonium moving in the cargo hold, sliding all the weight to one side of the plane. The pilot must've started to lose control then.

"Do you think this has anything to do with why we were so off course?"

"Maybe. I'm not sure how, unless he'd turned off navigation to not be tracked? I don't know, and the one person who does is dead."

Audra glanced at the cockpit in the distance and shuddered, seeing the pilot's body lying out of the wreckage. Luke came over and touched her arm.

"Look, this is worth a lot of money. The amount in there isn't for amateurs. Someone paid big for this to be moved and will be searchin' for it. I have a feelin' he got himself in deep with some type of underground group and this was planned to be used in a bad way."

"Like to make a bomb?"

"Somethin' like that, yeah? Nothin' good could come of this. If it was bein' used for energy, there'd be no need for secrecy. We need to get away from here because if they come for it, which they will, and we're found alive... we won't be for long, like. We visibly pried open the cargo door and saw what was inside. We can't undo that. I'll check the cockpit for any kind of logs with our names on them. You never found your bag or phone?"

Audra shook her head. They'd gotten sucked out with her but were nowhere to be seen when she came to. Her bag had her wallet, ID, and other personal info in there. However, no one knew if Luke and Audra survived and wouldn't know where they were if they were careful. "What do we do?"

"We get back to the cave to regroup. Trust me, they know the plane either went down or he ran off with it. Soon missin' person reports will be filed on all of us and dots will start to connect. We'll need to move in the next day, or so, as far away from here as we can."

They gathered everything they were taking onto the tarp, and Luke went to the cockpit to try and find anything that said how many people were on the plane. He found a logbook and a folder of papers. Nothing else was there, or at least wasn't anymore. Things could still be scattered anywhere. He walked back, scanning the area for any debris which might give them away. Nothing was apparent and he made his way back to where Audra was sitting.

Audra watched him approach, appreciating the way he deftly moved over rocks and fallen trees. She admired his lean build and ability to adapt to his environment. He was their only hope out of there. She stood up as he approached, and he smiled wearily.

"Let's get a move on. I'm knackered and need to eat," Luke said, rubbing his hand over his face.

They tied off the tarp and Luke grabbed one end to drag. Audra followed behind on her homemade crutch, making sure nothing fell out. It was slow going and by the time they made it back to the cave, she was exhausted and her leg was throbbing. Luke motioned for her to take a seat and he got the fire going. Once it was burning strong, he left to fill the bottles and canteens at the river. Now, she was really scared to be alone, hiding in the shadows when she heard someone approach until she saw it was him.

Luke pulled out some dried noodles and seasoning he'd packed with his gear and heated water over the fire. He had both his and Adam's eating utensils and collapsible bowls. He broke the noodles up into them, then poured over the seasoning. As soon as he poured the hot water over, the noodles began to expand and a delicious aroma filled the cave.

"That smells better than anything at this point," Audra murmured.

"Enjoy it while we can. This all will attract animals and people, so after tonight we're goin' to have to be careful with what we send out there. We'll need to move at least a distance in the next day, or so, to put as much space between us and the plane. We may have to skip a fire for a day, or until we're far enough away that it won't be smelled or seen from the crash site. Depends on how far we get."

He handed her a bowl of noodles and sat down beside her with his. She breathed in the steam and sighed. At least for that single solitary moment, she could enjoy something. It was the first thing they'd eaten since peanuts that morning.

"At this rate, I'll lose some of this weight," she joked.

Luke eyed her and shook his head. "What weight? You look healthy, like."

Audra blushed. "You don't have to say that, especially as fit as you are."

"I'm not just sayin' that, Audra. You are a perfect weight. Why would you think otherwise?"

"I guess, because I've put on a few pounds and James would always point it out."

"James? The guy who beat you, yeah? Perhaps his reasons were to prevent you from seein' your value and keep you there. You're absolutely beautiful."

He said it with such honesty and conviction, Audra turned away. James always picked at everything. Her weight, her hair, her clothes. True, she was only a little heavier than she'd been at twenty-two when they met, but the constant reminders had made her feel gross and worthless. She plucked at a thread on her shorts and thought about it. James was negative before he was positive. He constantly pointed out a flaw before anything else. She could've gotten her hair done and he'd point out a blemish on her skin. It was mind control to keep her from feeling good about herself. Then, when he'd offer a compliment, she'd feel unworthy of it. Grateful for his kindness.

Luke got up and rinsed the bowls, then stood on the other side of the fire, watching Audra. She met his eyes and instead of staring down, she smiled. He smiled back, lines forming around his eyes. He was very attractive in a rugged way. His hair was so curly it formed ringlets at his shoulders and his eyes were framed perfectly by thick, brown eyebrows. He'd been clean-shaven when he boarded the plane but already had a scruff of a beard forming.

Audra found herself staring a little too long and glanced away, feeling her ears get hot. Luke threw a log into the fire and reheated water, making them each a cup of tea in metal cups he and Adam had in their gear. He sat down across from her while they sipped.

"Tell me about growin' up? Are you an only child?" he asked to keep the conversation going.

Audra nodded. "The one and only. My parents are a little older and planned on one child. They did everything with me and were very encouraging."

"Did they know you were goin' to Boise, then?"

"No. I hadn't spoken to them in a while."

"Why's that?"

Why was that? Oh yeah, every time she did, James would find a way to pick a fight after. It became easier to avoid the call to avoid the fight. Audra shrugged, focusing intently on her tea.

Luke cleared his throat. "The sooner you talk about all it, the sooner it loses its hold on you."

Audra peered up and chewed her lip. "What about you? Family?"

"Parents still married, a sister, and two brothers. All back in Ireland."

"Why did you leave Ireland?"

"Rock climbin' competitions. It's all I wanted to do."

Luke wore a sleeve over the remaining part of his arm, which almost looked like was wearing a sock. Audra glanced at it, trying to imagine what it felt like. She met his eyes, her cheeks instantly blazing with shame for her blatant stare.

"I can show you if you want. I'm not uncomfortable with it," Luke said gently.

Audra nodded and Luke came over to her. He peeled off the sleeve. The arm ended above where the elbow would be and was round at the end. Audra reached out to touch his arm and was surprised at the muscles which led up almost to the end. Luke let her feel the arm and grinned, showing no sign of embarrassment or unease.

"I use every inch of it, as well. When I climb, I use the stump to brace meself and the shoulder to pull up with me other arm. Also me legs are really strong, as well, because I use them to catapult up and over to grab holds, like. It's different, but it works."

"Clearly," Audra replied, mesmerized. He could do more with his body than most people who weren't missing an arm. "Do you ever use a prosthetic arm?"

"Not really. I have one, but it doesn't serve the purpose I need. It doesn't help me climb. I guess, I'm used to movin' without it. I feel like maybe it's more for other people's comfort, you know?"

Audra didn't but that didn't matter. He'd adapted to what he needed. She glanced up from his arm to his face and met his eyes. Her eyes drifted down to his mouth and she shifted her gaze back to his arm. He pulled the sleeve back over and took a sip of his tea.

"You can ask me anythin'. I don't mind," he said, his words telling the truth.

Audra did have questions but didn't want to come across as insensitive. "What is the hardest part of this? Of not having an arm?"

Luke lay back and leaned over onto his elbow, resting his head in his hand. "Honestly? That most people avoid talkin' about it, yeah? I can see the questions in them but they turn away. They don't talk to me at all because they can't get past it."

"Are you angry about it?"

"Angry? No, it's all I've ever known, so. It's just part of me. Frustrated at times, but only because other people define me by it. I'm the guy with one arm to them, like. But I'm Luke, I'm a rock climber, I like pizza. This is one part of who I am, like me curly hair. It is not who I am as a person as a whole if that makes sense. It's not *me*, just one small element that makes up the many parts."

"I do like your hair," Audra said before she realized it came out. She immediately regretted it and swallowed the heat rising in her.

"Do you, then? I like yours, too," Luke replied and sat up next to her. "We're stuck together out here, Audra. You have to stop runnin' like a deer every time we cross a bridge."

Audra peered at him and smiled. Luke reached out and brushed a strand of hair out of her face. Was that what they were doing?

Crossing bridges?

Chapter Six

*T*hey took the next day to map out a course of action. The wound on Audra's leg was beginning to come together inside but was still deep enough to stick a finger in. Luke was concerned with it hindering her if they needed to climb or getting embedded with dirt. They'd stay at the cave through the day and night, then head out in the morning, creating some distance between them and the plane. By sunrise, they'd begin the journey toward the closest town... days away at best.

Much to Audra's relief, Luke made coffee using water he heated and ran it through grounds from the gift basket, using a silk scarf they found in one of the bags. They ate peanuts and tallied up their food. Just off what they'd gathered, they could make it through about five or six days if they were careful about rationing. By then for sure, they'd either be rescued or hopefully get somewhere safe until they were. Luke had limited knowledge of edible plants for the area and Audra had none. They'd check as they hiked but it was getting cold, options would be scarce. Luke eyed Audra's leg and sighed.

"I think we need to stitch up what we can, yeah? I can make you a sleeve out of a sock to go over the rest. To keep it secure and clean while we move."

Audra tried to not show the fear inside her. She was terrified at the idea of a needle and thread going through her skin without anesthetic. "I think it's fine, it'll heal on its own."

Luke took a sip of coffee, then shook his head. "Audra, we need to make as much time and distance as we can, like. You risk infection and openin' it up more. Even if I just suture the edges on either end, it will help draw the rest together and heal faster. I know you're scared. I'd be, too, but I promise I'll be careful."

"Is it going to hurt?"

"Well, yeah. I've had to stitch meself a bit and it isn't pleasant. Like gettin' a shot but a lot of them. Honestly, for me, it's the thread pullin' through the skin that's the worst. It doesn't hurt really, but feels disconcertin'. Sorry, probably not helpin', am I?"

He actually was. Audra was still scared but understanding what would happen, made her feel a little less chaotic about the process. She peered at the wound and could understand what Luke was saying. It was deepest in the center. If he could suture toward it on either end, it would pull the whole wound tighter, even where he couldn't stitch.

"Okay. Let's get it over with, I guess. Now, I wish we'd found booze in the luggage," Audra joked, her voice tight with worry.

"Eh, well, I don't have booze, but I do have somethin', yeah?" Luke went to a bag and took out what looked like a rolled-up cigarette.

Audra was confused. "I don't smoke, so not sure how that would help?"

"It's marijuana. It's grand for pain and distraction, so. Have you never tried marijuana?" Luke seemed slightly surprised.

Audra shook her head. Of course, she knew what it was and most of her friends had smoked, but she'd always avoided it. Mostly out of fear and societal expectations. At this point, she'd do just about anything to not have the sensation her leg being sutured.

"I'll try it," she said, feeling a little like the focus kid on an after-school special.

Luke gathered up the supplies to stitch the wound and made a bed of blankets and pillows for Audra to lay back on. She sat down as he lit the joint and handed it to her. She hadn't so much as smoked a cigarette in her life and wasn't ready for the fit of coughing which came from inhaling. Her eyes watered and she coughed until her throat was raw. He encouraged her to take another drag. She did, but this time was ready and drew it in slowly. She handed it back to him and bobbed her head as she lay back, holding her breath as long as she could. He put it out and spread out the needle, antiseptic, and suture thread.

"Audra, I'm about to start. Are you ready?"

Audra felt the effects of the marijuana and nodded. She wasn't, but her head felt slightly numb and disoriented, which she liked. It was like the moments between being awake and being asleep where every muscle in the body relaxes and the mind lets go. It was too quiet, though.

"Luke, tell me about Ireland."

He laughed softly and she felt the first stab of the needle. "It's beautiful and ugly at the same time. Americans prefer to show it as all countryside and rollin' rock walls. But it's like here in some ways. Cities and towns, rubbish and filth, too. I miss the sea because you're never terribly far from it there. Me family is from Cork, so in a way, I got the best of both worlds. We went into the city to do things; museums, concerts and the such. We went to the country to get away. I was lucky, I suppose."

Lucky.

Luke had a unique perspective on his life. He was born and had his arm amputated when he was a baby, however, he still counted himself lucky. Audra tried to ignore the feeling of the thread sliding under her skin but Luke was right, it was the worst part. Like an invasion. She glanced down and watched Luke bent over her leg, forcing the wound together, then trying to push the needle through with one hand. While seeing the needle press in through her skin was slightly horrifying, the deftness with which he did it solely with one hand was fascinating. His thumb and pinky finger acted as clamps as his middle finger pushed the needle through both sides, then pulled the needle and thread tight with his middle and pointer fingers.

He caught her watching and grinned. "Rock climbin', yeah? I can crack walnuts open with me fingers."

"I'm impressed. I can't even get the price stickers off of glass," Audra murmured lightly.

Luke chuckled and peered back down to work. Audra rested her head back, closing her eyes. Stab, stab pull. Stab, stab pull. She could actually feel her flesh coming together. She realized she was digging her fingers into her stomach and forced her hands to relax. Just about the time she was able to lose it and tell him to stop, he sighed and sat back.

"Good enough for now. I need to clean it up and bandage the open part. Are you doin' alright?"

Audra opened one eye and looked at him. "I think so. Can I look?"

Luke put his hand out and she took it. He guided her up to a sitting position and the wound appeared less intimidating. Either side was stitched as far as he could go without it pulling too hard against the sutures. It gave the impression of a giant eye on her leg. Luke rinsed it out and applied gauze and tape over the open part. He dug through the bags until he found a knee-length man's sock and cut off the foot with a knife. They shimmied it up her leg and over her thigh to cover the wound. Not having to see the wound made Audra feel better about it. It was still there but not staring back at her.

"That's better. Try standin' up and movin' around," Luke instructed.

Audra got to her feet and moved slowly around the cave. It still hurt and limited her movement, but with it being partially stitched and the compression of the sock, she was able to move without the wood stick. She sat back down and took a sip of now-cold coffee.

"Thanks, Luke. I think by tomorrow, I'll be able to move faster."

"You know, Audra, that was pretty impressive. I've seen grown-ass men cry, havin' to get that many stitches. You did grand, like."

"I think the marijuana helped. I felt disconnected from my body in a way. I still felt the needle but there was a delay in registering the pain. By the time it registered to my brain, it was over."

Luke chuckled. "Yeah, weed can do that."

"Do you smoke a lot?"

"Enough. Mainly to decompress. I don't when I need to focus, as it doesn't have that effect on me, so. For some people it does. For me, it helps let go."

Audra cocked her head. "Do you ever worry about being caught with it? Getting arrested?"

"Of course. In some areas of America, it's so vilified, yeah? It's illegal in Ireland, too, but usually get away with just a fine. It's ridiculous, really. Alcohol use is rampant in both countries but the focus is on weed, which has been proven to have medicinal and psychological benefits. Anyway, not gettin' on a pedestal. Just speakin' from me point of view."

Audra had seen firsthand the destructive effects of alcohol abuse and didn't disagree. James was at the most violent the more he drank. She met Luke's eyes and smiled. His demeanor was different than James's. No bravado or need to control the environment. Luke was soft-spoken, introspective. Like he had nothing to prove. For the first time in years, Audra didn't feel like she needed to be on guard. Luke was comfortable in his skin and created an atmosphere of openness she wasn't used to.

"Luke, can I ask you something?"

"Sure, anythin'."

"Do you have a girlfriend, or have you?"

"I have. I don't. Why?"

"No reason, really. I think I'm just coming to grips with a world where my every move isn't being watched, and I don't have to answer to anyone... or justify my existence."

Luke winced. "Ouch. That's no way to live. No one has the right to make you feel that way. For me, I like bein' alone. I mean, company is nice and one day I do want a family, but not at the expense of me own happiness. You were married nine years? Children?"

"No, we tried, but it didn't happen. James wasn't willing to find out why. Eventually, I was glad we didn't have any. The hell he would've put them through."

Luke watched her. She could tell he was trying to imagine her life before. He shook his head. "Longer than a prison sentence."

"Self-imposed, I guess. I could've left sooner."

"Could you have? Takin' into account the toll mental abuse takes?"

That was true. It wasn't just physical, the trap was in the mind. She'd feared for her safety, but also was ashamed for putting herself there. It made her feel guilty, small, and alone. And stupid. Oh, how stupid James made her feel. She didn't trust her own thoughts.

"You're right. Can we change the subject?"

Luke nodded. "Of course. I need to go refill the water containers. like. You alright while I go?"

"Yes. I was going to lay out on a rock in the sun for a bit. I'm tired."

Luke chewed his lip. "Be careful not to be seen. Be aware of any noises. Should I leave you the gun in case?"

"No. I'm scared to use it and have never fired a gun before. I'll be okay. I'll stay near the cave, I just need to get out into the sun to try and recenter."

Luke gathered the bottles and paused before he left. He looked like he was going to say something as he watched her. Finally, he lifted his hand in a wave and left. Audra cleaned up the area and sealed anything perishable before leaving the cave. She'd seen a large, flat rock about twenty-five yards away and wanted to lay on it to mentally refresh. She walked over, impressed by how much easier it was to move her injured leg. She stepped on the rock and eased herself down in the middle. The rock was still cool but the sun was warm. She closed her eyes and breathed deeply in and out. A few days ago she was planning a nice dinner and movie night with James. Now, she was in the wilderness, injured and on the run from more than James.

At least there was Luke.

Audra brought Luke to mind and allowed herself the freedom to think about him. In a weird way, she'd shared more intimacy with him over the last couple of days than she had with James in years. Luke had comforted her, listened, supported, and even medically treated her. James hadn't so much asked her how she was feeling in longer than she could remember. She'd forgotten what it was like to be nurtured by another human being and was grateful for Luke. She dozed off on the rock, thinking about what it would be like to touch his skin. To feel the warmth of another person who seemed to want her near to them.

She was woken up later by the sounds of movement approaching. She wasn't sure how long she'd been asleep but felt refreshed and ready to conquer their next journey. The steps came closer, the sound of leaves crunching with the weight. Luke must've made it back from collecting water. She yawned and sat up, expecting to see him coming through the woods. Instead, she made eye contact with the large, golden eyes of a mountain lion, poised to pounce on her. It bared its teeth and growled when she screamed at the top of her lungs.

She prayed it would be over quickly when it sank its fangs into her.

Chapter Seven

T ime stood still as Audra faced the mountain lion. She could almost hear its heart beating. Its eyes were locked on her and its haunches quivered with planned attack. Sweat beaded at Audra's brow as she had flashes of memories cross her mind. Playing in the backyard with her dolls when she was four, eating ice cream with her grandma when she was ten, her first kiss at fourteen, graduation with her friends at eighteen, her first date with James at twenty-two, their wedding at twenty-three, the first time he struck her at twenty-four, the last time four days ago, the plane crash, holding Luke's hand. All of the rage she'd been suppressing for years surfaced and she stood up and clenched her fists.

"Leave me alone, you motherfucker!" she yelled with all her might.

At that moment, the mountain lion seemed like it doubted itself and lifted a paw in confusion. Luke came running through the woods and saw Audra facing off with the creature. He grabbed the gun out of his pack, firing it in the air away from them. If the mountain lion had been unsure by Audra screaming at it, it definitely didn't want any part of the scenario with the gunshot and turned, galloping over the boulders and away. Both Luke and Audra stood in place, frozen by what just happened. Luke set the safety on the gun and slid it back into the pack. He moved toward Audra, who was staring at where the large cat disappeared.

Luke reached her and touched her hand. She glanced at him wide-eyed, her hazel eyes matching those of the mountain lion's. He nodded and wrapped his fingers around hers, helping her off the rock. She peered up at him and back to where the animal went. Luke could tell she was in shock and slid his arm around her, pulling her in close. She rested her head against his chest and didn't move.

"I will say, that badass woman I just saw standin' on that rock, tellin' a mountain lion to fuck off, is hands down the strongest thing I've ever seen in me life," he whispered in her ear. "I'd go to battle with you on me side."

Whether it was his words, scaring off the cat, or the years of being held down, Audra started to sob into his shirt. The adrenaline from the encounter with the mountain lion began to ease and she trembled uncontrollably. Luke held her while she processed what happened and rubbed her back with his hand. He guided her to the cave and they sat down on a blanket. He sat facing her and took her chin gently in his hand, meeting her eyes.

"Audra, I don't know how you can't see how tough you are. You survived a plane crash and scared a mountain lion away. James is a piece of shite. He was afraid of you, which is why he did that to you. He knew you were better than him and he didn't deserve you, so. You're the most amazin' woman I've met and I hardly know you. People hold other people down they know can and *should* leave them behind. From the first moment I saw you board the plane, I could see in you a fierceness most people don't possess. When you turned those fuckin' beautiful copper eyes on me, I was floored. Promise me you won't go back to him, yeah? He doesn't deserve you and will try to kill you, rather than let you go."

Audra watched him speak, the truth in his words heavy. She knew the draw back to James was there. She didn't know why and maybe it was part of the abuse, but he'd track her down. He'd beg her to come back, swear to get counseling. Part of her would believe him because that's who she was. The difference now... she wasn't isolated. She'd faced her own death and knew she was someone she wanted to fight for.

"I promise. If you promise me something," Audra whispered.

"Anythin'. Name it."

"Promise me you'll stay with me, stand by me. He'll find me and try to get me back. If that doesn't work, he's going to try to force me back. I know we've only known each other for a few days, but I trust you. I don't have many people on my side and James knows that. He planned it that way. I need whoever will stand with me to back me up."

Luke kept his eyes on hers, then nodded. "I can do that. When we make it out of here, I imagine we'll be connected for life."

"We already are. How many people can say they survived a plane crash together?"

"True. And faced down a mountain lion," Luke said, chuckling softly.

They ate some dried fruit and nuts from one of the gift baskets and fed the fire. It at least deterred animals. Audra thought about Luke firing off the gun and bit her fingernails as she thought.

"You don't think anyone will find us from the gunshot?"

"I looped around and checked the crash site but no one had been there. Animals had, yeah? But no humans."

"How do you know?"

"Animals are gettin' to the bodies, but the plutonium hadn't been touched. That will be the first goal for whoever it belongs to. Securin' that, like," Luke explained as he threw some deadfall on the fire.

Audra sighed with relief. She didn't want to be the reason they needed to move sooner. "So, we're still good until the morning?"

"I believe so. Tomorrow is goin' to be tough, so we need to try and sleep tonight. We need to cover as much ground as we can before nightfall tomorrow. We'll follow along the river to make sure we have water. When your leg is stronger, we can start the climb over the mountains."

Audra lay down and stared out of the cave. Tomorrow they'd be more exposed but moving farther away from the plane. On one hand, it would put distance between them and anyone who might want them dead for knowing about the plutonium. On the other hand, it would put them further from rescuers who might come. They only had a little food and she was slowing them down. However, Luke didn't make her feel that way. She glanced over at him as he was looking at the map.

"Luke?"

He met her eyes and smiled. "What's up?"

"Would you mind coming over here and just lying with me for a bit?"

Luke nodded and came over, spreading another blanket out beside hers. He lay by her side on his back. She shifted and rested her head on his chest as he put his arm over her. She listened to him breathe and could feel his heart thumping through his chest. She felt like her breathing synced with his and started to doze off. How could someone she just met seem to understand her better than someone she'd known for a decade? It didn't really matter. All that mattered right now, she wasn't alone.

When she woke up later, Luke had fallen asleep, too. She sat up, watching him. What must he think of her? She tried to see herself from his point of view and part of her saw herself as a determined fighter, the other part as a chaotic mess. He seemed so calm and patient. Even with the mountain lion, his reaction was precise and measured. She slipped over and fed the fire, putting water on for tea. Once the water was hot, she poured it over two cups with tea bags and let them steep.

She came back to the blanket with the cups of tea and said Luke's name. He opened an eye, peering at her. She motioned with the cup of tea and he smiled. Sitting up, he yawned and graciously accepting the tea.

"Went to sleep next to a beautiful girl and got woken up with a hot cup of tea. Almost like bein' on holiday, isn't it?" he joked.

Audra blushed and sipped her tea. She liked hearing him speak with his Irish accent, finding it comforting. Once they finished the tea, they packed up everything as tightly as they could. They couldn't drag the tarp the whole way, so they put as much as they could into bags that could be carried on their backs. Most of the luggage was traditional with handles but there were two duffles and Luke's pack, which could be slung over his shoulders. Audra would carry one duffle on her back and Luke would carry the other and his pack. They gathered the rest of the items they wouldn't bring and Luke scattered them in the woods to look like plane debris.

After they ate a simple late dinner of noodles and almonds, they put their packs by the wall of the cave to grab in the morning. They left out two blankets and airplane pillows to sleep on, then pack in the morning. The fire burned until after midnight, then fizzled out. They curled up together and slept as much as they could before the morning. By the time the sun crept into the sky, they were both anxious to get a move on. Luke helped Audra change her bandages and doused the rest of the fire coals with water.

Once the coals were totally out, he moved them to the back of the cave, so any passersby wouldn't see a fire had been there. They took one last look around to make sure they hadn't left any obvious traces and loaded up their packs. Luke stuffed Audra's with mainly clothes and pillows, carrying the heavier stuff in his.

They stepped out away from the cave and he put his hand out to Audra. She shifted the pack, taking his hand. They moved methodically along the river, stopping only to eat and rest for a few minutes. The day was beautiful and with the sounds of the river rushing by, it was almost easy to pretend they were just on a day hike.

That was until they saw a plane fly overhead. It was a small plane, maybe half the size of the one they'd been on. It was heading in the direction of the crash site and was unmarked. It wasn't Rescue. There was an off chance it was unrelated, but they both knew better. Someone had tracked the crash and wanted the cargo. They moved off the river under the tree line as it approached, hoping they hadn't been spied. Luke waited until it was gone and quickly filled their water bottles. They'd need to move away from the river until they made it farther.

They pushed on, even though Audra's leg was aching and her muscles burned everywhere. By nightfall, they found a crevice to tuck into and rest. They couldn't risk a fire, so ate energy bars and drank an electrolyte mix Luke shook up in a canteen. They pulled the blankets out, having just enough space to lay together in the opening. Audra was exhausted and began to feel her eyelids get heavy. She shivered and pressed closer to Luke. He was on his side and it became very apparent her pressing against him was causing an unexpected effect. He shifted to try and move away, which only made the friction between them stronger.

Luke sighed, frustrated. "If you could stop movin', Audra, it might make things easier, yeah?"

She couldn't help it and began giggling. There was nothing she could do and she couldn't deny feeling his apparent desire for her was causing a reaction in her as well. He slid his arm around her and chuckled.

"Fine, then. It'll go down on its own."

"Sorry," Audra replied, shaking with laughter which only made the issue last longer. She needed to stop but couldn't make herself.

Finally, after a bit, they began to drift off and Luke rested his head against hers. "I'm happy you're here, like. Well, as much as I can be happy either of us is here. At least I'm not alone," he whispered.

Audra laced her fingers in his and smiled. She understood what he meant. She'd been alone for a very long time. They slept until the sun came up and both were so stiff, they almost couldn't move when they woke up. No risk of fire, so no coffee. They quietly ate another energy bar and gathered up their things. They took turns looking out while the other one relieved themself and loaded up to go.

Luke paused, then turned to Audra. "Hey, about last night."

Audra shook her head. "No, it was my fault. I shouldn't have been shifting and rubbing against you like that. Don't worry about it."

"No, I liked that. Obviously. I guess, I just want you to know it wasn't just because we were close and simple logistics, yeah? It was because it was you," he explained.

Audra cocked her head and peered at him. "Because I was there?"

"Yes and no. Yes, because you were there and it felt nice. However, it wasn't the first time, you understand?"

She watched him. She furrowed her brow, then tipped her head.

"You're makin' this hard on me, Audra. It's not the first time you've caused that reaction in me. You've done it from across the cave. When you looked at me on the plane and our eyes met, I felt it comin' on and looked away, so I could control it. Now, do you understand?"

She nodded as it dawned on her. This time she did. Last night wasn't just because she'd pressed against him. He wanted her. A bubble of excitement rose in her and she blushed. She felt like she had as a teenager when a boy in school made eyes at her. She met Luke's eyes and chewed her lip. He smiled, glancing away.

"I wish you'd say somethin'," he said and laughed bashfully.

Audra reached out and took his hand. He rotated as she stepped on her toes to kiss him on the cheek. In his turning, she accidentally met his lips instead and they both pulled back in shock. Luke laughed as red spots formed on his cheeks.

"Movin' a little fast aren't you, then, Audra?" he teased.

"Maybe a little, Luke."

Chapter Eight

*O*ver the next series of days, Luke and Audra moved throughout the day and slept where they could at night. Food was running short and while they found a few plants they knew to be edible, it wasn't enough to sustain them with the energy they were expending. They saw the plane from earlier leave and come back, each time ducking out of sight.

On the last evening when they stopped, they ate the last of the peanuts and some dried apricots. Audra hated apricots but happily ate them to quiet the pains in her stomach. Luke built a small fire to heat water and quickly extinguished it once the water was hot. They still had plenty of coffee and tea left and would need to fill their guts with that until they figured out how to get nourishment.

"I guess I could try fishin' with the knife," Luke thought out loud. "I've never caught a fish in me life, but now's as grand a time as any, I suppose."

"How would you do that?"

Luke shrugged. "I've watched enough telly to figure it out. Not sayin' it'll work, but I can try."

Audra, too, had seen on television where people would take a knife and stick to make a spear and stab fish out of the water. She clearly remembered it not working very well. "What do we have left to eat?"

Luke dug through the pack to look. "An energy bar and apricots. That's it. Oh, yeah! And these, I forgot about them."

He pulled out the two candy bars he'd found under the pilot's seat. Audra's eyes lit up.

"Can we have one, now?"

"Maybe we could split half of one. The sugar will only make us hungrier in the long run," Luke replied and unwrapped one of the bars. He took the knife, cutting it in half, then cut that half again, handing Audra a small piece. She nibbled it and sighed. It was the most amazing piece of candy she'd ever eaten. She savored it between sips of tea and was sad when she took the last bite. Luke was watching her, grinning.

"What?" she asked.

"That was adorable, like."

"What was?"

"You eatin' the chocolate. You were like a wonder-filled child," Luke answered, chuckling.

"I didn't want it to end. You'd better hide the rest from me. I have a wicked sweet tooth," Audra said, not totally joking.

Luke stashed them back in the pack and kept it close to him. He brought out the sutures and needle to finish stitching up Audra's wound. It had come together enough, he could close up the remaining opening. While she wasn't looking forward to it, she was ready to finally get it closed. Like before, she took a couple of hits of the weed and lay back. They weren't smoking any other time to make it last, as well. The drawback was it made her hungry all over again, and all she could think about were the candy bars. Luke got to work on her leg and within minutes had it completely stitched up. He helped Audra sit up and she looked at the crooked but closed line. It looked like the fake wound stitches at Halloween stores. Still, all she could think about were the stashed candy bars.

Luke sat back and took a hit of the weed and snuffed it out. She hadn't seen him take one and knew he was conserving it as much as he could. He leaned against the rock wall where they were sitting, then let out a deep breath. He closed his eyes and pulled his knee up, resting his elbow on it.

"I needed that," he said quietly. "Nightmares."

Audra scooted up next to him. "Do you want to talk about it?"

Luke opened his eyes and smiled sadly down at her. "Not really, but it might help, yeah? I've been havin' visions and nightmares about Adam. Watchin' him die. Seein' his body. I keep seein' him reach out to me and hearin' him askin' me to help him. Then I wake up and he's just dead, so. I've been tryin' to push it down, so we can get the hell out of here. It's gettin' worse."

"How often are you having these nightmares?" Audra asked. She hadn't noticed. Then again, she was passing out every time they slept.

"Every time I close me eyes, like. I haven't gotten much sleep since the crash."

Audra peered at him. How had she not noticed? His eyes had dark circles under them and the lines around them were deeper. "Tell me about Adam. How you met?"

"I came to America when I was twenty-four. I'd been rock climbin' around Europe up until that point and wanted to come here to explore, get in on some competitions. I met Adam at one of the competitions in Colorado. That's where he's from. I was smokin' weed behind the bathroom and he asked if he could take a drag. We began talkin' rock climbin' and the rest is history. We've been best friends ever since. Started travelin' together and pretty much were inseparable."

"Does he have family or a partner that might be missing him?"

"I don't suppose, yet. He has family in Colorado but like me, they're used to him bein' gone and out of touch for weeks at a time. We were goin' to a competition, then rock climbin' at some different sites. No one will miss us for a while, yeah? He never had a serious girlfriend that I knew of. We were always together and while we hooked up with some girls here and there, neither of us cared about much more than climbin'."

Audra nodded. She'd never been passionate about anything like that in her life. She did the typical course. Went to school, worked, got married, worked some more. Children had been next in the plan but didn't come. Thankfully. She never would've escaped otherwise.

She turned to Luke, eyeing him closely. "How old are you, Luke?"

"Twenty-nine. You?"

"Thirty-one."

Luke laughed. "Really? I thought you were younger than me. Explains how you were married for what, nine years?"

"Almost. I was married pretty much right after turning twenty-three and it would've been nine years in two months."

"I see. When's your birthday?"

"Next month, October 9th."

"February 27th is mine," Luke said.

"So, we're pretty close in age, then. I always thought my life was over at thirty. Being around you, I see it differently, now."

"Thirty is nothin'. Just beginnin' life. I still feel like a kid most times."

Audra liked that outlook. She felt like she'd given up her whole life for James but she hadn't. Just a decade. "So, what do you want out of life?"

"Right now, to get the fuck out of here." Luke laughed. "Long-term, I want to keep rock climbin'. Longer-term, I do want to get married and have a family, yeah? I just don't know when that is."

"Me too. I want kids for sure. Everything else is up in the air. Starting over."

"Startin' over is good if it's at the right time. Granted, you picked a weird way to do it," Luke said, winking at her.

"True, but otherwise I wouldn't have met you," Audra replied, surprised by her honesty.

Luke eyed her and grinned. He had the best smile, it lit up his whole face. She resisted the urge to reach out to him, then glanced away. She vowed to herself to be more aware of his struggles and to pay attention when they slept. She thought about Adam, how he and Luke were excitedly talking before the crash.

He'd been so alive, laughing and joking with Luke. She let her mind rest on the memory. He'd been wearing a red shirt, she remembered. His Star of David around his neck. He had light brown, maybe blond hair. He had a big, broad grin and straight teeth. His eyes almost disappeared behind crinkles as he laughed. He was stocky and tan, using his hands when he expressed himself. He'd been so full of energy.

Her memory shifted to seeing him dead and she tried to shake it away. She'd only seen him alive briefly and dead for as long. Luke had known him for years alive and had to see him dead as he pulled off the Star of David. His best friend and constant companion. She couldn't imagine. Instinctively, she reached out, taking Luke's hand in her own, and squeezed it. He glanced over at her.

"I'm sorry, Luke. About Adam. I can't comprehend what you're going through. Yet, you've been here for me the whole time."

Luke leaned over and let his lips brush her cheek. "Honestly, Audra, up until I saw you alive, I'd nothin' to live for. I saw Adam's body and thought about figurin' out a way to just end it. I didn't and still don't want to live without him. But then there is you, so. You know, I need you as much as you need me. Not just to survive."

Audra nodded, resting her head back against the rock wall. If either of them were the sole survivor of the crash, they wouldn't have made it out. By both of them surviving, it forced them to not only fight for their own lives but also for each other's. She didn't believe in destiny but couldn't deny there was a reason they both walked away from that plane crash. She sighed and leaned her head against his shoulder. Now, they just needed to make it home.

After a fitful night of sleep with their stomachs waking them up repeatedly, they got up, made coffee, and ate the last energy bar and apricots. Now, all they had was the candy bars. Luke kept an eye out as they walked, searching for edible plants, and pointed them out as they went. Audra started to feel like a deer with how many random leaves and berries they were eating. Her stomach was cramping when she ate and grumbling when she didn't.

They stopped at lunchtime and Luke tried to spear fish, using the knife tied to a stick. It didn't work and he almost lost the knife in the water. They tried grabbing fish with their hands, but that also proved fruitless. It was hilarious and frustrating. Exhausted, they sat and ate the other half of the candy bar, leaving one for dinner. Nothing was like it was in the movies. It made Audra think about a book she read about Chris McCandless, a guy who went to Alaska to live in the wild and ended up dying in an abandoned bus either from starvation or some type of food poisoning. She couldn't remember exactly the details but recalled crying as she read the book, feeling his isolation and desperation at the end of his life. Fear gripped her as she thought about how easily they could mess up and die. She began chewing her fingernails and spitting them on the ground.

Luke came next to her and sat down. "Hey, we are goin' to be alright. We'll figure somethin' out, like."

They gathered up and headed on, Luke tracing their path on the map. They'd traveled about twenty-five miles over the last week and were picking up speed. The closest town was still at least twenty miles away, over the mountain range. They had no food and at least three to four days ahead of them. Eventually, they'd have to head away from the river and other than the water they had at the time, would have a hard time finding that, as well. Audra felt pretty hopeless. Not only would rescuers not be looking for the plane where it had crashed, they were moving away from that, too. They were ants under the grass.

Unseen and inconsequential.

She focused on Luke's shifting shoulders in front of her, the rhythm dragging her out of her downward spiral. They hadn't bathed in about a week other than splashing off in the river and were becoming part of the world around them. Luke's hair fell in corkscrews at his shoulders, brown with gold where it caught the sun. Audra was glad she'd cut off her hair to her chin as it stayed out of the way and she could run her fingers through it to keep it under control. Luke was doing the same and tied his back with bands he had in his gear when it got out of control.

They rinsed their dirty clothes in the river and put them in tree branches to drip dry when they stopped. Surprisingly, neither of them smelled. Sometimes to Audra, Luke smelled like pine and fresh dirt, which she couldn't deny gave her feelings.

The sun began its descent in the sky and they needed to find a place to camp for the night. Luke paused to scan the hills when something out of the normal vertical lines Audra was used to seeing from the trees caught her eyes across the river. She blinked and again saw the horizontal lines.

She reached out and put her hand on Luke's shoulder. He turned and she pointed at what she was seeing if it was truly there. Luke peered hard through the trees and began to smile.

It was a cabin.

Chapter Nine

*T*here was no clear path to the cabin, any roads or trails had long since grown over. They crossed the river at a lower point and cut through the brush. The cabin was dark, but they knocked, anyway, to be sure. It looked like it had been sitting abandoned for some time. After a minute of knocking and waiting, Luke tried the door. It was locked, so he circled around and tried the back door, which was locked, as well. He checked the window off the small porch. Also locked. He took the knife out and slid it between the top and bottom window. He jiggled it until he knocked the sliding lock, easing it over. He pressed up on the window with his one hand but it didn't budge. Audra came to help and they were able to shove it up.

Luke climbed in, then disappeared around a corner. Audra heard the bolt lock slide on the door and it swung open. Luke motioned her in, quietly shutting the door behind them. It was clearly someone's hunting cabin, and they hadn't been there for a very long time. Years, from what it appeared. There was one large bed to the left of the door next to a wood stove. A small bathroom off of that. A kitchenette with an island and four stools. The sitting area had two rocking chairs and on the far wall was a couch that pulled out to another bed. A coffee table made out of antlers and a wood plank sat in the middle of the seating.

Everything was covered with a thick layer of dust, and the roof had leaked above the kitchen floor where it warped the wood. Luke began rummaging through the cabinets and Audra nearly screamed with delight when he opened a cabinet filled with canned food. They checked for expiration dates. Most were still good but getting close... if they even had dates. It'd visibly been years since anyone stepped foot in the cabin. Maybe the owner passed and it was left to rot. Either way, it was shelter and food.

Luke tracked how far they'd come, estimating they were about twenty-six miles from the crash site. Safe enough to build a fire. Or, at least they hoped. He checked for cell service but there still wasn't any. Audra went through the food which was primarily beans, canned vegetables, and fruit. Presumably sides to whatever they killed during the hunt. Her stomach growled angrily at the sight. There were cans of something called brown bread, which she'd never heard of. She showed it to Luke, who took the can and smiled.

"I don't know about this, but in Ireland, we make brown bread." He flipped the can over and looked at the ingredients. "Hmm, it seems like it's a commercialized canned version of it, so. It's decent."

"What makes it brown?"

"Molasses and wheat flour. Sometimes dark beer or coffee, but not this one."

Audra shrugged, it didn't sound terrible but the idea of bread in a can was pretty strange. Food was food right now, so she couldn't be picky. "I'll try it."

Luke laughed, setting the can down. "Maybe one day, I can make you authentic Irish brown bread, yeah?"

"Well, let me try this first to see if I hate it."

Luke shook his head and went back to making the fire. Audra checked the drawers and found a can opener and pots in the island cabinets. She tried the small stove but it didn't turn on. She peered underneath and it had a line running to it that had been turned off. Hoping she wouldn't explode them, she turned the handle and tried the stove again. She could hear it hissing, however, nothing was happening. Luke walked over and lit a match by the burner. Flames jumped up in a circle.

"Propane. I'm surprised it's still in the tank," he said and helped her pour beans and vegetables into the pot. "There used to be a road over there, like. It's grown over, but at one point people were comin' here. There's a propane tank outside that had to have been brought in and filled by a truck. Lucky for us, there's still some in there."

Audra looked out the window and saw a large pale blue cylinder outside of the cabin. "Is there a town or houses nearby?"

"Not accordin' to the map, no. Me guess is this was family land and they used to come up regularly. Maybe as families got smaller and people died off, it became just a huntin' cabin. Perhaps it became too expensive to have supplies and propane transported here, so they stopped comin'. Maybe

got too old. I saw a magazine over by the bed that is from four years ago. I don't think anyone has been back since."

"That's sad, it's so pretty here. In time, it'll just be rubble."

They ate at the island, sitting on the stools. It was the first time since they met, they were doing something normal. Something people did every day. After, Audra turned on the sink but nothing came out. If there had been running water, there wasn't anymore. They took the dishes down and rinsed them in the river, then headed back in. The fire gave a nice glow to the cabin and Audra pulled the blankets and sheets off the bed to shake them out outside. She remade the bed and lay down, enjoying something soft underneath her. Her eyes closed and she felt the heaviness of sleep pulling her down. She rolled over and propped her head on her hand to stay awake.

Luke was sorting through their bags and had his equipment spread out on the floor.

"What are you doing?" Audra asked.

"Adam was me spotter and belayer. I was tryin' to plan out how to climb without one. I'm missin' some equipment that may have been in Adam's rack since we shared a lot of stuff. It was crushed behind the plutonium and I couldn't get it out. I have no quickdraws or chocks. I can boulder, which is climbin' without ropes, but doin' that with one arm is more than a challenge. Not to mention, this is more free-soloin' at this point."

"Could I be your... whatever you called it?"

"Belayer? We have to get you up, too, yeah? We'll be able to hike up a lot of it, but eventually we're goin' to hit rock walls we need to scale. Some pretty straight up. I was goin' to get up first to guide you to the top. However, without chocks, it'll be pretty much on me to not fuck up. I think you'll have to go first with me guiding you from behind."

"So, if I get to the top, is there a way for me to help from there?"

Luke considered it, then shook his head. "The reality is, if I start to fall while you were tryin' to hold on to keep me from fallin', I'd just end up draggin' us both down, like. You're so light."

Audra chewed her lip and thought about the situation. Ultimately, Luke was having to depend on only himself. "What if you got up and could attach the rope to like a tree or something?"

Luke laughed without humor. "Well, that would be ideal, but it isn't a cartoon, Audra. There aren't goin' to be random trees at just the right place."

She felt indignant at his comment and huffed. "Maybe there will be, Luke."

He met her eyes and shrugged, a smile playing at the corner of his mouth. "Maybe."

Once he packed away his things, he looked at the couch bed and pulled it out. It was musty and appeared like some animal had made a nest in it. He closed it back and Audra frowned.

"We have been lying next to each other for over a week, why would that change?"

"So, I can sleep without you distractin' me," Luke replied with finality.

Distracting him? Oh. Audra yawned and nodded. "Well, unless you want to fall through that ratty-ass mattress, I don't think you have a choice. We'll need to share the bed. I'll stay on my side."

They climbed into bed and as promised, Audra made a mental line down the middle and didn't cross it. Luke lay on his back with his hand resting on his chest and let out a deep breath. Within a few minutes, he was asleep. Audra watched the fire flicker for a while and let her eyes slowly close. For a moment, she forgot she wasn't at home in bed and rolled over, expecting to see James.

Instead, she made out Luke's outline. His brown, week-plus-old beard, his long straight nose, and thick eyebrows. His curly hair hovering around him like a halo. The opposite of James who kept his blond hair short and had more of a snub nose.

She'd grown accustomed to sleeping on the edge of the bed, never knowing when James would flip a switch, and dangled her foot off into the darkness. She wanted to move closer to Luke but had promised space. She closed her eyes and let sleep take her.

Later in the night, she could feel Luke shifting around and opened her eyes. He was still asleep but was obviously in a battle with himself. He took a sudden deep breath and his eyes opened blankly. He was having a nightmare. Audra scooted in close to him and wrapped her arm over him.

"Luke, wake up. Luke," she said and shook him.

He stared at her blankly and then his eyes came into focus on her face. Sweat dotted his forehead and she wiped it away gently.

"Hey, you were having a bad dream. I'm here. It's okay," she whispered.

Luke rolled over and pulled her tightly to him. She could feel his heart racing in his chest. He breathed in and out to calm himself and rested his face near the top of her head.

"Adam?" she asked.

He nodded. "Adam."

"I'm sorry. I know I promised to stay on my side of the bed, but you were clearly in distress," Audra explained.

She could feel Luke shaking. Was he crying? No, he was laughing. He met her eyes and shook his head.

"Really quite literal, aren't you, like?"

Audra didn't know what he meant by it and furrowed her brow. "I said I would, and I didn't want you thinking I wasn't true to my word."

"Audra, you truly are a piece of work. I'd hope that me bein' in distress was enough reason for you to break your word."

"Well, it was."

"Cheers." Luke ran his fingers through her hair and peered at her. "I don't mind this so much, anyway."

They fell asleep intertwined and Luke made it through until morning without any more nightmares. He had coffee ready by the time Audra woke up and for a moment everything seemed normal. Like they were a couple just staying at a cabin for the weekend. Audra held on to the moment for a bit, then sighed and got up.

"I need to go to the river and wash my hair today. How long do you think we'll stay at the cabin?"

Luke considered, then shrugged. "We've made it pretty far and are as safe here as we are hikin', so we can hold out a few days and get our strength back up before we head up the mountains. Once we do that, we really can't stop because we're goin' to need to shed everythin' except what we're wearin' and need to eat. I'll have me equipment and you'll carry the food. I've mapped out the lowest point to cross, but it's still high. Once we get to the top, we may be able to ring for rescue if the cell phones work, so."

Fear gripped Audra with the idea of having to traverse the mountains. It would be cold and they couldn't carry extra supplies. They'd need to move as fast as they could. Staying for a few days would be a welcome relief and give them time to remove her stitches. She wanted to be unhindered to make the trek.

Audra gathered the sample bottles of shampoo and clean clothes to change into. The cabin had a couple towels tucked in the bathroom, so she grabbed one and left one for Luke. He was staring at the map when she slipped out and went down to the river. She knew she was alone but still felt self-conscious taking off her clothes. Searching for a more discreet area, she found a place where the trees hung over the water. She pulled off her blouse and bra and rinsed them in the water, laying them on a rock to dry. She peered around and slipped off her pants and underwear and did the same. She poured water over her head, making sure to avoid it dripping on her sutures, and washed her hair. She rinsed her hair and quickly scrubbed the rest of her body, cascading water over her flesh, careful to direct it away from the wound.

It only took a matter of minutes, but she felt completely exposed. As she was slipping on clean clothes, she saw Luke standing on the porch, looking out toward the mountains.

He hadn't seen her naked, had he?

She was shielded by the trees for the most part, but if he'd glanced over from where he was standing, he would've seen her in all of her glory.

She walked up toward the house and caught his eye. He turned bright red and went back inside. He *had* seen her naked.

For Audra that wasn't the shocking part.

It was that she didn't mind.

Chapter Ten

*L*uke left to wash in the river shortly after Audra came in, not meeting her eyes. She evilly thought she kind of liked having this effect on him and ran her fingers through her hair. He grabbed a change of clothes and slipped out the door without a word. After a bit, she peeked out to see him swimming in the water, admiring his strong chest and ability to move with the current without being taken down. She couldn't see any more of him and wasn't trying to spy or disrespect his privacy.

She went through the cans of food, deciding what to make them to eat. The choices were beans and veggies, beans and fruit, or fruit and veggies. Oh, and the brown bread she'd been too afraid to try. She opened the can and sniffed it. It smelled sweet like molasses, and she tried to figure out how to get it out of the can. After banging in on the counter with no luck, it dawned on her to use the can opener on the other end and push it through. It came out in the shape of the can with the ridges indented on the sides. She was fascinated as much as she was mortified.

Luke walked in, slipping a shirt over his head, and saw her staring at the canned bread. He came over and tore a small piece off, then ate it. "Yeah, tastes sort of like what brown bread would taste like if you shoved it in a can and let it sit on a shelf for years."

"Do you think they cook in the can? I mean how else would it fit so perfectly?" Audra asked, poking the lump.

"I've no clue. Maybe they cook it, then use the can like a cookie cutter to cut the bread into the can?"

They both started laughing at the image. Some way or somehow, it was fully cooked in the shape of the can. She sliced it and put it in a pan to toast. The other choice was decided. Beans and canned pears. When it was all done, she put it on plates and sat with Luke at the island. She nibbled the bread, surprised at how good it was. It was sweet with raisins, and toasting it made the flavors make sense. Luke ate a couple of plates and lay on the bed, his hair still wet from the river.

"I saw you swimming out there. Looked like fun," Audra said to get the conversation going.

"It was, you should join me. After you get your stitches out, yeah?"

Audra nodded, thinking about the possibility. "Maybe. I don't have a suit, so it would be in my bra and underwear. Or I guess I could wear shorts. The water was chilly when I was bathing earlier."

Bringing up her bathing earlier made Luke's ears turn red and he made an effort to change the conversation. "I could try catchin' fish again, like."

"Leave them be unless we need to. I'm kinda digging communing with nature here."

Luke bobbed his head, watching her. She knew what was on his mind and sat down on the bed next to him.

"You saw me? In the river?"

Luke glanced away and swallowed. "Sorry, I didn't see you at first and thought you were further down, so. I was lookin' at the mountains and glanced over, then saw you. I'm really sorry, it was inappropriate."

"I don't mind. We all have bodies," Audra replied, attempting to make light of it.

Luke stared at her, then sighed. He sat up suddenly and walked out of the cabin. What had she said? When she went out to talk to him, he abruptly cut her off.

"Just let me be alone for a bit, Audra."

She went back inside with her feelings hurt. There wasn't much to do in the cabin. Without Luke to talk to, she started feeling a little stir-crazy. They'd been on the move since the crash and now thoughts were beginning to settle in. What would happen when, or if, they made it to safety? By now, everyone had to have been reported missing. James would've gone to the police as the dutiful husband. If even to cover his own ass if she ended up dead. It was going on two weeks. Search and Rescue were probably scouring the wrong area, but eventually, they'd see the plane wreckage from the sky. What about the plane they'd seen? It'd come and gone a couple of times. Well, it had gone once and come twice. So, were they still there? Were they following them?

Audra started to pace with her thoughts, feeling frantic. This was no vacation. Luke wasn't her boyfriend and they weren't on a weekend getaway. He was her only chance at survival and he was shutting her out. The familiar feelings of isolation and disgust with herself started to creep back in and she fought off the feeling to bury herself under the blankets. She was capable of keeping it together. She needed Luke to get out of there but he also needed her, she reminded herself. They were a team. Why wasn't he acting like it? Anger rose in her and she stepped outside, slamming the door behind her. Luke was gathering wood and stopped to watch her. She stormed up to him and poked her finger to his chest.

"You don't get to shut me out. We're the only two fucking people out here and you're obligated to talk to me," she hissed.

Luke set the wood down firmly. "You don't get everythin' you want, Audra. I'm a person, too, who has things I want I can't have, yeah? Can you not just give me some damn space?"

Audra glared at him and didn't move. "Fine. What is it you want?"

Luke met her eyes and looked away, clenching his jaw.

"Luke, tell me what you want and I'll give you space."

He muttered something she couldn't understand and she reached out to touch his arm. He yanked away and took a step back.

"I couldn't hear you, Luke," she said softer to try and diffuse the situation.

"Nevermind." Luke gathered up the wood and walked into the cabin, letting the door bang shut behind him.

Audra thought to follow but knew he needed the space he was asking her for. She owed him that and sat down to stare

at the river. They'd been together the whole time and maybe he needed some time for his own thoughts. That was fair. She waited about an hour and went inside. He'd stoked the fire and was lying on the bed, staring at the ceiling. They were back to where they started. She found things to mess with in the kitchen, wanting him to just speak to her.

Finally, he sighed and sat up. "Will you come over here, Audra?"

She went over and sat down across from him. He met her eyes and she could see an apology in them.

"Have you ever wanted somethin' so much it hurt? When you didn't get it, it destroyed you a little?"

Audra nodded. Month after month, when she wasn't pregnant in the beginning, she felt like tiny pieces of her were being torn away. "When I couldn't have children."

Luke took her hand and squeezed it. "That must've been hard. One day you will. I'm sure of it. I don't mean to be short with you. I'm just fightin' with that feelin', right now."

"For what?"

Luke turned red and shook his head. "You, yeah? I want you. And I can't have you."

Audra considered this, then tipped her head. "Why's that?"

"Why I can't have you? One, you're married, like. Two, you're your own person and may not want me the same."

"Luke, I'm not married. Maybe on paper, but James destroyed that years ago. I've been alone a long time. As soon as I can, I'm filing for divorce. I just need to be safe, first. Second..." She cleared her throat and took a deep breath. "I want you, Luke. Like, really want you."

He watched her for a moment, taking in her words but didn't move. Audra leaned in and kissed him, allowing her lips to linger on his. He slid his hand around her back and drew her in close. She let her fingers trace his shoulders and rest against his upper arm. They pulled back to see how it felt and smiled. Luke brushed a strand of hair out of her face and stared at her intently with his green-brown eyes.

She furrowed her brow and laughed nervously. "What?"

"Nothin'. Just this, like. I want to hold onto this."

Audra reached up and twisted one of his curly strands around her finger. It was enough. They could take it slow now that they crossed the bridge. The remainder of the day, they gathered wood and washed the rest of their dirty clothes in the river. By dinnertime, they were happy to eat more brown bread, beans, and veggies this time. They held each other in bed and allowed kissing to express their desire. It was the gentle, quiet moments that fed their connection. Audra fell asleep with Luke's curls tangled in her fingers and his hand on the small of her back. Like it was easy and meant to be.

It'd never been like this with James. James pressed for sex almost immediately and used it as his form of affection. If he took her hand, it meant he expected sex. If he rubbed her shoulders, he wanted sex. She'd become afraid to reach out to him because it usually meant he'd push for sex. She forgot what simple intimacy was like. It was everything.

Later that night, Luke was thrashing in the bed from a nightmare, so Audra woke him to comfort him. He sat up and ran his hand through his hair. "I can't fuckin' take this night after night. I'm watchin' Adam die over and over and he is askin' me to save him. I'm goin' to lose me mind," Luke said, his voice choked with emotion.

Audra rubbed his back, not knowing what to say. Time might make it better or it might not. He needed to process Adam's death in a way that was final. Leaving his body strapped in the plane was making part of Luke wonder if he'd left Adam behind, suffering and alone.

Audra moved to face Luke and took his face in her hands. "I want you to tell me about the crash in your own words. What you remember from that day? What happened to Adam."

"Audra, no. It's fuckin' terrible."

"It is. But until you tell your brain what happened, it is going to doubt it."

Luke met her eyes, then dropped his head. "We were talkin' and felt the plane shift. We fly a lot, so we both knew somethin' wasn't right. It felt wrong, yeah? The plane started to dip to one side and lose altitude. I heard the tip of the wing hittin' the tops of the trees and knew we were goin' down, like. There was nothin' we could do, then the wing ripped off the plane on your side. I looked at you and saw the hole form on that side of the plane. Your seatbelt was unbuckled. I unbuckled mine to reach out to you, then you disappeared out of the plane. I was bein' pulled out and glanced back at Adam as we hit the mountain. I saw him get crushed on one side. He was starin' at me, then his eyes went blank. I reached for him but was dragged through the hole and out, so. When I came to and got up, I headed back to the crash site. I went in to try and get him out. He was trapped in the twisted metal... I couldn't free him."

"He was dead?"

"He was, or at least appeared to be. I left to try to get help and look for other survivors. I heard you and came back. I went in again and Adam was still there with his eyes lifeless. Then I wondered if he'd actually been alive the first time and only unconscious. I checked for a pulse but there wasn't one. But what if there had been one the first time and I was too thick to check?"

"Luke, there wasn't. I was in there and everyone was dead," Audra whispered.

"How do you know, Audra? What if he wasn't?" Luke asked, unconvinced.

"Because they were. Adam was lifeless, then. He died on impact. He didn't move from when I was in there until you went back or since. He didn't die, hoping for you to save him. He died when the plane hit the mountain. You know that, your brain is playing tricks on you. It's part of grief. Denial, guilt, anger. I can't remember the rest. You're feeling guilty because it's easier than accepting Adam is gone. If you blame yourself, you don't have to officially bury him."

Luke started to cry, gut-wrenching sobs. Audra held him while he mourned his best friend and the life they were never going to have together. The brother who he'd never let go and would never get to see again. He held onto her and released the pain he'd been denying. When his tears ran dry, he lay back and pulled her onto his chest. They fell asleep and woke up with the sun.

A few days later, Luke checked the wound on Audra's leg and felt it was safe to remove the stitches as long as she kept it clean. He snipped them and quickly pulled the thread back

through the skin. They headed out to the river and Audra took off her clothes and jumped in, the cold water catching her breath for a moment. She waved him in. Luke stripped down completely and her breath was caught for a second time. He stood on the bank, getting up the nerve to jump in and she was stunned by how beautiful he was. Every ounce of him was muscle and lean. She wanted to touch him and swam toward him when he leaped in. He came up, gasping with the cold and she moved in close to him. She slid her arms around his waist and pressed his lips to his. She could feel his body pressed naked to hers and felt a desire she never had. She slid her hand down to his buttocks and around the front. He grabbed her hand, his eyes locking on hers.

"If you do that, we won't swim, yeah?"

She moved her hand and grinned. She swam away, diving under the water. When she came up, she saw Luke floating on his back and watched with appreciation.

Now, it was her that wanted him. With every ounce of her being.

Chapter Eleven

They stayed more than a few days. They were enjoying their newfound connection and decided to stay longer for Audra to gain more strength in her leg. It was probably a mistake, but they'd been on the go since the crash and needed to recover. They stayed in the cabin for a over week, swimming every day. Though they were sick of beans, it was guaranteed food. They set a day to leave and mentally prepared for the trek through the mountains. It'd take a few days to get high enough to hopefully get cell coverage and call for rescue. If the phones weren't dead by then, or if there was a cell signal even there. Nothing was guaranteed. It was well into September and the nights were getting cold. They'd move as much as possible and only stop to nap and eat, keeping their bodies moving and as warm as possible.

They'd managed to resist doing more than holding each other and kissing, but it was getting more difficult. They chose to remain clothed in bed to try and keep any barriers between them. It wasn't that they both weren't wanting to take it further, it was that they were savoring each other, the small intimacies. They wanted to get back to civilization and figure out who they were; where to go from there. Now, they just needed to make it out.

They never saw the plane leave again. It could've gone the other direction, though. It'd been weeks since the crash and it was time to move on. Luke was still sleeping when Audra woke up and stepped outside to use the bathroom and rinse in the river. She didn't even see the man approaching through the woods until he was just yards from her. She was slipping on her clothes and turned around to go back to the cabin when she saw him standing at the woodline, watching her. He was a tall, dark-haired man in slacks and a matching olive-green shirt, almost like a park ranger... but not. Something was off. She gasped, instinctively putting her hands to her chest. He moved toward her methodically and smiled.

"You live here?"

Audra nodded, to not give away who she was. "Yes, this is our home. Can I help you?"

He glanced at the cabin and back at her, not believing a word she said. "I'm with Search and Rescue, we're looking for survivors of a plane crash. I'm sure you heard it go down, being so close."

She shook her head, attempting to appear confused. "No, we didn't see a plane crash. That's terrible. Is everyone alright?"

He was irritated with the game but went on. "Nope. Most died. We think a couple of people survived and maybe went for help. Have you seen anyone come through?"

"No, sir, no one has come through. Maybe they went the other direction?"

"Hmm, maybe. That's some cut you have there," he said pointedly, eyeing the still-fresh scar on her leg.

"Rock climbing," she countered.

"So, what do you do up here? No towns nearby."

"Family land. But that's not any of your business now, is it?" Audra replied indignantly, trying to cover her fear.

He eyed her with underlying anger. "I suppose not. You have a nice day, Ma'am."

Audra chewed her lip as he started to walk away. She was frozen in place and began to relax as he appeared to be leaving. She moved toward the cabin and heard him clear his throat. She turned to face his direction and saw he was holding something in his hand.

"You dropped this," he said with a tinge of sarcasm in his voice.

She peered at the item in his hand. Fuck. It was her driver's license. Which was in her carry-on bag she never found. She met his eyes and bolted for the cabin, hoping to lock the door behind her before he reached her. She screamed Luke's name just as the man grabbed her and threw her to the ground.

"Stupid bitch," he muttered.

She kicked him as hard as she could in the knee, causing him to buckle, then scrambled to her feet as Luke ran out to see what was going on. The man had gotten back up and pulled a gun out on them. Audra was by Luke's side and saw he had the pilot's gun in his waistband at his back. The guy laughed at them, shaking his head.

"You should've kept moving. I was able to track you because you're sloppy."

"Why would you be tracking us, asshole?" Audra spat at him, surprising even Luke. "I thought you were with Search and Rescue?"

"Shut the fuck up. I know you saw what was in the cargo of the plane since you pried it open. Dead people don't pry doors open."

"Yeah, and what was that?" Luke asked, acting confused. He hid his accent to be on the safe side. "What was in there?"

The guy had more than lost his patience with the pair of them and cocked his head. "Well, this has been real fun, but I need to get a move on. We're transporting the cargo and just need you to be dead, so there is no trace. Wrong time, wrong place, and all that."

He put his finger on the trigger and Audra had just about enough of men controlling her life.

"I don't think so, fucker," she said quietly and ran out at him, throwing him off his guard.

He went to fire but she dove and tackled him in the stomach. They fell to the ground and he knocked her in the head with his gun. He scrambled up and went to shoot her as Luke brought the gun out from his waistband and landed a bullet in the guy's skull. The guy crumpled to the ground, not moving. Neither Luke nor Audra budged for a moment and stared at the guy, half expecting him to sit back up and come at them again. He didn't. Luke stepped over to Audra, helping her up and they stood waiting. Finally, convinced they were safe, Luke turned Audra toward him firmly.

"What the fuckin' hell is wrong with you? He could have shot you, girl!" His accent came through strongly with the surge of emotion.

Audra rubbed the newly forming knot on her head and started to cry. Luke gathered her close and squeezed her tight.

"I'm not mad. That was brave as hell. I just can't lose you. We need to go, yeah? He said 'we' which means he's not alone and they'll wonder why he isn't respondin'. Where did he come from?"

Audra pointed to the woodline. Luke went over to check the area. There was a pack and radio but the guy had been on foot. They couldn't risk using the radio as he was obviously communicating with others and they didn't want to be picked up on that channel. The pack contained food and a compressed sleeping bag. Luke snagged the pack which was easier to carry than anything they had and came back.

"Let's get our stuff together and go. He was alone from what I can tell. For now. We can put distance between us and them if we leave now, like. Are you injured?"

"My head hurts, but I'll be fine. I'd rather just go."

They went in and gathered everything they'd need. They left everything else, knowing it didn't matter. They'd already been discovered and now only movement was on their side. Audra sat on the side of the bed and stared around. She started to shake, the image of the man pointing the gun at them on repeat in her brain. Luke came over, kneeling on the floor in front of her. He met her eyes.

"We're alright, yeah? You absolutely saved our lives. It was crazy and when I saw you go toward him, I thought you were gone for sure. But you weren't and he's dead. Audra, I love you. Please know that."

Audra met his eyes and nodded. She placed her hand on the side of his face. "I wasn't going to let him take you from me. We have come too far with all of this shit. I love you, too."

Luke sat up on his knees and kissed Audra deeply. She pulled back and unbuttoned her shirt, not breaking eye contact. Luke watched as she slipped off her blouse and bra.

"Luke, I need you," she whispered and drew him toward her. They moved onto the bed and took off all of their clothes, lying next to each other naked. Audra ran her hand down his chest and kissed him firmly.

"Now."

Luke shifted on top of her and she let him in. He moaned and pressed his mouth to hers as he moved inside of her. She arched toward him, needing to feel him deeper. She was desperate to be consumed, clawing at his back as he fulfilled a need she'd never had met. Luke rhythmically drove into her depths until she twisted her fingers in his hair and cried out in release. He whispered her name in her ear as he shuddered. He braced up on his arm to meet her eyes. She opened her eyes and felt a reflection of her soul in his. Luke gently placed his lips on hers and they stayed with him inside her until they both felt they could let go and still be a part of each other. Luke rolled off and pulled Audra close as she rested her head on his chest. There was no going back.

Audra got up and put her clothes back on as Luke watched her. He put his arm behind his head and closed his eyes for a moment. When he opened them, they were hooded with honesty.

"Audra, I promise to protect you with me life. I'll never hurt you intentionally and will never lay a hand on you, except out of love."

Audra stared at him, considering the weight of his words. She climbed into bed, straddling her legs over either side of him, and leaned down close to him. "I know, Luke. You're one of the good guys."

Luke pulled her down to meet his mouth and she could feel desire rising in her again. She drew back and shook her head.

"We have to go."

Luke sighed, then tipped his head. "You're right."

They finished dressing and gathered what they were taking. Luke fastened his pack with rock climbing equipment, gun, map, and sleeping bag on his back and Audra took the dead man's pack and moved the food they were bringing over to it. It was heavy but she could manage. They needed to eat. As they passed the dead man, they paused and checked his pockets. There was no identification but Audra grabbed her ID and slipped it into her pack. His uniform was weird. Not quite military, not quite park ranger. There was a patch on the sleeve she didn't recognize but took a mental picture. Snake, flag, crossed guns.

They traversed the river at a shallow point and stopped to fill their water containers, tying them off to their packs. One last look at the cabin and they headed straight for the mountains. The town on the map was almost directly across from where they were, however, the only way to it was over the mountains. Luke mapped out a trail between peaks they should be able to cut through. Audra immediately felt the burn in her legs as soon as they began to ascend and knew it was going to be tough. She rubbed her thighs and pushed on.

Luke took the lead and grabbed her hand to pull her up as they started climbing over larger rocks. He moved across the rocks like they were nothing, seeming to know exactly where to place his feet. His strength kept her moving and he made sure to spot her to keep her from falling. By the end of the first day, they'd made it a good distance and could see back down to where they'd been. They stopped to eat and Luke built a small fire behind some rocks. They had tea and beans. Even removing the one can made Audra's pack noticeably lighter. It was already well after dark, so they curled up together to sleep for a few hours. The sleeping bag came in handy as it was much warmer than the blankets and zippered closed. It was just big enough for them if they spooned together, which they didn't mind.

It was still dark when they got back up to continue on and Luke held Audra for a moment against his chest. Each day would get tougher and the climbs steeper. They tried the phones but there was still no service. The mountains were likely blocking any signals from the town, so until they crested them, they wouldn't get service. They drank their coffee quietly and Luke checked the map. His sense of direction was impeccable and his connection to the hills almost eerie. The fire was out and they loaded up, making their way through the darkness. Luke fastened a rope around his waist with a carabiner and had Audra connect it around hers as well. That way if she slipped, she wouldn't go far. He had shoes meant for climbing and hiking, but she quickly learned her Converse-style sneakers basically had no grip.

By the end of the second night, they were so high up, it made Audra nervous to look down. She was grateful for the line connecting her and Luke. They'd paused midday for him to show her some rock climbing basics on a flatter wall. He showed her how to discover toeholds and hand placements where there didn't seem to be any. He worked with ropes dropped from the top and without, not knowing exactly what they'd be facing, aware they had limited equipment. Within an hour, her arms and legs were shaking from the exertion but she liked when she'd find a placement and be able to move up. When she got to the top, she stood up and threw her arms in the air, grinning. She glanced down at Luke, who was smiling knowingly.

"You want to be me partner?" he asked, winking.

Audra stared down at him, feeling more powerful than she ever had, then nodded. "I think I already am."

Chapter Twelve

*T*hey heard the rumble of the small engine before they saw the plane. Seeing it off in the distance, they tucked themselves under an overhang and watched the approach. It was the same plane as before. They must've discovered the dead man and were searching for Audra and Luke. As it came closer, they could see the pilot and a passenger. Both men appeared to be donning the same uniform the man Luke shot was wearing. The plane made multiple passes and went on. It'd be back and they wouldn't stop until they found the two survivors. Once it was clear, Luke drew out the map to see how much farther they had to go. Another day at least, probably two. He sighed, setting the map down.

"We may have to travel at night, like. It's harder to see and more dangerous, but we don't have the veil of trees anymore durin' the day."

Audra was sitting under the overhang and rested her chin on her hand. The climb was difficult when she could see where she was going. It would be almost impossible when she couldn't. The benefit they had was that the plane couldn't land near them, so even if they saw Luke and Audra, they couldn't get too close immediately. Luke sat down next to her and rubbed her back.

"I know it's a lot, however, if they see us, they can shoot at us from the plane," he said.

She hadn't thought of that. Of course, they could. During the day Luke and Audra would be easy targets. Moving targets, but targets nonetheless. Luke dug through his pack and pulled out a headlamp. It was small but when he clicked it on it was bright.

"Won't they see that?" Audra asked.

"Sort of. If I hear the plane and click it off, we'll become part of the dark. That's even if they bothered lookin' for us at night, like. I can wear this and lead the way. We'll have to move slower, but I think it's the only way, Audra."

Audra sighed. Luke was right. They needed to stay put until nightfall, then move. They had a couple of hours until then. Not wanting to draw attention to themselves, they ate cold beans and brown bread, using up the last can of the bread. Audra thought that when they got out, she'd never eat beans again. Tired, she climbed into the sleeping bag and yawned. Luke sat peering out and for a moment she watched him. His back was to her as he perched on a large rock, surveying the area.

Regardless, with Luke, she felt safe. He used every ounce of his body and mind to make sure what he did was for the better good. *He's one of the good guys,* she reminded herself. Had she not met him, she wasn't sure she would've

even understood what that meant. He turned, smiling at her and she gave him a small wave, then closed her eyes.

A little while later, he climbed in next to her and she slid her arm around his waist. He held her hand and rubbed his thumb across her fingers.

"One day I'm takin' you home to Ireland, yeah?" he whispered.

"I'd like that," Audra whispered back.

After a few hours of rest, they got back up and readied to push on. Audra was scared and tried to shove it down inside of her. Luke made sure they were clipped together and clicked on his headlamp. It reminded Audra of coal miners she'd seen in movies, going down into the earth. She and Luke were going up, but it still felt as claustrophobic and foreign as she imagined it was for the coal miners.

She slipped and fell repeatedly, skinning her knees and bruising her ego. Luke moved slowly and methodically, but Audra couldn't see more than a few feet in front of her. She pictured taking a wrong step, dragging them both off the mountain to their deaths. Exasperated, she stopped. When Luke felt the tug on the line connecting them, he turned around. Audra was on the verge of a breakdown.

"I can't fucking do this, Luke. I'm going to end up killing us both," she said, choking back tears.

Luke clicked off his light and came back to her, putting his arm around her. "You won't."

"I will. I can't see anything and keep falling. I don't know where my feet are going."

"You're thinkin' about it too much, so. You need to feel it, like. Start trustin' your instincts."

Trust her instincts? Audra was pretty sure she'd proven those were terrible if not non-existent. She laughed bitterly and Luke sighed.

"Audra, you have this. Fuck James and his bullshit. He took advantage of you because you have a big heart. But you are also one of the most intuitive and determined people. Trust yourself. Trust me. We can do this."

He didn't wait for her to respond and clicked back on his light. He moved forward and she reluctantly followed, not having much choice since they were bound together. Trust her instincts. She stopped trying to see with her eyes and paid attention to the way the ground felt. Instead of trying to think of where to step, she allowed her feet to just move forward. Before long, it seemed like the moon was offering more light, or she'd become accustomed to the dark. She could make out Luke's outline in front of her and matched her expectations to his movements.

Soon they were deftly moving over boulders, her hands finding finger holds and her feet firmly stepping on any variation in the rock. Instead of being tugged along by the rope between them, it fell slack and she was moving with Luke rather than against him.

They climbed until the sun tinted the sky and found a place to tuck into. Audra was tired but exhilarated from finding her connection with the mountain. Luke built a tiny fire and heated up water. They ate fruit and had coffee as they watched the sunrise. Making sure they weren't visible, they spread out the sleeping back and climbed in. Audra faced Luke, resting her head against his chest.

"Thanks for not giving up on me... for pushing me."

Luke laughed softly. "I can't very well leave you behind, can I?"

She smiled. "I suppose not. You're stuck with me. At least until we get back to civilization."

"Why would that change anythin'?"

Audra considered the question. Out here it was just Luke and her in their own world. A messed-up world but theirs nonetheless. Once they got back, though, she was still married. James would be after her and she had nowhere to go. Luke was more or less transient, going where the climbing took him.

"Do you have a place that is home here in the States?" she asked.

"No, I suppose not. Adam and I would just crash at his apartment between climbs. Now that he is gone, I don't know what I'm doin', so. I think I need to go back to Ireland for a bit and regroup, yeah?"

Audra felt panic tug at her. If he went back to Ireland, that would leave her alone to fend against James. She nodded, however, didn't speak. Luke had his life and she had hers. Luke stiffened up and drew back.

"Audra, I'm not leavin' you, like. You need to finalize things with James, but I want you to go with me."

"To Ireland?"

"Yeah, I told you that earlier."

"I thought you meant some random time in the future."

Luke laughed, eyeing her. "I mean, it will be some random time in the future, yeah, but when I go, I want you to go with me."

"Oh."

"I won't make you go, but I'd like to share that part of me life with you."

"Luke, I want to. Out here everything makes sense. I'll still have to face James and file for divorce. He may try to kill me."

Luke was silent for a moment, then tightened his arm around her. "Neither of us will let that happen."

The image of Audra running at the man with the gun and Luke shooting him in the head came to her mind. She knew he was right. The days of James controlling her life were over. She'd kill him if she needed to, but she wouldn't go back to that abuse. She'd survived a plane crash, faced off with a mountain lion, and taken down a man with a gun. James's little bitch ass was no match for her, now.

She reached up and wound her fingers in Luke's curls and fell asleep against his chest. She dreamed they were being chased over and over. In one of the dreams, she turned and saw the man with the gun leering at her, his mouth in a twisted dark grin as he raised the gun to shoot her. All of a sudden, she felt herself transform, morphing into the mountain lion. The man's eyes grew wide with fear as she pounced on him and ripped out his throat. When she woke up, she felt a sense of urgency to get back and confront James.

Luke was still asleep, so she peered up at him. His eyelashes created little arches against his lower lids and he breathed peacefully. He hadn't had nightmares since that night they talked about the crash and Adam dying. She unzipped the sleeping bag and started to slip out when his hand reached out and pulled her back in.

"Not yet," Luke said sleepily and opened his eyes.

Audra met his eyes and knew. They slid off their clothes and wrapped into each other, the warmth of their bodies heating up the sleeping bag. They kissed until their bodies demanded more and Audra climbed on top of Luke, feeling him fit inside of her. She moved, placing her hand on his chest and leaning her head back as he matched her rhythm. He ran his hand over her breasts and drew her down to his mouth. She was on the verge when he flipped her over and thrust until they both released. Audra rested her hands on his buttocks and stared up at him.

"I love you," she said simply. It hadn't been long since they'd first laid eyes on one another, and they only knew each other out there, but she meant it.

He brushed the sweaty hair from her face and kissed her forehead. "You and me, Audra. It's us now, yeah?"

Not hiking during the day gave them time to talk and relax a little. They napped when they could and practiced rock climbing, making sure to listen out for the plane. It came by a couple of times during the day but they ducked under covering until it passed. They made love as often as they wanted, taking time to explore each other. A thought hadn't occurred to Audra and when it did, she knew she needed to bring it up to Luke.

"I'm not on birth control."

He glanced over, raising his thick eyebrows. "Oh, yeah, that's probably somethin' we should think about."

"I never got pregnant with James, so I didn't use any. I didn't think about it because of not being able to get pregnant, but I guess there is always a risk."

"In nine years you never used birth control and didn't get pregnant?"

Audra shook her head. "No. I really wanted a family, so we tried right off the bat, but it never happened. After a while, I kind of just thought it was me."

Luke considered this. "If you don't mind me askin', when was the last time you had a period?"

"I guess a few weeks before the crash. I haven't since and was due before we were together the first time. I should've had it, but it never started."

"Maybe the crash stressed your body so much it threw it off?"

"I guess. I've heard with athletes and any major trauma a period could stop for a while."

"Are you worried?" Luke asked honestly.

Audra thought about it, however, with so many years of disappointments over having kids, she hadn't even considered it as an option. "I don't think so. I think the chances of me getting pregnant are pretty much non-existent. Are you worried?"

Luke shook his head. "Not about that. To be honest, if we make it out alive and in one piece, I think a lot about me life is goin' to change."

"Like what?"

"Like livin' for only meself and rock climbin'. Rock climbin' is still of the utmost importance, but I don't want to do it by meself, like. I want to explore the next phase of me life."

"I understand. I think we're both on the cusp of some pretty big changes. What do you want the next phase to be?"

"I want to move back to Ireland. Not just a visit, I'm ready to go home and I can travel for competitions. I want to think about a family, so."

Audra listened and thought about their earlier conversation about her going to Ireland with him. She'd assumed he meant for a visit. What did this mean for them?

"Luke, I-"

"Audra, I don't want to be without you, yeah? I want you to move to Ireland with me."

Chapter Thirteen

*A*s they climbed, Luke told Audra about growing up in Ireland. His family history and how some of his extended family moved to the States. However, his grandparents on both sides wanted to stay and raise their children in Ireland. His parents felt the same. He wanted to eventually raise his own children there, as well. He talked about how other countries viewed the United States and how while he loved the land and expanse, he didn't feel it was the ideal place to live. Audra never thought about it that way. Being raised in America, she was always told that it was the best country in the world, but could see Luke's point. Americans had become so obsessed with consumerism, it was hard to step outside of it. He didn't press her about moving to Ireland, but never denied he wanted to spend his life with her. She was sure she loved Luke, but she needed to face her current situation before she could know where she wanted to be.

Or *who* she wanted to be.

The one thing she knew for sure, was that Luke had become the closest friend she'd ever had in her life. She confided in him like she'd never confided in anyone. He listened without judgment, however, also reminded her when she needed to look inside herself. He offered alternative views for her to consider and presented questions she hadn't thought about. After a night of hiking and climbing, they stopped but weren't ready to sleep, so Luke made them tea and they watched the sun come up. He eyed Audra and stretched his legs out in front of him, leaning against a rock.

"What are you goin' to do about James?" he asked without leading the conversation.

"I don't know exactly. I'll file for divorce immediately, then figure out how to protect myself. I don't know how he'll react, but he probably won't just take it. I can get a restraining order... not sure that would stop him. I need to stand up to him. I think it's the only way to end this." The words sounded right, but she wondered how she would carry them out.

Luke nodded and took a sip of his tea. "I won't tell you what to do, or intercede unless you ask me to, but I won't let him hurt you either, Audra."

"I know you won't, but you can't be around me twenty-four seven. Eventually, he'll find me alone."

"Do you have any reason to stay in Spokane, or Boise for that matter?"

"Not really. I was only going to Boise to get away from him. I had a job at a daycare in Spokane, but I'm not committed to it. My parents are in Oregon now, so there isn't anything to go back to. I guess I need to stop running to be able to know where I belong."

"Fair enough. You haven't had a chance to figure out who you are, yeah?"

"I haven't."

"What are things you dreamed about as a child or things you like to do?"

Audra thought about it. She was a really active child, always playing some sport. She liked pushing herself to the brink. However, that wasn't a career. She loved children and working with them but didn't love daycare as it was all about cramming as many children into a space to make a profit. She shrugged, wrinkling her nose.

"I don't really know. I wanted to have children and I like rock climbing with you. Otherwise, I guess I saw work as something I *had* to do. To pay the bills, you know? What about you? Other than rock climbing, what do you want to do?"

Luke laughed, shaking his head. "Nope, that's it. I have been singularly driven to rock climbin' since I was a child, like. I've thought about openin' a climbin' school, focusin' on adults and children with disabilities."

Audra liked that idea. It was the best of both worlds. It piqued her interest and she raised her brows. "That sounds amazing. Now, that is something I'd love to be involved with."

Luke grinned. "I want to do it in Ireland."

Audra got the hint and snickered. She licked her finger and made an imaginary line in the air. "That's one for Ireland."

"Well, I'll be there, too."

"Okay, that's two for Ireland."

Luke rubbed his chin. "I'll think of more, won't I?"

"I'm sure you will," Audra replied, hoping he would.

They bedded down and Luke sighed into her hair. "We should get over the top tonight. Maybe get cell service."

Audra glanced up at him, feeling butterflies in her stomach. "Really?"

"Yeah. Only issue from what I can tell, is the last leg is straight up and we can't use any equipment."

"Why?"

"Because I'd need to go up to anchor at the top since I'm missin' equipment. There honestly isn't a safe way to do that. I'd need to free-solo to get up there, anyway, and not sure I'd be able to set a sturdy top anchor once I did. Then you'd be stuck at the bottom, so. I know I can do it free-solo and you're goin' to have to, as well. I want to make sure I'm right behind you in case you slip. We'll be connected by a rope, like. I can guide you from below."

"What if I fall?" Audra asked, terrified.

"Then we're both goin' down because while I can get up the wall, I can't hold us both."

"Is there another way?"

"Not that I can figure out," Luke answered, meeting her eyes.

Audra chewed her lip. "So, we're just looking for places to put our hands and feet with no safety net?"

"Pretty much," Luke said quietly. He knew she was afraid but there was no other way.

"Okay."

He hugged her tightly and she allowed herself to trust they could do this. If they could, she'd never doubt herself again. After all, she was doing it with two arms and he was doing it with one. He'd be right behind her, guiding her the whole way. Because of the risk, they agreed they'd have to do it with some daylight, especially with her going up first. They insisted they still be connected with the line, despite the fact it wouldn't be able to save either of them. If one went, the other was going, too. It was more symbolic of their journey and neither wanted to go on without the other. Luke had already lost Adam and Luke was all Audra had in her life. They slept while they could, then fueled up with coffee. When it was time to conquer the hopefully last leg of their journey, nerves drove them into silence.

Audra sat down next to Luke while they had coffee, placing her hand on his leg. She wanted to feel him close and knew once they started the climb, even though they'd be close in proximity, they'd be on their own. Luke smiled at her and tucked her hair behind her ear.

"You can do this, Audra. I believe in you. I've seen you conquer everythin' thrown your way since we first met. It's one placement at a time."

"Have you ever done this before?"

"Not like this. Adam and I did free-climbs but not with so much at stake. They were fun, like. We scoped them out prior and practiced with equipment. This is new, but I know we can do this, yeah? We can take our time and I'll be right there with you."

"I know you will. I guess we don't really have a choice, so there's no point worrying about it. There's only one way out and it's up," Audra said.

Luke grinned at her. "Spoken like a true rock climber."

They pushed nerves aside and began to plan their ascent. Even if they got to the top and there was no cell service,

the rest of the way to the town was down which was easier and faster. They risked being seen while they were climbing, however, they needed to be able to see to spot any textures and rock formations they could use to get ahold of the rock. Luke would primarily use his feet, using his one hand to brace himself and his legs to push up. Audra, being less experienced, felt like he was still going into it with a better chance of not falling. She tried not to think about it.

They moved in the dark before sunrise as far as they could, so they'd arrive at the wall right as the sun came up. Audra could see the rock wall looming in front of them as they drew closer, growing bigger and bigger. There was no way they could scale it. Maybe Luke could, but she couldn't. She paused and stared, totally psyched out.

Luke stopped, giving the rope a tug. "This is the worst part. Bein' close but not close enough, yeah? You're seein' the big picture of what we'll be climbin' in increments. Trust me. Once we get closer and you tune in, you'll see nothin' but the variations and textures on the rock you can grip onto. You'll be face to face with the opportunities."

"If you say so," Audra muttered, irritated at his confidence.

"Hey, I'm scared, too. It never isn't dauntin' but once we start climbin', you'll be too focused to be scared."

Audra nodded and trudged forward. As they got closer, Luke peered at her shoes, appearing concerned. "Those shoes are goin' to be detrimental. They're too flat and hard, like. You won't be able to grip as well."

"They're the only shoes I have."

"We can go barefoot."

"Barefoot? That's crazy."

"Think about it. We use our bare hands, so we can feel the slightest bump and fissures on the rock. Our feet are the same, Audra. I'm goin' barefoot, as well. These are fine for hikin' and the climbs we were doing, but I'm better off barefoot, so. We both are."

"Fucking hell, Luke. Anything else you want to tell me before we get there? Am I going to have to climb upside down, also?"

Luke chuckled. "That's the spirit."

"Haha."

They continued on, each in their own heads as they approached the wall. When they got to where they could no longer climb with their shoes, they stopped and removed them. Audra tied hers off to her pack and peered up. It was fucking straight up. It was still dark, so they sat and talked for a bit. Audra needed to work out tension and went over, grabbing Luke by the hand.

"Before we do this and risk our lives, I need you."

She kissed him on the mouth, placing her hand on his groin. It didn't take more than that and they took each against a rock. Luke unbuttoned Audra's blouse to expose her to himself and nature. Audra gripped his hair and pulled him to her. Fervent, desperate, and all-consuming.

They allowed the fear and anxiety inside of them to be expressed on each other, grasping and trying to become one. Luke covered her mouth with his and as he let go of himself, he bit her lip gently. She responded in kind and could taste the metallic tang of blood on their lips. They lay gasping on the rock next to each other, half-clothed and fully spent. Luke rolled to face her and rubbed his thumb across her lips, wiping away a mixture of their blood.

"Sorry," he whispered.

"Don't be," she replied, gently kissing his bleeding lip.

They knew it was time as the sun was rising above the trees. They fastened their clothes and made sure their packs were securely clamped on their backs. If anything fell, there was no going back. They made sure they had their chalk bags, powdering their hands and feet. Luke ran his hand along the wall to feel for areas to start the climb. Audra watched and wondered how Luke planned to stop her from falling if she did. There really was no way, he just knew he wouldn't keep going if she did. That's why he wanted to be underneath her, to try and if he couldn't, they'd go together. It wasn't romantic, it was not wanting to be the one left alone.

Audra saw Luke do a quick sign of the cross in front of him and cocked her head. "I didn't know you were religious?"

"I'm not but was raised in the Catholic church, yeah? Part is tradition, part is *why the hell not* if I might die?"

Audra nodded and repeated the motion he did. Why the hell not? She moved to the wall and found her first finger holds. Her bare feet quickly found the first lip and she started up the wall. Part of it was exhilarating, most of it was terrifying. Luke was right, very quickly her only focus was finding her hand and foot placements, then pushing herself up. There was no energy for anything else. She was clipped to Luke and felt the rope get taut as she moved and loosen as he followed below her.

No matter what, they were together in the fight of their lives.

Chapter Fourteen

*E*ach step was a marathon. Audra could feel the sweat dripping down her back and falling from her brow. She kept her eyes forward and up, only glancing down once to check on Luke. He was expertly finding crimps and holding on to the rock with his one arm. He used his other shoulder and stump to create leverage and his feet to push. She was in awe but couldn't pause to take it in.

It was slow and painful, each movement up felt like an accomplishment. Luke shouted words of encouragement which she took to heart. He pointed out variations in the rock she didn't see initially. They each were facing their greatest challenge. She prayed they both make it to the top. If they did, she'd never let him go. She'd go to the ends of the earth with Luke. She'd move to Ireland.

There was no place to rest, no chance to stop. Her arms were exhausted, however, she'd found a rhythm and pressed on. Find finger holds, grip, foot placement, push. Pause, breathe,

do it over again. And again. And again. The rock was the earth, everything else was just air.

One slight misjudgment and she'd lose the earth until she found it in falling, taking Luke with her. She tried to think of something else. She remembered being a teen and running track, how the hurdles freaked her out. Over and over, she'd run toward them, then chicken out last minute, picturing herself tripping and crashing to the ground. It wasn't until she looked past them to the finish line, she was able to clear them. They couldn't exist to her. The finish line was all that mattered.

The finish line. She peered up and tried to see the crest but it was still out of view. It wasn't the finish line, yet. Every ascension step was. It wasn't one race, it was hundreds. Each time she pushed up, she gave herself a gold medal in her mind. She wanted to pause to rest her arms, however, even stopping was taking every muscle in her body. She felt tears streaming down her face and let it out. This was the hardest thing she'd ever done and probably would ever do. Luke heard her crying and yelled out.

"I love you, Audra. You're the strongest person I know, and you're blowin' me mind. Keep goin'. When we get to the top, I'm goin' to hold you forever, and I'm takin' you to Ireland."

Audra laughed through her tears and took another step. "If we make it to the top safe and sound, you can take me anywhere."

"*When* we make it to the top, I'm holdin' you to that, yeah? Now, get a move on, girl," Luke teased.

"I love you, Luke," Audra whispered, as she pushed on.

It seemed like hours and Audra glanced up, surprised to see she could view the edge of the top in the distance. They were so close. It was full daylight and now they risked being seen, as well. She took every bit of energy in her body and pressed toward the end. When her fingers finally gripped the edge, she almost couldn't believe it and cried a different kind of tears. She used her feet to push herself over the edge. Once she was safely up, she leaned over and watched Luke in his ascent. He was nearing the edge and she mentally took a deep breath.

A moment too soon.

She felt the rope tug at her and looked down. The foothold he'd been balancing on gave way and the bits of rock crumbled beneath his feet, leaving only a sheer wall. He had his feet pressed against the wall and his hand was clinging to the finger hold. That was it. He had no way to push up and his strength was going to give out, having to hold his weight primarily with one arm. He was using friction to brace himself in place but sweat was making his feet slippery. She could see his arm straining to grasp on, and his feet were beginning to slide. He'd pull one up at a time to get a better grip, but it would only help for a few seconds. He stared up at Audra with fear in his eyes. He couldn't hold on much longer. He met her eyes, defeated.

"Unclip."

"What? No, Luke. You can do this."

"Fuck, Audra, I'm slippin' and if I do, I'll drag you over the edge. Fuckin' unclip."

"No! You go, I go," she replied adamantly.

Luke shook his head and tried to adjust his feet. In the distance, Audra could hear the plane engine. Shit! After all, they'd done, it couldn't end like this. She was being dragged by the rope connecting them, giving her an idea. She rotated to reduce the length between them, wrapping the rope around her waist tightly. She was right up to the edge now and the line was taut. She braced her legs, determined.

"Luke, I need you to listen. When I count to three, I need you to push up with all your energy, everything you got. I'm going to use my body to pull backward at the same time to try and get you to the edge."

"Audra, you're too light. If this doesn't work, then I'll be killin' us both, like."

"I know. Trust me."

Luke bobbed his head, his arm shaking with exertion, every vein visible. "Right, when you say three, I'm givin' it everythin'. It's heaven or hell from there."

Audra knew what he meant and could see the plane in the distance approaching. She took a deep breath and yelled, "One, two, three!"

On three, she dug her heels in and yanked back with all that was in her. Luke pushed as hard as he could with his legs as his feet slipped on the smooth service. He used his arm to pull up, using the weight against the rope to project himself upwards. It wasn't much and Audra started to feel herself being tugged forward when she saw Luke's fingers grasp at the edge. She wanted to reach out and help, but her weight against the rope was the only thing keeping them from going back over the edge.

She threw her full body weight against the rope, leaning back comically. Luke found a small lip to get his feet on and shoved upwards and over the edge, Audra's weight catapulting them backward to safety just as the plane came clearly into view. Luke got up and grabbed her hand, guiding her to the nearest covering as the plane flew over. The pilot looked right at them and turned to the passenger.

The plane circled back as Luke and Audra scrambled into a group of boulders and hid between two. They'd been seen, but the plane couldn't land too close. The plane came back, however, not seeing them, went away. They knew it was going to land and they'd be followed, but they had time to move. Luke gazed at Audra and they started to laugh. Almost maniacal laughter from the stress. Luke hugged her and kissed her as hard as he could. He drew back, shaking his head.

"You're insane, yeah? Thank God you are, but you're totally fearless."

"It's like this, Luke. Do you think if you'd fallen to your death, I would've had any reason to go on?"

"You really feel that way?"

"You know I do," Audra insisted.

"Good. Me too," Luke replied, meeting her eyes.

"Can we rest for a minute? My legs are jelly."

Luke peered around. "Let's just move from where they last saw us. I could use some coffee."

They walked for about twenty minutes, found an area with trees, and sat under them. They made the last of the coffee and checked the phones. Still no service, but they were on the other side of the mountains and the town was only about twelve miles away. Hopefully, as they got closer, service would come through before the battery died. One phone was already toast, leaving them the last one. They ate cold beans and let their arms and legs rest. It was a small reprieve, knowing they needed to keep moving, but Audra felt like they'd climbed for days. They finished and got ready to head on. They slipped back on their shoes, both of their feet raw and blistered. Audra winced in pain. When she stood up, her legs buckled and Luke caught her before she fell.

"Damn, I'm spent," she muttered.

"I got you. Let's move slow and I'll grab you if you start to fall," Luke promised.

"How are you able to move?"

"At this point? Sheer determination to get out, so."

Audra could understand that and walked forward. Each step was excruciating and she tried to focus on Luke's hand on her waist. They heard the plane overhead and stayed out of view. Now, it truly was a race to the finish line. By evening, Audra was on the verge of collapsing and they decided to check the phones again. No service. Audra was ready to lose it and began to bawl. Luke held her while she cried.

"Audra, we're close. Let's stop for a bit and regroup. Even if we never get service, we'll make it to the town."

"What if they find us first?"

"Then I'll fuckin' shoot them, yeah?"

Audra nodded and wiped her nose. She knew he meant it. They'd had just about enough of other people's shit.

"You really are a badass, Luke."

He laughed, wiping a tear off of her cheek. "Takes one to know one, right?"

They bedded down and held each other tight. Before the sun rose, they woke and sat up.

"My God, every muscle in my body is screaming," Audra griped. Her hands were raw and her feet were swollen.

Luke was about the same. They were out of coffee, so he made them tea and they ate a can of green beans. It was disgusting, but Audra was past the point of caring. She was so bruised and battered, everything was going through the motions. Eat to shut the stomach up, move to stay safe. She'd lost track of time and couldn't remember basic things. Much longer and she felt her brain would totally slip.

"Luke, when was the crash?"

He looked at her weirdly, thinking about it. "I don't remember. A month maybe? More? Fuck, me brain is fried."

So, it wasn't just her. She couldn't form a timeline. Day and night were only defined by sunrise and sunset. It was all becoming a blur. Now, it was just her and Luke in an alternate reality. If someone said they were still in America and people were somewhere in a coffee shop miles away, talking about the latest movie they'd seen, she would've laughed. It felt like they were in another country or another time. Separated from their own world. Luke took her hand and flipped it over, peering at the blisters. He rubbed his thumb across her palms and squeezed her hand gently.

"You ready to go?"

"No," she replied honestly. "But this is our new reality. We'll spend the rest of our lives just walking and eating canned food."

Luke laughed. "The canned food is about to run out, but you may be right about the walkin', yeah?"

"Not funny."

He leaned forward and kissed her. "No, it's not. We have a few hours before the sun comes up. Let's see if we can find cell service."

Audra sighed and forced her shoes back over her swollen feet. They managed to get upright and slip their packs on. The packs were almost empty and the water down to just a bit at the bottom of one bottle. It was lighter but for the wrong reasons. Audra ignored the pain and took Luke's hand as they headed in the direction of the town. As the sun came up, they stopped and drank the last of the water. It was beautiful and in any other circumstance, it would've taken their breath away. Instead, they watched for a moment and pushed on. Daylight wasn't their friend and they were tired of running.

As they made their way down the mountain, Audra turned on one of the cell phones and blinked. She stopped, causing Luke to turn around.

"You alright, Audra?"

She held the phone up so he could see and he moved closer, his eyes wide.

She peered at the screen again, it was there. It was only one bar, but there was service! It was password protected, however, had the words *emergency calls only* on the screen. She dialed and put the phone to her ear. She almost screamed when a voice came on the line.

"911, what's your emergency?"

Chapter Fifteen

*A*udra stumbled through, explaining who they were and where they were located when Luke took the phone and gave coordinates from the map. He let them know they were being chased and they needed medical and police assistance. Search and Rescue were being sent. Fearing stopping would put them in danger, Luke told the 911 operator they were going to keep moving along the route to the town. There looked to be a highway they were heading toward and could meet the emergency vehicles there. Audra wanted to stop but Luke was right, stopping made them a target. Knowing they were just moments away from safety, gave her the push she needed and they picked up the pace.

They could see the highway a distance away through the trees and headed for it as they heard the plane circling overhead. There was a clearing between them and the highway they'd have to cross. They paused under the trees, hearing sirens in the distance. Surely, the plane would leave, now. It didn't, so Luke and Audra knew they were going to need to make a run for it. An ambulance was coming down the road and they didn't want it to bypass them. As it drew closer, Luke met Audra's eyes, then nodded.

They bolted across the clearing and were about halfway when shots rang out from the plane. Audra kept her head down and continued running with Luke behind her. She heard him curse and glanced back. He was hunched over but still moving across the field. They made it to the highway just as the ambulance was about to miss them and started yelling. It hit the brakes and veered over to the side of the road. A Search and Rescue vehicle came behind and police after that.

The plane was gone.

Luke collapsed at the edge of the road and Audra went back to him. He'd been shot. Paramedics rushed over and checked him out. The bullet had ripped through his right shoulder but exited fairly cleanly. They helped him up and got him to the ambulance. Another paramedic for Search and Rescue checked Audra out, but she was trying to talk to the police officer.

"Did you see that plane?"

The officer peered into the sky and shook his head. "Not really. Why?"

"Uh, they were shooting at us?" she replied, impatient and frustrated.

He looked at Audra like she was delirious. "Why?"

"Long story, but there was cargo in the plane we were in that crashed, they don't want people to know about."

"What kind of cargo?"

"Plutonium."

His eyes grew wide and he stepped away to make a call on his radio. Audra was escorted to the ambulance where Luke was being treated.

"Your friend insists you ride with him in the ambulance," the paramedic told her.

Audra climbed in and Luke was sitting on a gurney, trying to reach out to her. He'd been shot through the shoulder with the arm and couldn't lift it. She slid in next to him and took his hand.

"What are the odds, am I right?" he joked.

"Not funny, Luke. Good thing you have me."

The ambulance jolted as it pulled onto the highway, knocking Luke into Audra. She leaned against him and wound her arm around his waist. They watched through the back doors of the ambulance, as where they came from got smaller and smaller in the distance. They'd made it out alive.

Once they got to the hospital, Luke was whisked away and Audra was brought into a curtained room in Emergency for a full check-up. The nurse checked her vitals and asked about any injuries. Except for feeling beaten from head to toe, Audra didn't have anything specific. The doctor came in shortly after and checked her over. The leg wound was healed over, however, they wanted to make sure the muscle repaired correctly and wouldn't cause excessive scar tissue which might restrict movement in the future. Audra asked about Luke but no one seemed to know.

A police officer came in later with a man in a suit and asked a lot of questions. About the crash, about the cargo, about the people following them. Audra described the plane and the uniforms the people were wearing. She told them about the man attacking her and Luke at the cabin, and how they had to shoot him. She remembered the patch and sketched on a notepad the best she could. The man in the suit, Agent *Somethingorother,* seemed very interested in that and stepped out of the room. The police officer leaned back and eyed her.

"The plane you were on crashed way off course. Any idea why?"

"Why would I know that? I didn't even know what our course was supposed to be until Luke showed it to me on the map."

"Lucas Riordan? Your companion?"

Audra nodded. She didn't even recall Luke's last name prior to the cop saying it. "How is Luke?"

The cop looked at his notes and shrugged. "In surgery, I think."

Surgery? For fuck's sake, she needed to see him. She watched the door anxiously. The cop continued writing notes as he asked her to repeat the details of their experience since the plane crash. Audra was ready to scream.

The man in the suit came in and said something in the police officer's ear, not meeting Audra's stare. The cop got up and left as the man sat down.

"Audra, Letsky right? I see that from your intake paperwork."

"I prefer Banner."

The man frowned but nodded. "So, you weren't listed as a passenger on that plane?"

"No, my friend booked the ticket for me."

"May I ask why?"

"I was going to stay with her and didn't want anyone to know," Audra answered honestly.

"Is there a reason you didn't want anyone to know?" the man asked, seeming suspicious.

Audra sighed. "Look, I don't want my personal business out there, but I was leaving a bad situation. It was for my safety."

The man eyeballed her and made a note on his pad. "Do you want to tell me about it? Strictly confidential."

"My husband liked to beat the shit out of me, okay? I was running for my life."

"Your husband? Is that James Letsky?"

Audra nodded, swallowing hard at the mention of his name. She almost expected James to pop out from behind the door to grab her.

"He reported you missing. Has been on the news and leading the way in searching for you," the man replied.

"It doesn't mean anything. He's one person in front of the world and another behind closed doors," Audra insisted.

The man looked up and squinted his eyes at her. "How do you know Lucas Riordan?"

Audra laughed, almost too loud. "How do I know Luke? Our fucking plane crashed and we were the only survivors. That should already be somewhere in your notes, shouldn't it?"

"You didn't know him before the plane crash?"

"How would I have known him prior? We were total strangers when we boarded that plane. He was going rock climbing with his friend Adam, I was running from an abusive husband. We didn't even speak a word until after the crash."

"No one is accusing you of anything. We're just trying to define why there were people using a passenger plane to transport plutonium."

"I think the question goes the other way. Why was there plutonium on a plane transporting passengers?" Audra spat.

"That too."

"Did you get it? The plutonium? Why was it there?"

"I can't get into details, but the people you saw are a homegrown terrorist group. They were planning to use the plutonium for nefarious reasons."

"Nefarious reasons? What does that even mean? Like a terrorist attack? Here in America?"

The man watched her but didn't respond.

Audra sighed, frustrated. "If it wasn't for me and Luke, you wouldn't even know about it. What is going on?"

"Long story short, we got the men in the plane that shot at you and most of the plutonium. Looks like they may have shifted some already. Mr. Riordan was able to provide coordinates to the crash in the ambulance and we caught them on site. As soon as you sketched the patch, we knew who we were dealing with. They've been on our radar."

"So, now what?"

"Day in the life for us. You prevented a lot of deaths, though. This was planned to be large scale."

"Like a bomb?" Audra asked, her blood running cold. That couldn't be it.

The man shrugged. "Something like that. You'll probably hear more later. This is a big deal to national security, so you may be required to testify."

He stood up and shook her hand. "We'll be in touch. You'll need to stay local for a bit until this gets sorted out."

Local? She didn't even know where she was. He gave her his card and left. A nurse came in to check on her and Audra asked about Luke.

"I think he's just coming out of surgery, now. I can take you to the recovery room if you'd like?" the nurse offered.

"Please, I want to be there when he wakes up." Audra stood up and winced, the bottoms of her feet feeling like someone had used an electric sander on them.

The nurse led her down a series of hallways and showed her to a small waiting room outside of recovery. "I'll let them know you're here, waiting to see him."

"Thank you," Audra said and sat down in a corner. She almost dozed off when a nurse came to the door.

"Miss? You're here to see Lucas Riordan?"

Audra nodded and rose. She moved painfully toward the door on her bandaged feet, following the nurse into the recovery room. Luke was at the end in a bed by the window. He was still out of it and Audra pulled a chair up next to him. His shoulder was bandaged and his head cocked to the side, unaware of her presence. His hair was tangled and she reached up to loosen it with her fingers. He stirred and opened his eyes, meeting her own.

"Audra," he whispered.

"Hey, you're out of surgery. No one has told me anything."

Luke nodded and grinned. "We made it, yeah?"

"We did."

"Ireland. You promised."

"I did. But, hey, those guys chasing us? Terrorists. The plutonium? Bomb. Or, something like that. I'll tell you more later, but we can't leave town yet. As soon as we can, though? Ireland."

Luke tried to move his shoulder and winced. Audra squeezed his hand.

"Stop doing that, Luke. Let it heal."

Luke laughed weakly. "Easier said than done, like."

They moved Luke to his own room which also had a fold-down bed for visitors. More police came, with more questions. Luke and Audra repeated everything they knew, over and over again. It almost felt like *they* were on trial. Finally, visiting hours were over and everyone left. Audra tried lying on the fold-down bed but had been next to Luke for a month straight and missed his presence. She gazed at him lying in the bed.

He looked over and smiled. "Come on then, love."

She got up and climbed into his bed with him. He smelled like home to her. She buried her face in the curls at his neck and rested her hand on his chest. She leaned up to kiss him and they held their mouths together, not wanting to be apart. It was at this moment the door opened, and the nurse from earlier spoke.

"Mr. Letsky, your wife is in here."

Audra felt fear grip her stomach as the voice she hoped to never have to hear again rang out.

"What the fuck do you think you're doing, Audra?" James said with venom in his words.

Chapter Sixteen

*A*udra bolted out of the bed and stood in the middle of the room like a child caught with their hand in the cookie jar. James glared from her to Luke, clenching his fists as his face turned a dark red. Audra froze, fear keeping her stuck in place.

Luke spoke low and clear from the bed. "If you fuckin' touch her, I'll kill you."

James laughed and sneered. "I sincerely doubt it."

Audra moved to the door and opened it. James followed her out, giving Luke a dirty smirk. They faced off in the hall, the nurses' station far enough away to not notice them.

"Are you fucking kidding me, Audra? I've been distraught and beside myself with worry about you. Then I drive for hours to find you in bed with a cripple."

"Don't call him that!" Audra spat, her earlier fear giving way to rage.

"I'll call him whatever I damn well please."

"If he hadn't been shot, he could beat your ass, James."

"Well, lucky for me he got shot then, huh?" he retorted, smug satisfaction crossing his face.

Audra felt heat rising in her cheeks. "I want a divorce."

"Fuck you. You're coming home with me and that's final. You're *my* wife and I don't need this shit from you, right now. Stop all the drama, Audra."

"I want a divorce," Audra repeated more firmly.

"Well, I won't give you one," James said and grabbed her by the arm, digging his fingers in. "No one would want you, anyway. You look like shit with your hair like that."

Audra felt doubt creep in and took a step back. She remembered what Luke told her about how James was using mind games to control her, then laughed. She yanked her arm away. "Go to hell, James. Luke wants me, I want me. That's all that matters. You can't control me anymore."

James leaned in close, his blue eyes sparkling with intent. "You want to bet? I'll hunt you down and I'll murder you."

The image of turning into the mountain lion in her dream came to mind and she chuckled. "I fucking dare you."

James made a move toward her and she reeled back, slapping him as hard as she could across the face. The sound of her hand hitting his skin echoed in the hallway and a nurse peered around from the station to see what made the sound. James jerked back and the expression on his face was almost comical. He put his hand to his cheek, glaring at her. The nurse watched, trying to determine if she should step in and James waved her away. She looked at Audra for confirmation and

Audra put one finger up in the air to have her hold on. James had no moves left at this time. He glanced from the nurse to Audra, then set his mouth in a small, tight line.

"This isn't over. You either go with me or I *will* make sure you can't be with anyone else."

Audra leaned toward him, forming her eyes into slits. "Oh, you're done, James. I have pictures and videos of what you did to me. I'll send them to your work. If anything happens to me, I have friends who'll make sure they go public. I'll send them to your parents, to your coworkers, to anyone you know. I have years of pictures of bruises and black eyes. The finger marks and cuts. Every goddamn mark you ever made on my body. You'd better fucking run and hope I never get the urge to share them out of spite. You *will* grant me the divorce and quickly. I'm filing in the next day, or so, and every week that passes that you don't sign them, I'll send the pictures with a play-by-play of the abuse to someone you know. Starting with your parents. Let them see their son isn't the golden boy they thought he was."

James flinched at this. The world thought he was a hard-working, loving husband. His parents had no idea he beat his much smaller wife. Audra could see the shift in his eyes from wanting to kill her, to wanting to cover his own ass.

"You're such a bitch. I fucking hate you, anyway," he said quiet enough, so the nurse couldn't hear.

"Good, it'll make this that much easier. I'll have the papers sent to our home. If I don't get notice you got them, I'll have them served to you at work. As soon as we are done here, I'm filing a restraining order against you. So, unless you want me to go to the news about your tendencies, I'd recommend

going on and driving back home to be there for those papers. I don't want anything from our life, so do with it what you want. Don't ever speak to me again, James."

He paused, thinking of something to say but saw all the cards had been dealt. He glared at her and turned to walk down the hall. He stopped and turned back. "I hope you die. I hope your cripple dies."

Audra laughed forcefully. "That's all you have, James? Go fuck off."

He turned crimson and continued down the hall. She watched as he pressed the elevator button and waited, knowing she'd won. The elevator was taking a long time and she leaned against the wall, enjoying he was the one in the headlights. Finally, he stormed off and headed for the door to the stairs. He threw the door open and went down. Audra waited outside of Luke's room for a bit to make sure James didn't reappear. After a few minutes, she walked to the nurses' station.

"I need to speak to the police. That was my soon-to-be ex-husband and he threatened to kill both me and Mr. Riordan. I need to place a restraining order on him. I was on that plane escaping from his abuse. He can't be allowed anywhere near us."

The nurse nodded and picked up the phone. After she called the police, she set the phone and eyed Audra. "Are you okay?"

"I will be. Once I know he can't be around us."

"I'll make sure. I'll let security know as well, in case he shows back up at the hospital."

"Thank you. I don't think he will, but it's better to be safe at this point."

"Please let me know if you need anything else," the nurse said kindly.

Audra smiled and went back to Luke's room. She knew he wanted to be able to help, to intercede, but was unable to with his arm strapped to his side. She opened the door and slipped in. He met her eyes with apology.

"No, Luke, this was my battle all along. If you'd been able to step in, he'd never have been convinced. I needed to stand up to him. You've been my strength all of these weeks and reminded me I have something to live for. That's what I needed to be able to face off with him."

"Is he givin' you the divorce?"

"I believe he will. I threatened to expose him to everyone. Can we not talk about this, right now? Can I just lay with you?"

Luke motioned with his head for her to come next to him. She climbed into the bed and rested her head on his non-injured shoulder. He freed his arm enough to put it on her and leaned his head against hers. She felt the shakes coming on as the nerves she'd pushed down to stand face-to-face with James started to come up. Luke stroked her arm with his finger and talked softly to her.

"Audra, the fearless. No one can hold you down, yeah? Thank you for lettin' me in and lettin' me love you. It's been the best gift of me life and I'm grateful to have found you. I never want to let you go, so. It's you and me forever if you'll still have me."

Audra peered up and met his eyes, his kindness and vulnerability breaking her heart just a little. "Have you? I want you, Luke. For the rest of my life."

He smiled and kissed her on the forehead. They fell asleep, holding on to each other gently. They were awoken by a soft knock at the door.

A female police officer poked her head in. "Hey, I was told you wanted to file a restraining order?"

Audra nodded and sat up. "Yes, thank you. Against my estranged husband. He has threatened my life. And Luke's."

"Okay, so two restraining orders?"

"Yes, and can I file a report of the threats he made?" Audra asked.

"Of course. That pretty much goes hand in hand with the restraining orders. Why don't you tell me what happened between you and Mr. Letsky?"

"This time or the time he beat me before?"

"Let's start with this time and backtrack."

Audra started to speak her truth, beginning with the incident in the hall and going back to the start of their relationship. She was still sitting on the bed with her back to Luke. He had his fingers resting against her back for emotional support. She didn't cry like she thought she would. It was replaying a movie of who she'd been. She wasn't that girl anymore. *She* was her protector. The officer took notes and had them sign the papers for the restraining orders. She glanced up at Audra, her face serious.

"I just have to let you know, in my experience, the restraining order doesn't always stop them. You need to get somewhere safe. Maybe a shelter?"

"No, I'm not running anymore. I told him I'd expose him if he came near me again. That if anything happened to me, I had a friend who'd release the pictures of what he did to me to his work, his parents, and everyone he knew. That I had pictures of all of the injuries."

"Oh, that's good. Can you show them to me, so we can put them in the report?"

Audra started to laugh and the officer looked confused. Audra shook her head. "No, I can't."

"Why? It doesn't have to be right now," the officer explained. "Whenever you can get them to me."

"No, it's not that."

"Oh? What is it then?"

"They don't exist. I was lying to him."

"Ah, I see. So, there are no pictures of your injuries?"

Audra shook her head. "No, but he doesn't know that. I scared him enough into believing I do. Using the tools I have to get free."

The officer nodded, smiling slightly. "I'll put that you said you have pictures in the report and leave it at that."

They finished the paperwork and she handed Audra the copies. "I wish you the best. If anything else comes up, please let us know. I saw what you went through from the previous reports and I have a feeling you'll be alright. Really impressive."

After she left, Audra sat on the bed and faced Luke. She put her hands on either side of his face and kissed him. He put his head back and cocked his head slightly, drawing his eyebrows together.

"How could you ever have doubted yourself? It was hard hearin' about what James did to you, but that was not the Audra I know. To be honest, I'm intimidated by you. By your strength, yeah?"

"Don't be, Luke. You're part of the reason I'm this me. You helped me see I was worthy. James broke me down systematically over years until I didn't know who I was. You allowed me to find myself again. I did it, but you held my hand the whole way. You were my partner."

"I hope I still am."

"Whether we're climbing mountains, chasing off wild animals, fighting off strangers, or not strangers, I want to be with you."

"Well, I hope maybe it's not all that. Maybe just climbin' and raisin' a family, like," Luke replied, then chuckled.

A family? Audra watched him carefully. She'd started her period that morning, which was for the best. She wanted time with Luke. Alone. She nodded and chewed her lip.

"Maybe one day. Right now, I want to go on adventures with you."

"Fair enough. Me too. A family can happen whenever and however. I'm in no rush. Besides, a family starts with two," Luke replied.

She'd never felt that with James. They were married but they weren't family. He didn't have her back. Luke would die for her, she knew that. They had proved that to each other. She leaned against him and rested her hand against his thigh.

"First, we heal. Then we can decide what is next. At this moment, all I want to do is appreciate being here with you," Audra murmured, feeling his warm breath against her shoulder.

"With your hand on me thigh," Luke whispered in her ear.

Chapter Seventeen

*A*udra told her parents everything. Her mother cried. Her father wired her money for an apartment. She filed for divorce. As it came up on a week, she worried James would call her bluff and she had nothing to expose him with other than her words.

On the seventh day, the signed papers arrived at her lawyer's office. It was over. He didn't contest anything, however, she didn't ask for anything, either. Except for her freedom. So, why didn't she feel free? A thought tried to push to the forefront of her brain but she could never catch it. Luke was released a week after his surgery. He'd have gone sooner, but the physical therapist wanted to work with him since he only had one arm and it was in a sling. Luke played along, knowing he could use his feet if he needed to. He humored her until she signed the release form.

After his release, Audra took him to the apartment she'd secured. It was within walking distance and since they didn't know what the future held, it was the only month-to-month rental she could find. It was a dump.

It was about the same size as the cabin they'd stayed in and didn't have much to offer. The floors were all linoleum and it was unfurnished except for a stove, where only half the burners worked, and an old, very loud refrigerator. Audra bought an air mattress, a folding table, and a couple of camping chairs. It was temporary. Once the police didn't need them anymore, they'd be on the move again.

Other than the money her father had wired her, she was broke. She and James shared a bank account but she no longer had access to it. Her car had been impounded in Spokane for unpaid parking tickets. After paying the deposit and month's rent on the apartment, she was down to a couple hundred dollars and put a dent in that for groceries. She'd have to look for work as soon as she could.

She opened the door to show Luke and could see what was either horror or humor on his face.

"I know it's not much, but it's month-to-month and all I could afford. I got us chairs, a table, and an air mattress. I didn't figure we'd be here long."

Luke started to laugh. "It's perfect, yeah? We don't need much and I want to get out of this town as soon as possible."

"About that. I only have a little over a hundred dollars left, so I'll need to go get a job," Audra said, helping him in.

"Audra, I have money, too."

"You do? From what?"

"From competitions, sponsorships, that sort of thing," Luke explained.

"I don't follow. For rock climbing?"

Luke nodded. "Yeah. I make an income between placin' in competitions, appearances... stuff like that."

"I didn't know that was a thing."

"Not for everyone, but I've made a name for meself, so. I do pretty well," Luke answered.

"So... do I need to go get a job tomorrow or are we okay for a month?"

"We're fine for a month. Longer, yeah? As I said, I didn't have a home, so I was stashin' that money away. We are goin' to be alright."

"Oh. Well, either way, that's your money. I need to figure out how to make ends meet," Audra replied, getting flustered. She didn't want Luke to think she expected him to cover her bills.

"Audra, I need your help right now until I can use me arm fully again. If you leave me alone, I may not be able to open a door or make food, like. While we're here, can we put a pin in you gettin' a job, so you can assist me? I really need your help. Once I'm healed, and we're allowed to leave, I'd like to get the hell out of this town and go from there. Start our lives together."

"I can do that. I guess I hadn't considered that. I brought your rack here and bought some dishes and clothes from a thrift store. I think we're okay for now. We can take it a day at a time."

"Just so you know, I have thousands of dollars saved. I'd like to open the rock climbin' school with most of it, but we have money to live on. I don't want you worryin' about anythin'," Luke offered.

Audra blushed and looked away. She didn't want to be dependent on anyone again. Have anything held over her. Luke read her mind.

"Remember, if you weren't here, I might lock meself in the bathroom and never be able to get out. You're me arm, at the moment."

Audra met his eyes and could see he was trying to not laugh. She smiled and kicked him lightly with her foot. "Fair. We don't want that happening. Do you need anything, now?"

"Actually, I do need to use the bathroom, yeah? You mind helpin'?"

Audra walked to the bathroom door and swung it open. "Do you, uh... need any other help?"

Luke shook his head. "No, it's awkward, but I can manage. I'd like to have a shred of dignity left."

He went in and Audra shut the door behind him, leaving it cracked so he could push it open. She went to the kitchen and made them sandwiches for lunch. When Luke came back out, he sat in one of the camping chairs and grinned at her, leaning back in the chair.

"Livin' the high life?"

"Haha, very funny. I worked with what I had. I didn't know you were flush with cash."

"Not flush, but I do alright, so. Get paid for what I love the most. Well, now the second most."

Audra placed the sandwich in front of him and sat in the other chair. Luke was struggling to lift the sandwich to his mouth but compensated by leaning down close to it. He adapted. He always did. His shoulder was still in a loose sling but the physical therapist devised it in a way Luke could still move his arm as much as the injury would allow. Which meant he could raise his elbow to about halfway, then needed to twist his fingers up to get closer to his face. His shoulder was still immobile. Audra wanted to help but knew he'd only let her when he absolutely had no other option.

By bedtime, it became apparent he was unable to get his shirt off. Audra stepped in and slid it off his left shoulder, over his head, and down over his arm, being careful not to pull or bump the injured shoulder. He didn't have to sleep with the sling, so she helped take that off, as well. The surgery had been to remove bone shards and repair injured tissue, so he had a bandage on both sides of the shoulder. Audra ran her fingers over his collarbone and down his arm gently, avoiding the bandage. Luke flinched and tried to move his hand to take hers, but he couldn't reach. Audra rubbed her fingers across his palm and met his eyes. She pushed him back on the air mattress carefully and unbuttoned his pants, sliding them off. Luke watched in silence, unable to stop her if he wanted to, which he didn't.

Audra paused at his underwear and raised her eyebrows for permission. He nodded and she slipped them off, running her hands up his thighs. Injured or not, his body responded. She stood back and took off her clothes. She lay next to him and ran her hands down his body. He attempted to touch her but was limited. Audra put her hand on his arm.

"Just let me do this, Luke. I want to."

Luke let his arm drop and gazed at her. Audra took in the beauty of his body, every inch of muscle that was used. Countless scars from climbing and lines showed he used his body to its full extent. When neither of them could take her

hands wandering over his body, Luke whispered her name with desire. Audra eased her legs over him and guided him inside of her. It had been since before the free-climb that they'd been together. Even though she didn't want to rush, they both were brought to climax quickly. Audra collapsed on his chest. He rested his hand on the small of her back, breathing out deeply. No words needed to be spoken.

Audra eased down next to him with her hand on his chest. She could feel Luke breathing rhythmically and realized he'd fallen asleep. She pulled the sheet over them and listened to the sounds. The fridge humming, Luke breathing, sirens not too far off. He'd been in the hospital for a week and she'd gotten used to the constant interruptions and questions. She'd been anxious to get into their own place, however, now the irrelevant sounds were giving her anxiety. She sighed and got up, slipping on her clothes. The silence was too thick. She went to the window and stared out. She got the feeling she was being watched and spun, expecting Luke to be up, but he was still in a deep sleep. She couldn't shake the feeling and peered out at the road below. It was empty, except for cars going by. She closed the blinds and stood out of the window view. It was nothing, she told herself and climbed back in next to Luke.

The next morning, she went to look out the window and was greeted with a benign city street view. Nothing out of the ordinary. People going to work, waiting for the bus, chatting about the weather. No one was watching her. Luke was up and joined her at the window.

"What are you lookin' at?" he asked, peering out.

"Nothing, really. I just had a weird feeling last night and am reminding myself it was all in my head."

"What was the feelin'?"

"That I was being watched," Audra replied, the words feeling heavy in her mouth.

Luke turned to her, his face concerned. "Did you see anyone?"

"No, it was all in my mind, I think."

"Wake me up next time, like. I don't want you feelin' like that alone."

"I will, Luke. It's nothing, really. Just processing everything we went through."

"Yeah, there's that. Still, I'm here for you."

Audra smiled up at him and placed her hand on his cheek. "I know you are. Let's change those bandages."

Luke sat and let Audra switch out the bandages. The wound was healing nicely and Luke tried his shoulder out, being able to move it a little more each day. He put it back in the sling and thanked Audra. She kissed him on the top of the head. In another week, he'd be able to use his arm and they could plan the next move. They knew about the investigation around the terrorist group and plutonium but weren't privy to any more information than that. Still, they were asked to stay local until charges were filed and proceedings were in place. They were the only witnesses since everyone else died and it put them in a precarious situation. Ireland would have to wait.

Audra headed down to the convenience store at the corner for some cleaning supplies. As she was walking back, enjoying the sun, she got the same feeling from the night before and glanced around. No one seemed familiar or was paying her any mind. Fear gripped her stomach and she picked up the pace back to the apartment. As she rounded the corner into the apartment breezeway, she thought she saw James standing across the street and started to run. She threw the apartment door open and slammed it shut, startling Luke.

"Audra, what the flyin' fuck? Are you alright?" His voice was confused and concerned.

"I thought I saw James!"

"Where?"

"Out there, across the street," Audra said, her voice wavering.

Luke peered out and shook his head. "I don't see anyone. Do you think you were followed?"

"I don't know."

"Let me just take a quick walk out there. I'll be right back." He checked the breezeway and street where she came from. He came back, shaking his head. "I don't see him or anyone that looks like him. Could you have been mistaken?"

"I guess. I was already freaked out, thinking I was being followed and maybe I got myself worked up," Audra replied, feeling foolish.

"Come here, yeah?"

Audra walked over as he drew her in the best he could.

He rested his cheek against the top of her head as he spoke. "It's goin' to be fine, like. You just got spooked for a second, that's all," he assured her.

Audra sighed and bobbed her head. He was right. She was just worn out from everything. That was all.

That night, when she woke up screaming in terror and clawing at the air, it became very apparent to her that wasn't, in fact, all.

Chapter Eighteen

*T*he nightmares continued night after night. Audra was always being chased or finding Luke murdered. Sometimes, she was being chased by the mountain lion, sometimes James. Other times, it was countless random people in vans in the shadows. At times, she'd think she was awake and would roll over to find Luke dead, his eyes gazing at her, hollow and lifeless. She felt knives, gunshots, and assault from all angles. It got to the point where she was afraid to sleep and would hold out until her eyes refused to stay open. Luke tried everything with her. Meditation, calming tea, holding her while she slept, however, nothing changed. She felt like she was losing her mind.

During the day, violent thoughts haunted her. She checked the door was locked a couple of times an hour and was afraid to stand in front of the windows. She refused to leave after about a week of the nightmares, so Luke took over any errands they had. Even inside with the blinds closed, she felt like she was being watched. Luke was concerned and asked if she wanted to talk to someone.

She shook her head. "No. They may think I'm crazy and want to lock me up. I just need to work through this."

"Audra, they won't lock you up. Maybe it would help to talk about what you went through, yeah?"

"I can't, Luke. I just can't. Not with strangers."

He stared at her, his eyes worried, then nodded. "I'm here for you, so. I hate seein' you go through this."

Audra smiled at him blearily. He'd been there for her, but the intrusive thoughts were taking over. Before long, she felt like that was all she might be. It was getting worse, she was slipping farther away from him. It didn't help that the police were still asking questions and the people chasing them had only partially been charged. It was a huge organization that believed the country was falling to hell because of moving away from conservative values, and they intended to take it down from the inside. The guys who shot at them were arrested, however, not the heads of the organization. For all Audra knew, they could be tracking her and Luke, planning an attack.

Then there was James. He completely fell out of the picture, which wasn't like him. She would've actually felt better if he was around making threats because at least then she'd know where he was. Now, he was like a ghost. A ghost who might be right around the corner. Waiting, planning. Every time Luke went out, she sat in one spot clenching her fists until he came back, convinced he wouldn't. Every time a door opened or closed in the hallway, she was sure someone was coming after them. Even in the shower, she left the curtain half open, so she could see out.

She and Luke hadn't been intimate since the nightmares began. She felt like she was trapped inside an outer shell, which she couldn't connect to. Luke held and kissed her, but she couldn't find her way to the surface. He didn't press, however, she could see he was growing increasingly concerned. As he should... she was slipping into the madhouse. At one point, he found her staring from the corner of the blinds and came up behind her. She involuntarily flinched at his touch and he turned her around to face him.

"Audra, if you shut me out, I can't reach you, like. What is it?"

"I don't know. I just have this feeling. We're being followed, they're waiting until everything dies down and are going to kill us."

Luke sighed, then peered out the window at the street. Nothing was amiss. "Audra, it could be in your head. I'm not sayin' it is, but I haven't seen anyone followin' us. I think because we needed to run so much to save ourselves, your brain still believes it's happenin'. I've been out, yeah? I don't think anyone is watchin' us. You're sufferin' trauma like I did after Adam died, except it continues in your wakin' hours. You need to find a way to let this go and set yourself free."

Audra turned to him and stared. It wasn't that simple. What if he was wrong and they were being tracked? What if she let her guard down and it cost them their lives? Maybe he was the one being unaware and foolish.

"Luke, you don't know that. We could be in danger! They know we have information against them. You're making assumptions because you want life to go back to normal. That's stupid and arrogant."

Luke seemed genuinely taken aback by her words. "Audra, that's not fair. I went through all this, too, and I'm not bein' stupid or arrogant. That's hurtful and I don't deserve you givin' out to me. I'm tryin' to move past this and have a life with you. We can't do that if you're locked in what happened to us. I can't seem to reach you and it's breakin' me heart."

He put his hand out to her, but she pulled away.

"Maybe that's the problem, Luke. Maybe *you're* delusional and putting us in harm's way. We can't have a life together if you can't see what is truly going on."

Luke eyed Audra, his expression pained. He shook his head as he walked over to the small kitchen counter, grabbing his wallet. He turned back to her. "I won't dignify that with a response, yeah? I think it's best if I go out for a bit."

He went to the door and waited for her to say something. She didn't. He opened the door and left. Audra wanted to run after him or cry, but she was frozen by the window, feeling numb. She saw him walk down the street, then disappear around a corner.

While she waited for him to come back, she paced the floor, replaying scenarios in her head. Who was following them, how they'd be tortured and killed. How the police were in on it. She cleaned the apartment from top to bottom and paced some more. It had been a couple of hours and Luke still wasn't home. Had they caught him? She thought about calling 911 but worried that would give her away.

By nightfall, she was frantic and watched the street for Luke. He was nowhere to be seen and she was sure he was never coming back. She realized she was scratching her arms until they bled and went to the kitchen to put the kettle on. She began telling herself he was going to be fine. Pictured him walking in the door. This helped her move from only shallow breaths to deeper ones. She sent him messages in her mind and willed him to walk through the door. He didn't.

After a cup of tea and some more pacing, she lay in bed and stared at the ceiling. What if he'd given up on her? For the first time in over a week, she felt tears come to her eyes and experienced something other than fear. She felt regret. She ran her mind over the feeling and pictured Luke. She allowed herself to feel shame for her words and knew she didn't truly mean them, though, at the time she thought she did.

Hours passed and Audra dozed off from exhaustion. She didn't hear Luke come in and set bags down. He made his way to the bed and watched her sleeping. Audra was woken up by his arm covering her and pulling her to him. She murmured his name. He whispered gently to her.

"Audra, I'm not givin' up on us. I know what you're experiencin' is very real to you, and you're not willin' to step outside yourself to see that it isn't. At least some of it, like. So I'm forcin' you to. Sleep now, in the mornin' we'll talk."

Audra listened, knowing there was no response. She laid her cheek against his chest and slid her hand over his waist. She didn't know what was in store in the morning, but for now, she was glad he came back. She fell asleep holding on to him and praying the nightmares away.

The mountain lion's teeth were sinking into her arm as she jolted awake. A scream caught in her throat. Luke sat up next to her and held her like he always did. The sun was starting to inch into the sky. Once he knew she was okay, he climbed out of bed and made coffee. Audra came over and sat in one of the chairs, eyeing Luke. He handed her a cup of coffee and sat across from her.

"I'm goin' to talk and need you to listen, Audra. First, we need to address the cycle you've gotten yourself locked into. You can't get out, so I want you to smoke with me. To let your brain calm down, like."

"Smoke? Weed?" Audra asked, confused.

"Yeah, you need to give your brain a break, so. It's firin' on all cylinders and it's like a car about to hit a wall at full speed. Will you do that with me?"

Audra nodded. That's exactly what it felt like inside her head and she needed relief. They finished their coffee and Luke packed a glass pipe with marijuana. He lit it and handed it to Audra.

"Take one hit and see how you feel. We'll go slow until you feel like your brain is calm, but not so much that we can't work this out."

Audra took a hit and handed the pipe back to Luke while she held it in. Within seconds, she could feel the grip on her brain loosen a little. He motioned to the pipe to see if she wanted to take another hit. She nodded and he handed it back to her. She drew in a small one and knew she was good. She was still clear but her brain was no longer a spinning firecracker. Luke sat the pipe down and leaned forward.

"Are you alright to talk about this?" he asked gently, reminding her of when he first found her at the crash site.

Audra bobbed her head, clasping her hands together tightly. Luke reached out and covered her hands, helping her to relax. She met his eyes, waiting for him to speak first. Luke smiled and rubbed her fingers.

"Yesterday I went for a walk after we argued. I was hurt, then realized the words you said had less to do with us and more to do with the fear cycle you were in. So, I tried to think of other ways to reach you. I thought a lot about Adam. How when we'd come to new challenges and fear would overtake us, we'd psyche each other up, darin' each other to take the first step. Adam, he really was me brother, you know? Losin' him put me in a downward spiral. Had it been other circumstances, I don't think I would've pulled out of it. The image of him dead, like. Had I not had our survival to focus on, I may have lost me mind or me life. Do you understand where I'm comin' from?" Luke asked firmly.

Audra did and she didn't. Luke lost Adam which made him crazy, but since they needed to be on the run, he couldn't let it take him down. However, she didn't have that. They'd stepped back into an almost normal, mundane life. She had no refocus, nothing driving her away from the fear and mental spiral.

"I mean, I understand that survival saved you after Adam died, but what the hell am I trying to survive, Luke? Getting groceries?"

"Inherently that's the issue, yeah? You went from a hundred miles an hour to zero, and your brain can't comprehend it. It is still in fight or flight mode and there's nothin' to fight or flight against. So, it's creatin' things, scenarios to feed that void."

"That doesn't make sense. Why would it be doing that? That seems counterproductive."

"It is counterproductive, but when you're used to bein' in that mode, the chemical in your brain reacts to it. Your

162

chemicals, your brain, are still reactin', so. I think. I mean, I'm no doctor, but it makes sense. It's like adrenaline junkies, they get accustomed to that feelin' or chemical balance and have a hard time comin' out of it. You're stuck in a perpetual state of fight or flight, like."

"How do I stop being in that?"

"Outside of goin' to a doctor and them tryin' to adjust your brain chemically?" Luke asked.

"I won't do that. Since something caused my brain to react this way, there has to be some way without medication to get it to stop reacting that way," Audra insisted.

"Is there no part of you willin' to go the traditional route and talk to a doctor?"

"None. I don't trust they'd be able to help and don't want to be dependent on medication. It's just not who I am," Audra replied.

"That's fair. I'm the same way, yeah? I was just makin' sure before we moved forward."

"Move forward how?"

"I have an idea. It goes back to what I was sayin' about Adam and me. In order to get over the intimidation of a new climb, we had to face it. Once we started climbin', we saw that the fear holdin' us back was just that, fear, and could be overcome. We called it *catchin' the earth*. Makin' the abstract fear turn into concrete power by usin' our bodies to connect to the rock. Steppin' outside of our thoughts. It was the abstract, the unknown, causin' us to be afraid. The moment we touched the rock and caught it in our minds, the fear slipped away, like. The exhilaration of accomplishin' the climb was more powerful than the fear."

"Okay. So, what are you getting at?"

"Do you trust me?" Luke asked, locking on her eyes.

Audra nodded, that had never changed. Luke stood up and went to the bags he'd brought in the night before. He handed one to Audra and she opened it, peering in. There was a fresh rack of climbing supplies and a pair of climbing shoes in her size. She stared up at Luke, thinking she understood what he was getting at. He grinned at her and tipped his head.

"Believe, trust, conquer."

Chapter Nineteen

*A*udra watched as Luke went through the equipment, explaining how each thing worked. They'd climbed when they'd been on the run, but that was just the basics to move with the limited equipment he had, then. Now, he wanted her to understand the proper technique for safety. He was in his element as he laid everything out and went over different uses, knots, and adjustments. For him, it was an extension of himself. For Audra, it was a lot of things to keep track of. However, she wanted to do it. Needed to.

To find a purpose and a distraction.

Luke showed her how to load the rack and went through the different types of shoes. Though, he pointed out, her regular shoes were shite and barely worthy of walking on the street. This made Audra laugh. They both stopped when she did and Luke's mouth hung open.

"I've really missed that laugh," he said as he touched her cheek.

Audra hadn't truly laughed in weeks. She smiled at him and glanced away, feeling vulnerable. They changed clothes and loaded up to head out for the climb. Audra was fine until they went outside, then panic rose in her. She must've appeared off because a lady on the street stared at Audra attempting to catch her breath until Luke gave the lady the evil eye. He put his arm around Audra.

"Hey, you're alright, yeah? Here, I have somethin' to show you."

Audra peered up at him and furrowed her brow. What could he possibly have to show her? He firmly grasped her hand as he led her to a side street. He pointed and she glanced to see at what but didn't understand.

"Luke, stop messing with me. What's going on?"

"See that little silver truck at the end with the dented bumper?"

"Yeah?"

"I bought it. We need to have transportation and it was the right price, so."

Audra stared at the truck. It was a two-seater with a small bed that had seen better days. "It runs?"

"No, Audra, I bought us a truck that doesn't run, so we can just sit in it, like."

"Haha, very funny. I take that as a yes."

Luke kissed her and rattled the keys. "You ready? Let's go climb!"

They loaded in the truck, throwing their packs in the back. The inside seats were cracked but the radio worked. Luke turned it to a station playing a mixture of music and fired up the truck. It ran rough, but it ran. Audra glanced at Luke's shoulder. The bandages were off and he was moving it. Not as much as he had before being shot, but enough to function. He grinned at her. He was thrilled to go climbing again and his excitement was infectious. Audra smiled and peered around. The feeling crept in as they drove out and she kept checking the rearview mirror, expecting to see them being tailed. If the middle-aged, blond woman behind them was following them, she didn't act like it. Audra chuckled to herself at this thought.

It was a distance out, and before long they were outside of town by themselves. Audra took a deep breath, it'd be easier to see anyone watching them out here. She relaxed and gazed out the window at the mountains. It was a clear day and cool. It was going to be okay. A car passed them, coming the other way and Audra casually looked at the driver. The driver seemed to glare back at her and she grabbed Luke's leg. He frowned at her, confused, and she pointed at the car. He glanced at it, then shook his head.

"Audra, that's nothin'. Just a guy and his family on a drive."

Audra looked again and noticed children in the backseat. She sighed. "You must think I'm off my rocker."

Luke laughed. "Well, maybe not off your rocker, like, but for sure rockin' away."

Audra stared at him, then burst out laughing. "Fuck off, Luke."

Luke met her eyes, winking. She sat back and left her hand on his leg, gentle this time. The windows were cracked and his curls were blowing around his face. She reached out and caught one in her fingers.

He cocked his head at her. "What?"

Audra blushed. "You know, when I first got on the plane and saw you, I was pretty enthralled by your hair. It corkscrews at the end."

"Me sister was so mad I got this hair and hers was straight. She said boys shouldn't have such pretty hair. Truthfully, I fight it turnin' into dreads all the time."

"It's beautiful. I like that you leave it long," Audra confessed.

Luke watched her. "Cheers, Audra. I'm glad you like it. I like yours, too. I love the rich, coffee color."

Audra remembered how for years she'd done everything to change that color. She secretly called it turd brown, but Luke's description was better. She glanced in the side mirror and considered it. Her hair fell well below her chin now and she liked how it swung at all one length. James had always made her feel so plain.

"Luke?"

"Yeah?"

"Can you tell me about the first time you saw me? What you thought?"

Luke chewed his lip, considering the question, then nodded. "I first saw you in the little airport space. You were clutchin' your bag and avoidin' everyone. At one point, you were watchin' the door and I was able to truly see you, without you noticin', like. You pushed your hair out of your face. For the first time, I saw your eyes and was caught by their beauty. Your eyes are like a lioness's. A golden copper. With your dark hair, you were so strikin', I couldn't stop starin'. Like no one I'd seen before. I wanted to talk to you. You didn't notice me then, though."

She hadn't. She'd been so afraid James would come through the door, she'd stayed focused and ready to run. She hadn't even noticed the other passengers until they boarded. Then, she was ashamed to remember, she'd been focused on Luke's one arm. But she *had* noticed his hair, and like his sister felt, thought it was too pretty to be on a guy. Now, she wanted nothing more than to wrap her fingers in it.

"I'm embarrassed to say, I stared at your missing arm. Does that make me a terrible person?"

Luke laughed. "Only if you and everyone on earth are terrible, so. It's natural to notice, at least you're open to talkin' about it. Most people stare, turn red, and won't talk or even make eye contact with me. You made eye contact on the plane. I remember. You gazed at me with those soulful eyes and smiled. I looked away, so I didn't make a fool of meself."

Audra glanced down, smiling to herself. She remembered that, as well.

They drove in silence until they pulled into a lot and parked. Luke had scoped out a good easy climb to start and looked at the trail map. Audra got out to stretch, relieved they were the only ones out there. She grabbed her rack out of the bed of the truck and got everything on. She'd switch out her shoes right before the climb. Luke came around and wrapped his arm around her.

"Can I ask you somethin'?"

Audra looked at him, cocking her head. "Sure?"

"Does it bother you?"

"Does what bother me?"

Luke laughed softly and shook his head. "Audra, me missin' arm, like."

169

"Why would that bother me?"

Luke stared at her for a moment, then leaned in to kiss her. "See? That's why we work, yeah?"

Audra smiled, a little confused by what he meant. He took her hand and they hiked to the climb. Once they were there, Audra felt a familiar panic and stared up. It wasn't the climb, it was that the last time they had, they were bargaining with their life. She shook it off and listened as Luke explained the process. He'd lead, creating a path and she'd clip in behind him. It sounded simple enough, though she knew it wouldn't be that easy.

Luke got on his gear and peered up to map out the best course. He started up the wall, using his one arm to grip and the other shoulder to brace. He was fluid and made it appear flawless. Audra waited until he started getting chocks in, then followed behind. The rock was cool and rough, with lots of finger pockets and lips to climb on. As soon as her feet were up, she felt a shift in her as her focus honed in on the rock. She clipped in as she got to the anchors and continued up. Nothing mattered except the next section.

Luke peered down at her. "You alright?"

"Doing great. Easier than last time," Audra joked sarcastically.

"Understatement of the year," Luke quipped back.

Audra could see the injured shoulder was giving him trouble and he couldn't fully extend it yet. Even so, she was still moving slower and more clumsy than he was. They climbed for a couple of hours before she realized she hadn't felt like she was being watched since they began. She knew as soon as they got back to the apartment, that feeling would come back but was relieved for even a small reprieve. They stopped for lunch at the top and decided to hike the rest of the day. Both of them were beginning over in a way and there was no rush. Luke was out of competitions at least until his shoulder fully healed, possibly longer.

Audra gazed out over where they had come, then sighed. Maybe they should just stay out there. Luke finished off a sandwich and stood up, stretching his arm up toward the sky.

"That felt grand. Like comin' home," he said.

It had felt good. Powerful. Audra stood up beside him and they put their arms around each other.

"Thanks, Luke. It was good for my brain to have to focus on something else."

"I know it won't change overnight, but we can come out as much as we need to. And when we're allowed to leave, we can go find other places, so. There is a whole world out there, Audra."

Audra stared out across the mountains and trees, nodding. This had been their world since the crash but it didn't have to be. They could leave, disappear. Start a new life, just the two of them. That alone gave her some hope out of the cave she was in.

"Ready to go down?" Luke asked.

"For sure!"

He helped her get ready to rappel down. She was nervous putting her feet at the edge, however, as soon as she let go a bit it was exhilarating, hopping and sliding down to the bottom. Luke climbed down, removing any of the equipment they'd used. He wanted to leave it as they'd found it. They packed up their racks and switched out shoes. They hiked until dinner time, then headed back to the truck. They hadn't seen another person all day and Audra was grateful for it.

The ride into town was nice with the sun setting and they picked up a pizza on the way in. Once back at the apartment, Audra felt claustrophobic and peered out the corner of the window at the street. She knew it wasn't going away after one day of climbing, but she hated it overtook her when she walked back in the door. The empty street stared back at her, but she didn't believe it.

Luke set the pizza on the counter and clicked on the radio. He came over to Audra at the window, moving her away. He drew her in close to him and began to sway to the music with her. She smiled gratefully at him, resting her head against his chest.

"I don't know what I'd do without you, Luke. You put up with a lot of shit."

Luke chuckled, his chest vibrating. "True. But for you, I'd climb mountains. Oh wait, I already do that, yeah? For you, I'd fall out of a plane. No, done that, too. For you, I'd fight off wild animals. Hmmm, got that covered, so. Let me think. For you-"

Audra slapped him playfully. "I get it!"

"Hey, for me you were willin' to take a bullet, so I think we're even," Luke teased.

Audra gazed up at him and smirked. "I didn't know it was a competition."

Luke leaned in and kissed her, rising feelings in her she'd shut down for the past couple of weeks. Her mouth responded and they danced to the music with their lips connected. Breathless, Audra let go and rested her eyes on

Luke's face. His eyes were so kind and open as he moved his hand to her cheek.

"Audra, if this is a competition, then I'll always win because at the end of the day, I have you. You're mine. That's the ultimate prize."

Chapter Twenty

The nightmares continued and Audra was existing on fumes. Luke encouraged her to smoke when she was anxious, which helped during the day hours. At night, she could fall asleep easily but was awoken in the early morning hours in a panic. Then, afraid to go back to sleep, she'd sit up for hours. She learned to scream into her pillow, so she didn't wake up Luke every time. He'd insist on staying up with her and they both were running out of energy. One night, after a particularly bad dream where she found Luke murdered and his other arm sliced off, she couldn't take it anymore. She bolted out of bed and went to the kitchen to hide her sobs. Luke heard and followed, pausing by the refrigerator, his brows knitted in concern.

"Audra, come here."

He held her while she cried, but she was too afraid to tell him what her dream was. She shook her head and pushed him away.

"I'm a fucking lost cause, Luke. You'd be better off without me."

"Since that's not an option, let's just talk about it, yeah? What was the dream?"

Audra knew she'd either need to lie or just tell him because he wasn't going to let it drop. "I was being chased down the street and trying to get home," she stammered.

"By who?"

"It's always the same. I don't know. I just know someone, or something, is after me. And I run. This time, though, I made it home and ran in."

"That's good, isn't it?" Luke offered.

Audra shook her head, staring at the wall. "No. I ran in and shut the door. It was dark, so I turned on a lamp and you were dead on the floor. Your eyes were open, looking at me."

"Yeah, that's scary. However, I'm here and I'm safe, so."

"There's more. Whoever killed you in the dream had cut off your arm."

Luke winced at this. "That's a little gory. Why do you think that was in your dream? Because I'm missin' me other arm, like?"

"I don't know. Maybe so you couldn't protect me? Maybe because it was the most sadistic thing my brain could think of?" Audra responded miserably.

It *was* sadistic.

Luke nodded and pulled her to him. "Perhaps. So, in these dreams, you feel out of control and alone?"

"I guess. If you're in them, you've been murdered," Audra whispered, not wanting the words to carry weight.

"Which puts you back to bein' alone, yeah? I think you haven't faced how you feel like your life is not within your control. That if I leave, you're on your own."

Audra thought about it. That seemed about right.

Luke sighed. "Let's give you back some control. Tomorrow on our climb, you lead the way up and tell me what we're doin', step by step. I won't help at all. You're the guide. Alright?"

"Okay."

Audra peered up at Luke and felt a need to feel close to him. They still hadn't been intimate and Luke hadn't pressed, knowing she needed to make the first move. She was scared to bridge the gap now that it'd been so long. She sighed, frustrated, then pulled away.

"What's goin' on?" Luke asked, meeting her eyes.

"It's nothing. Just my stupid shit."

"What specifically? Talk to me," he persisted.

"I just fucking want you and don't know how to get back there."

Luke watched her, then tipped his head. "You tell me. You're in complete control and I'll do what you ask."

Audra felt silly and blushed. She took a deep breath. "Hold me."

Luke moved in and pressed her to his chest. She could feel his heart beating through to hers. She placed her hand on the small of his back, which settled her breathing. She glanced up at him.

"Kiss me. Hard."

Luke leaned down and took her mouth with his. He didn't let her up for air and she started to feel her knees buckle

as desire washed over her. She gripped his back and moved toward the bed.

"I need you to take me. Don't be gentle," she commanded huskily.

Luke took her hand and guided her to bed, pushing her back on it. He slipped off her underwear and hovered over her, watching her face for assurance. She placed her hand on the side of his face.

"I need this, Luke, to feel you. To feel alive. Safe."

Luke bent forward and kissed her softly as he entered her. Audra pulled him fiercely in. He was not gentle but respected her body in ways she couldn't understand. He put his mouth on her breasts and thrust continuously until she felt like she couldn't breathe. She felt consumed by him and let herself go to every motion, every sensation. She wanted to tell him to stop but didn't want him to. It was the cusp of pleasure and pain she wanted to go on forever. She could feel him close to climax and grasped his buttocks forcing him in even deeper as she cried out with the waves that washed over her. Luke shuddered and met her mouth. He braced on his elbow, running his fingers through her hair. They were saturated with sweat and breathing heavily.

Audra stared at him and wouldn't let him look away. "You're mine, Luke. No one gets to take that away from me."

Luke smiled. "I'm not goin' anywhere."

They lay side by side, holding hands as they let their bodies cool down. Audra turned and put her leg and arm over Luke's naked body. She gazed down in admiration and ran her fingers down his stomach. He laughed, grasping her hand. He turned to meet her and put his arm over her, sliding his leg between hers. It fit perfectly. Audra moved in as close as she could and kissed his shoulder.

"I love us," she whispered.

"Me too, Audra." He sighed with contentment. "Me too."

They fell asleep and Audra was relieved when she woke up again and the sun was up. Luke was sleeping, so she slipped out of bed and threw a t-shirt and underwear on. She put coffee on to brew and watched him from the other side of the room. He was sleeping on his side with his arm outstretched to where she'd been beside him. His hair was past his shoulders with wild curls going in every direction. He seemed so peaceful and innocent, she found herself turned on and went over to the bed.

"Luke," she murmured as she took off the clothes she'd just put on. She reached over and rolled him on his back, running her hand down between his legs. Luke opened his eyes and grinned.

"So, it's like that, is it?"

"It is," she said as she felt him get hard in her hand. She put her leg over him and guided him inside of her. She controlled the movements and if he tried to kiss her or touch her, she shook her head and pushed him back, keeping her hand on his chest. She ground her hips down hard on him and moved steadily until she was shaking with exertion and release. She felt Luke let go inside of her and she collapsed down to his chest, every part of her vibrating.

"Damn," was all he said as he wrapped his arm around her and kissed her neck.

"Coffee's ready," she whispered into his hair.

They climbed out of bed and her legs gave a little. She'd be sore from that. She threw back on the shirt and underwear and Luke slid on his boxer briefs. He came around behind her and slipped his arm around her chest, drawing her close to him. He placed his chin on her shoulder.

"You're mine, Audra, yeah? No one gets to take that away from me."

Audra leaned in against him, then turned around to fit into his chest. "I'm not going anywhere."

They had coffee and got ready for their climb. Audra thought about showering but knew she was going to get sweaty and liked smelling Luke on her. They packed food and water and drove out to the mountains. Once there, she looked to Luke for guidance, but he shook his head and put his hand in the air.

"All you, Audra. You've seen me do this, I've shown you the steps. You're the lead today, so."

The last time she'd been the lead was the day they free-climbed to be rescued. That was different. It was survival and she didn't have time to think. This time she was having to map out the course for both of them. Set the path. Find cracks for the anchors. If she did it wrong, Luke might fall. She might fall. She took a deep breath, stared at the rock, and muttered to herself.

"What's that?" Luke asked, not hearing what she said.

"Believe, trust, conquer," she repeated.

Luke grinned, brushing a strand of hair off her face. "That's me girl. What does that mean to you?"

"I need to believe in myself. Trust that I know what I'm doing for us. And conquer this damn rock."

Luke kissed her deeply, then nodded. "I'm so fuckin' proud of you. I believe in you, trust you know what you're doin', and am ready to conquer this with you."

Audra bobbed her head and stepped up to the rock, running her hand along it to feel for finger holds. She found her edging and placed her fingers on to grip. She pressed up with her foot and grasped with her hands. As she got higher, she placed the first anchor. Before long, she was focused on the course and moved steadily up. When she was unsure, she yelled down to Luke for guidance.

"You have this, Audra. Use your hands as eyes, it's there, you just have to find it."

She ran her hands along the rock and what her eyes didn't see, her fingers found. It was incredible and she felt like she'd discovered a sense in her she'd never known existed. It was almost like she felt the rock vibrating, telling her where to go. They made it to the top in a couple of hours and Audra stared back down in disbelief. It made more sense to her, now. She wasn't conquering the rock, she was conquering what was in her which was preventing her from climbing it.

"Luke! I get it. The rock was talking to me if that doesn't sound weird."

Luke laughed. "Not at all, the rock is your companion. Almost like a lover, yeah? You need to find its secrets and it will let you in."

Audra smiled, she liked to think about it that way. Like her and Luke naked and intertwined. She raised her eyebrows at him. He met her eyes and shook his head with a smirk as he unpacked the food. She came over and joined him, starving from the climb. They finished everything and lay back on the blanket to watch the clouds. Audra felt more at peace within herself and gratitude to Luke for sticking by her. They started in tragedy and had grown like flowers through the cracks in rocks.

"What's next for us? Soon we can leave this town and go anywhere we want. Start over. Where do you want to go, Luke?"

"Honestly, it doesn't matter now that I have you. There are rocks to climb everywhere, so. Eventually, I want to go back to Ireland, but mostly I want to be on whatever land you're standin' on, Audra."

"That is the most romantic thing I've ever heard." Audra sat up and stared at Luke.

He shifted and sat on his knees to face her. "Come hell or high water, I want you in me life, Audra. I've never met anyone like you and there is nothin' that could tear me away from you."

Audra nodded and reached out to touch his left shoulder, resting her fingers just above where the arm stopped. "I'd go anywhere with you, Luke. As you said, there is a whole world out there. But you are where home is."

Luke smiled and reached into his bag. He pulled out a small box and gazed at Audra. "I didn't know where or when I'd do this, but I knew pretty much from the first time we laid together, I would. I've been carryin' this around since soon after we left the hospital. I found it in an Irish shop in town."

He opened the box and inside was a silver ring with intricate knotwork and a pale green stone in the center. "It's Connemara Marble from Ireland, like. I didn't think you were a diamond kind of girl and wanted to give you somethin' from where I'm from. So, what I'm askin' is, will you spend the rest of your life with me? Be me rock climbin' partner and the person I share me secrets with? Will you be me wife?"

Audra met Luke's eyes and in them saw what she'd been seeking outside of herself. She nodded and touched the ring. "It's symbolic because you've been mine for a while. Yes, Luke, I'll be your wife and you'll be my husband."

Chapter Twenty-One

*A*udra shifted uncomfortably on the hard metal chair. She peered around the office and found it remarkable how every police station had about the same aesthetic. They'd been asked to meet with the special agent on the case involving the terrorist group and plutonium cargo. While it had been a request, the urgency with which they were asked made Audra nervous. They'd been in the apartment for a couple of months and both she and Luke were ready to move on. To start a life they chose, instead of others controlling their every move.

Her birthday had come and gone, with Luke making her a nice dinner and birthday cake to celebrate. As promised, he whipped up homemade brown bread which put the canned stuff to shame. He bought her a matching Star of David necklace like Adam's he wore. She understood the symbolism. They were all interconnected even though she and Adam had never spoken. They still shared a love that made them family.

They'd skipped over Thanksgiving, it not meaning anything to either of them. It was now early December and heavy snows prevented too many climbs. They'd waited patiently to be allowed to leave but it dragged on and on. Now, they were being asked to come in on the case and Audra hoped it was finally reaching a resolution. They waited almost an hour before the agent showed up and by then Audra was hungry and irritated. He shook both of their hands and sat down at the desk across from them. In a padded chair, Audra mentally noted.

"Thank you for coming in. I'm sorry for my delay. We had some information I wanted to make sure was valid before meeting with you. How are you doing today?"

Audra tried not to glare at the small talk. "Fine. So what's the news?"

Luke sensed the agitation in her voice and held her hand in his. The agent took notice, seeming surprised. He cleared his throat and glanced at the folder he was holding.

"Normally we don't divulge this much information to witnesses, but since things have come to light about the group we've been watching, we need to make sure you're aware of what's going on. The group that paid for and was transporting the plutonium, is known as the Brotherhood of the Serpent Strike. I know the name sounds ridiculous but they're a homegrown terrorist group that considers themselves a militia for the people. The people, being white supremacists. They *are* dangerous. Long story short, we've been aware of them from smaller attacks in America. Mainly against liberal groups, events, and buildings like churches of people of color and other cultures."

Audra listened, her fingers digging into Luke's hand. Why were they telling them this and what did it mean? She chewed her lip and couldn't think of what to say when Luke spoke.

"Beg your pardon, but since I'm not from here, can you explain what this all means?"

"Ireland, right? So, you're familiar with groups who attack other groups over beliefs?" the agent inquired.

"More or less, yeah?" Luke said uncomfortably. Ireland's past was no secret to the rest of the world.

"So, this time, instead of attacking a specific group, they planned to attack a specific city to make a statement against what they perceive to be the downfall of the US. The city being Boise. Why Boise? Who knows? Their mindset is very skewed. It could have been accessibility or something as benign as an art exhibit that was against their beliefs. The men who were following you were lower-level drones. They were to transport the plutonium and remove any risks. Which were you two."

Audra considered what he said. "They gave you this information, or how do you know all of this?"

The agent met her eyes and tipped his head. "Right. One turned state's evidence. Pretty young kid, actually. Nineteen, I think. He got caught up in the whole militia idea and turned pretty quickly when we laid out what the charges were for being part of a group with plans to carry out a terrorist attack in the US."

"Do you have what you need now to pursue charges against the organization?" Luke asked, trying to get to the point of them being there.

"We do. However, there are a few problems. First, in this type of situation, you can cut off the head but a new head will grow. We can charge those currently running the organization and anyone we can directly tie to the plans for the attack. However, that's only a few and they'll be immediately replaced by others. That's the first issue."

"What's the other?" Audra asked, afraid she already knew the answer.

"Well, they know who you are. Even though we now have enough evidence to not need you to testify directly in person, they know you provided information that led to us uncovering their intent and presence behind the attack. We need to move you into a protected state."

"Like witness protection?"

"Yes."

Audra shook her head. "I don't want to do that. Luke is a professional rock climber and needs to be able to compete. I have parents who I'm their only child. I can't do that to them. Will this blow over?"

The agent watched her before responding. "Probably in time. They're a big organization but pretty scattered. If you could disappear for a while, they'd likely move on. Our goal is to infiltrate and start breaking them down from the inside. You're small potatoes in the long run. It's a vendetta more than a mark if that makes sense."

"They're angry at us for now, but don't see us as a threat, yeah?" Luke replied.

"Exactly. You made things inconvenient for them and they'd love nothing more than to make an example of you, but they aren't going to climb mountains to do it."

Audra laughed at the analogy because it is exactly what they didn't do. The agent cocked his head at her, confused, but Luke met her eyes knowingly.

"So, we could've been followed all of this time, like?" Luke inquired for Audra.

"It's conceivable, but I think they would've struck if you'd been."

"Even if they thought you were watchin' them, too?" Luke asked.

"True, they could have been tracking you to make sure they didn't lose your trail."

Audra met Luke's eyes and bit her lip. Some of what she was sensing may have been real. It oddly made her feel better. She was aware a lot was her brain dealing with trauma, however, maybe not all. Luke nodded, an apology in his eyes.

"Now, what?" she asked.

"Since you don't want witness protection, do you have somewhere you can go no one knows of?" the agent suggested.

Luke squeezed Audra's hand. "Does it have to be in this country?"

The agent rubbed his forehead, considering, then shook his head. "I'm not a hundred percent sure. We do want you available if needed but could bring you back. Where are you thinking?"

Luke looked at Audra for confirmation and she bobbed her head.

"Ireland?" he offered.

The agent cleared his throat. "Let me check with the powers that be. I think it could be arranged." He excused himself and left the room.

Luke turned to Audra. "Me grandparents' house is in the countryside. It's been empty since me grandma passed. We could stay there, like. It's remote, we'd be off the map completely. It's been mine if I wanted it but haven't seen the need up to this point. What do you think?"

"What do I think? Luke, you have a house in the Irish countryside. I think that sounds like a dream come true," Audra answered truthfully.

"It needs some work, however, it's on some acreage. I always planned to build a rock climbin' facility there, so. I want to compete, but now more than anythin' I want to have a life with you. I want you... our family to be safe."

Audra nodded. It was time. "I'm ready."

The agent came back in and sat down. "Here's the deal. Ireland is approved if you agree to come back if needed for the case. We will pay for all travel and accommodations."

He said travel and accommodations like it was for a vacation. They agreed and he stared at them sternly. "Do you feel like you've been followed?"

"Yes," Audra replied. "We never saw anyone for sure, but there was always this feeling of being watched. Of being followed."

He made some notes, then peered back up. "You never saw anyone out of the ordinary?"

Audra shook her head, doubting herself.

"Even so, it's better to be on the safe side," he answered. "We can send some out to your apartment to gather your belongings and set you up somewhere until you leave for Ireland."

"What about our truck?" Luke asked.

"If you *are* being followed, they know it's yours. I wouldn't recommend using it anymore. We can cover whatever it's worth."

So, that was it. They'd leave from the police station to an undisclosed location and then on to Ireland from there.

"Just make sure they get all of our equipment, yeah?" Luke instructed.

"We will. You won't need furniture or anything like that. You'll receive a stipend to get situated in your new home for a period of time, as well."

It took the rest of the day to get everything in order, but by dinner time a car arrived and picked them up. They were brought down into an enclosed garage, so no one would see them leave the station. Their belongings were in the back and Luke did a quick check to make sure nothing of value had been left behind. They were given dinner to eat on the drive and were a little surprised when they saw the Boise city signs approaching. Luke chuckled, sliding his arm over Audra.

"I bet when you boarded that plane in Spokane back in late August, you didn't think it'd take you almost four months to get to Boise, yeah?" he joked.

"No. No, I didn't," she replied. "However, the journey took me somewhere better. In a super messed up way."

Luke grinned and kissed her. "You have a strange way of lookin' at things."

They pulled up to a small nondescript house and the driver let them know they'd be staying there until flights were arranged. Probably just a few days to a week. They were told to stay inside as much as possible, and that all of the cabinets were stocked with food and supplies. The driver helped them unload and unlocked the door to the house. They were allowed to call family from the untraceable phone in the house but not to let them know where they were. The driver handed them the key and left.

The house was furnished and very basic. No pictures on the walls, nothing personal. A couch, chairs, table. Places to sleep and cook. The fridge and cabinets were full and had been done so according to the foods Luke and Audra said they ate. There was cable and a bookshelf full of books and games. It was obviously a temporary safe house, making Audra wonder how many people had passed through there on the way to their new lives.

To keep down curious neighbors, the house had a sign out front listing it as a vacation rental with a number that went to a controlled line for a fake vacation company. That made the people staying look like short-term vacation rental guests and didn't raise too many eyebrows. They were told if asked to say they were in town for a conference. The story was probably different for each occupant. They were given fake names to use as well and Luke was told to try and cover his Irish accent. Mike and Jessica Denson from Boulder, Colorado. Most importantly, they were instructed not to leave the area or answer the door. Not even for girl scout cookies.

Neither of them could sleep, having woken up in one home and finding themselves in another. They watched TV, made love, and had tacos after midnight. They showered together and played cards until they were exhausted. In bed, they held each other and teasingly called each other by their fake names. Sleep came and Audra rested her head against the chest of the man she'd been on an adventure with pretty much

since the moment they laid eyes on each other. James had become a distant memory. A mistake she could put behind her.

The sun woke her and she hadn't had any nightmares. Luke was sleeping peacefully because when she was able to sleep, so was he. He had a scruff of a beard and she ran her fingernails through it. He opened his eyes a slit and pressed her fingers to his mouth.

"Good mornin', Jessica."

"Good morning, Mike."

"I love you, Audra."

"I love you, Luke."

"First, I'm goin' to have me way with you, then I'm goin' to cook you breakfast, like," Luke murmured.

"Mmmmm, I'd actually planned the same."

Luke did as he promised and after breakfast, they sat in the small glassed room off the back of the house, looking out over the backyard as snow gently fell. Audra realized something and turned to him.

"You know we have to get on a plane, right? To get to Ireland?"

"I'm aware. It'll be fine. What are the odds two planes in a row will crash, yeah?"

"What are the odds we'd be on a plane that crashed carrying plutonium for a terrorist group who wanted to blow up Boise and are now after us?" Audra replied sardonically.

"Touché," Luke said, squeezing her hand.

What were the odds?

Chapter Twenty-Two

*T*he car came to take them to the airport and Audra did her best to push her fear down. She and Luke woke up early and smoked on the back porch to quell their nerves. It was a commercial jet, she reminded herself, those hardly ever crash. There were multiple legs, as well, and the journey itself would take over fifteen hours. Ultimately, they'd land in Cork, Ireland, where Luke's parents and siblings lived, then make their way out to the country to his grandparents' house. By the time they got there with the time change, Audra was unsure what day it would be.

First step, don't crash.

The car ride to the airport was silent and they made sure they had their passports with their fake names for the flight and their real ones for once they landed. The driver was young and she chatted with them the whole way. Probably used to people being a little shell-shocked going onto their new lives, so she didn't seem to expect them to respond. Once they got to the airport, she jumped out and checked their bags as they showed their tickets and passports to the man at the counter.

Audra noticed something she hadn't been aware of as they made their way through the terminal to their gate. People stared at Luke... at his missing arm. Openly. It was shocking to see and she felt ire rising in her. Luke ignored them and kept his eyes straight ahead. It wasn't necessarily that people were looking, as much as *how* they were staring. Some whispered and pointed, some seemed horrified. Some of the worst were the sorry ones. They openly showed pity and treated Luke as if he didn't have a brain in his head. He was, *"Oh poor thing"* and, *"What a shame"* to them. Audra wanted to confront people but felt Luke squeeze her hand and draw her in close.

"Not worth it," he whispered in her ear. "These people don't have the brain-power to see things differently, so."

Audra peered up at him. "I want to punch them in the face."

Luke laughed and touched her face. "Me defender. Still wouldn't change anythin'. I like to blow people's minds with what I can do, instead of them decidin' what I can't. Like kissin' the most beautiful woman in the airport."

Luke turned her toward him, grabbing her around the waist and kissing her until she felt woozy. That made people turn away. Audra blushed and grinned up at him. What those people didn't know, was that she was the fortunate one. Luke was everything she could've ever wanted in a partner and more. She stepped on her tiptoes, kissing him gently.

"I can't believe you chose me," she said softly.

"What choice? It was set in stone from day one, yeah?"

They made it to their gate and sat by the window, watching the planes take off. One after another. They'd all make it safely to where they were going. At least, Audra hoped so. When their flight began boarding, she panicked and refused to get up when their row was called. Luke rubbed her arm and waited.

"Think of it this way. We know people are after us here. We don't know if the plane is goin' to crash. The likelihood of it crashin' has to be less of a percentage than us bein' found and killed by terrorists here. Weird to say, but I'm guessin' the odds of gettin' on that plane are in our favor," he reasoned.

He was probably right, Audra realized. She sighed and stood up. Plane crash or murdered? Plane seemed like a safer bet. They handed their tickets to the airline attendant and made their way onto the plane. Audra scanned for the emergency exits, eyeing everyone on the plane. They got to their seats and Audra stood frozen. If she sat by the window, she could get sucked out. If she sat by the aisle, she might get trapped and trampled. Luke saw her dilemma and leaned in.

"There is no fuckin' way I'd let anythin' happen to you no matter where you sit. If you sit on the aisle, however, I can put me arm around you, like."

Audra smiled wobbly, watching his face. "My defender. Aisle it is."

They sat in their seats and waited for the plane to take off. As promised, Luke put his arm around her and she rested against him. The captain came on and way too chirpily introduced himself and the co-pilot. The flight attendants went through the emergency drills and made sure everyone was buckled. Luke double-checked Audra's, then winked. She pinched him on the leg as he laughed.

As the engines ramped up to a high pitch whir, Audra took deep breaths and closed her eyes. They were going to Ireland. They were going to get there safely. She had Luke. He was her family. The plane started to taxi down the runway and she grasped his hand tightly. He laced his fingers through hers, then sighed. He was nervous, too. Last flight he took, he lost his best friend and had been on the run ever since. Audra kept her eyes closed as she felt the wheels leave the ground and the plane lift off into the sky. Once it leveled, she opened her eyes and peered around. Most of the other passengers were reading or chatting comfortably.

The image of seeing the mountain smash into Adam's side of the plane jolted into her mind and she began sweating. Luke pulled her in, kissing the side of her head. Audra turned to him and stared at Adam's Star of David. She reached out to touch it. It was warm from Luke's chest. She ran her fingers over the points.

"Did you ever talk to Adam's parents after the crash?" she asked.

"I did. I asked the police for their number since I knew him. I rang them one night to let them know how much Adam meant to me and what a grand lad he was. They, of course, knew of me and I'd seen them at a few competitions, but we'd never spoken face to face. They told me how often he spoke of me, how he looked up to me. Which is crazy because he was the put-together one out of the two of us, like. They're devastated, he was their only son. They'd fought him on rock climbin' because of the danger and couldn't believe it was a plane crash that took him. They told me once we make it to Ireland and settle down, they've some of his things they'd like me to have."

"Wow, I didn't know. That must've been hard."

"Oh, I cried like a babe when I got off the phone, yeah?" Luke confessed.

"Where was I?" Audra asked, confused.

"It was the day we argued and I left. I walked for a bit and Adam kept poppin' into me head, tellin' me to go back to you. I was hurt and frustrated. I didn't want to fight with you anymore, so I rang his parents. After that, I bought a truck and drove out to climb. It's when it came to me. About you climbin'. I knew you were trapped inside and the only doors you recognize are ones you're forced to open, so," Luke said it in a teasing manner but he was right.

Audra needed to be pushed to the edge to make a change. She'd stayed with James for years, after knowing it wasn't working and he was destroying her. It wasn't until she knew he'd kill her that she left. She didn't want to be that way anymore. She was worthy of more and had the power inside herself to go further.

"Believe, trust, conquer," she said firmly, shifting to face him.

"Believe, trust, conquer. Exactly. So, I came home to you. Not that I could've ever stayed away from you, yeah? However, I was determined to help you fight, to show you that you aren't alone in this world. Audra, you need to know I'd never leave you."

"I know. If you haven't by now..." she joked.

"I never will," Luke finished and brushed a strand of hair out of her face. "I can't wait for you to meet me family.

They're goin' to love you and be utterly shocked I found someone to spend me life with."

"Why's that?"

"I think they'd resigned themselves to me lovin' rock climbin' more than anythin'. That I'd go to me grave livin' alone."

"I'm thrilled you love me as much as rock climbing," Audra replied with a twinkle in her eye.

"Don't get me wrong, I love rock climbin'. It's in me blood, like. But I'd die for you. That's the difference."

"Well, please don't die for me, and I love rock climbing, too."

Talking made the flight less scary and before they knew it, they were landing from the first leg. They switched planes and had a little time to wander around the airport. Luke bought a couple of trinkets to bring to his nieces and nephews and they grabbed coffee. When it was time to board the next plane, Audra was more confident in its safety.

By the time the second leg was done and they were on the third, they were flying over water. Audra peered out the window at the ocean. She'd been born in a landlocked state and even though Washington touched the ocean, she'd only seen it once on a school trip. Seeing the massive expanse with no land in sight was both terrifying and exhilarating. She sat back in her seat and yawned. This was the longest part of the trip. The next landing would be in Dublin, Ireland.

Then on to Cork.

Luke's family didn't know he was coming and the agent told them to stay somewhere as Mike and Jessica Denson for at least the first few days to a week. This would avoid the appearance of them disappearing in the United States and showing up immediately in Ireland.

Audra tried to picture Ireland, but it was just from snapshots and shows she'd seen. Seeing it as home would be entirely different. She rested her head on Luke's shoulder and started to fall asleep, hoping she wouldn't have a nightmare on the plane.

The plane bumped from turbulence, shocking Audra awake and causing panic in her. She glanced around but no one else seemed to notice. She bent over Luke who was sleeping and gazed out the window. The plane was cruising alone in the clouds, no trouble in sight. She sighed and sat back. Luke slipped his arm around her.

"It's alright, *mo anáil*. Just a little turbulence," he murmured.

Audra leaned on him, placing her hand on his leg. "What does that mean? Those words you just said."

"*Mo anáil*? It's Gaeilge for *me breath*. You are me air. The reason I kept breathin'. *Mo anáil*."

"Fucking romantic," Audra whispered and kissed his cheek.

Luke chuckled but kept his eyes closed. By the time they touched down in Dublin, both were so excited to be in Ireland, they forgot they were worried about the plane crashing. They quickly made it to their connecting flight for the last leg to Cork where Luke grew up. They had a hotel room there for three days, then he'd ring his family.

They checked in as Mike and Jessica Denson. Even though it was the middle of the day, they were so exhausted, they slept for the next nine hours. They woke up around midnight local time and slipped down to the hotel pool to swim. Audra didn't have a bathing suit, so she wore a sports bra and shorts. They were the only ones at the pool and it reminded her of when they swam in the river at the cabin. Except now, they were free.

For the next three days, they treated it like a vacation. They made sure not to go out, as Luke might be recognized by friends or family. They stayed in, swam, ate too much, and explored each other like they were on their honeymoon. The morning of check-out day, Luke dialed his parents to let them know he'd arrived in Ireland. They were surprised and ecstatic, asking if he needed a ride from the airport. He let them know he and his fiancé were coming in and didn't need a ride. After he said fiancé, he didn't speak for some time, listening to the other end. Audra got nervous and watched him as she chewed her nails. He told his parents he loved them and hung up.

"Well?" Audra asked impatiently.

"Well, they're pretty shocked but excited to meet you yeah?" Luke replied with a mixture of humor and consternation crossing his face.

"When?"

"We check out here as Mike and Jessica Denson this mornin', so I imagine we'll need to meet with them sometime today. We can't stay here and I don't want to book anythin' under our real names, like. I was thinkin' we could stay with me parents for a couple of days before we head to me grandparents' house?"

Audra could see he was unsure about her reaction. She was spooked about not only meeting his parents but also staying with them. Now, she was the outsider. The American.

Everything between them happened so suddenly... what if his parents didn't approve of her? Of their relationship? She couldn't imagine parents of Luke would be judgmental, knowing his open and loving personality. She hoped not.

"I trust you," Audra replied quietly, attempting to hide her anxiety.

"I promise, they'll love you as much as I do."

Chapter Twenty-Three

W hatever Audra imagined Luke's family to be like, she was way off. She pictured a little, round, gray-haired mother and a curmudgeon father, smoking a pipe in a wingback armchair. She couldn't have been more wrong. His father was tall and thin like Luke, with graying, smooth, black hair and Luke's eyes. His mother was athletic with crazy, golden-brown, curly hair and gray eyes. They were younger than Audra expected and super friendly. Luke walked right into the house when they arrived, then straight back to the kitchen where everyone was gathered, drinking coffee and laughing. His mother grabbed him in a tight hug, kissing him on the cheek. His father was next and embraced Luke, patting him on the back as he kissed him the same.

"This is me fiancé, Audra." Luke grasped her hand and drew her in close to him.

Luke's mother came forward and hugged Audra, giving her a peck on the cheek.

"A pretty little thing, aren't you?" she said and grinned, Luke's grin.

Audra blushed, not used to such open affection. Luke's father hugged her more gently and lightly kissed her cheek.

"Welcome to our home and our family," he expressed kindly, then turned to Luke. "You did well, boy. She puts up with you?"

"Yeah, Da. She does." Luke squeezed her hand.

His parents' accents were much thicker than his and they talked fast, so Audra quickly lost track of the conversation and wandered around the living room, peering at pictures. She couldn't remember how many siblings Luke said he had, but it was easy to spot him in the pictures. Not just because of his missing arm, but because of how his eyes met the camera. Almost in a challenge. The family pictures had three boys and a girl. The girl with straight, black hair, one of the boys had golden-brown smooth hair. The other boy had black, kind of wavy hair. Nothing like Luke's. Then there was Luke. Three boys and a girl. It must've been fun growing up with so many kids around. She'd been alone and read a lot, playing by herself. School changed everything once she could participate in sports and make friends. She was drawn to sports because of the team camaraderie.

Luke joined her and laughed at some of the pictures. There was one of him climbing at about twelve and he was leaning dangerously back, bracing with his knees and giving a peace sign with a big grin. His hair was shorter but corkscrewed out from his scalp, making him look wild. Audra reached up and pulled one of his curls straight and let it spring back into place. Luke winked at her and peered at another picture. It was his mother holding him as a baby, his hair going in every direction, as was hers. Audra touched the picture when she realized he had two arms in the picture.

Luke nodded. "Before the amputation. They didn't know until I was about six months old. Me arm below the elbow stopped growin', like. The bones stopped developin'. It was amputated before I was a year old."

"Was it dangerous? I mean, would having kept the arm caused you any harm?"

"I don't think so, no. I think the idea was if it was amputated when I was a babe, I could be fit for a prosthetic then and be able to adapt to that before I ever knew anythin' different in me life."

"Did you ever use one regularly? A prosthetic?"

"In school for a bit. It didn't really make a difference for me. I just learned to use me remainin' arm faster and stronger. I guess with the new ones they have now, it might be different. However, I kind of like freakin' people out with me one arm," Luke joked.

Audra laughed, shaking her head. "Such a rebel."

"Seriously, though, I'm not opposed to prosthetics but have gotten this far without one, so. What's your feelin' on it?"

"My feeling? I don't have one. It's your body and it's perfect to me as is. You're stronger than anyone I've met and don't seem to need any help. But it's your call."

Luke smiled at her. "Cheers, Audra."

A gaggle of children came running in, clamoring around Luke's legs. Luke bent down and scooped up the littlest one, a girl with golden hair and big, green eyes. She stuck her fingers in her mouth and grinned at Luke.

"This here is Saoirse. Me older brother's youngest. Then there's Brendan, Siobhan, Michael, and Donal. These three are me sister's and these two are me older brother's. Me younger brother is still single."

Audra had already lost track of who belonged to who and shook her head, watching the children run around. "What are your sibling's names?"

"Patrick is the oldest; Saoirse and Brendan are his. Cara, me sister, is the next in line and Siobhan, Michael, and Donal are hers. Then there's me. Last, is me younger brother Liam. He's twenty-five. To be honest, he doesn't seem all that interested in findin' a girl quite yet."

Audra felt like she should be taking notes on all this. The parents of the children came in with their spouses and Audra began to feel overwhelmed. After a quick round of greetings, she eyed Luke for escape. He nodded and led her out back to a small porch with a couple of rocking chairs. They sat and he rubbed his thumb across her palm gently.

"It's a lot, I know. It's been just us for months and now you have twelve people descend on you all at once, like. Well, eleven, Liam hasn't arrived yet."

"I like them, it's just... very stimulating."

Luke laughed heartily. "That's one way to put it, isn't it? Me family can be very stimulatin'. Over-stimulatin', yeah? Trust me, as a lad, rock climbin' served many purposes for me. It was silence, as well."

"Does no one else in your family rock climb?" Audra asked.

"No, me older brother first took me when I was young because he wanted to impress a girl. He did it once, but I was hooked. Me parents wanted to encourage me, so made sure I went as much as I wanted."

"You have a nice family. My parents are great, however, maybe having just one kid, it was always calm and quiet at home. We talked and they spoke to me like I was an adult most times. Discussions about books, politics, things like that. I liked it growing up because they respected me as a person, but I did miss just being a kid."

"That's fair. Our house was fuckin' wild growin' up. Not only because there were four of us, but because me parents let us run amok for the most part. I'm surprised the house is still standin'."

One of the little boys about four or five years old came out and climbed onto Luke's lap, laying his head against Luke's chest. "Uncle Lucas, are you stayin'?"

"I am this time, Mikey. Me and your Aunt Audra," Luke replied, smiling at Audra.

Watching him with his nephew hurt her heart, knowing they may never be able to have children. Luke read her eyes and shook his head.

"We will. One way or another."

The little boy climbed off of Luke's lap to come over and climb onto Audra's. She was surprised at his comfort level. She'd worked with children for years and they always took a bit to warm up to a stranger. She wrapped her arms around him and began to rock. It felt nice. He sat for a bit and then clambered down to play with the other children. Audra stared off, thinking about family and children when Luke came over to her, putting his hand out. She took it and he drew her up close to him.

"We *will* have a family. I know that to be true, so. Right now, I want you and that's enough. I know you want children and it'll work out in time."

Audra slid her arm around Luke's waist and leaned against him. He tipped her chin back, and placed his mouth on hers, making her knees buckle a little.

"Get a room, like," a voice said sarcastically behind them.

Luke laughed and turned. "I was wonderin' when you'd show up, boy. Audra, this is me little brother Liam."

Audra glanced over, startled by how striking Liam was. His hair was black and wavy, his gray eyes twinkled with mischief. He had a long straight nose like Luke and his mouth curved up at the edges, giving him a daring look. He grinned, showing a broad mouth and straight teeth. *Girls must fawn all over him,* Audra thought to herself.

"Nice to meet you, Audra," Liam said and took her hands in his. His hands were warm and a little rough. "I didn't think Lucas would ever care about anythin' other than rocks. You must be somethin'."

"Well, rocks come in many different forms," Luke said honestly.

"Nice to meet you, Liam," Audra mumbled, more focused on what Luke said.

"I'll let you two get back to it, yeah? Ma wants me help in the kitchen. Good to have you back, Lucas." Liam stepped back into the din of the house and Luke put his arm around Audra.

"He's an odd one, our Liam. Maybe bein' the youngest."

"He's nice. I can see him causing some trouble though," Audra replied, watching Liam disappear out of view.

"That's an understatement, like. Me parents have bailed him out more than once," Luke said with a chuckle.

Audra leaned in against Luke, knowing they would have to go in shortly. She ran her fingers up and down his spine and sighed. "What did you mean about rocks coming in different forms?"

"I meant you are me rock, Audra. The thing I hold on to when everythin' else is in chaos. I know you're there for me and depend on your strength to get me through."

Audra had never seen herself that way. Where someone could depend on her strength. She definitely felt that way about Luke. She gazed up at Luke and smiled. "I like that."

"Me too," Luke replied.

They were called in and found seats at a long table near Luke's father. There was no kids' table, everyone sat together and was treated as equals. Food was passed around and after a short grace, the family prepared to dig in. Luke's mother stood up and raised her glass. She rested her eyes on Luke.

"To havin' the whole family together again. Havin' our Lucas home for the holidays. For good this time, yeah? To our family growin' once again with our new daughter, Audra! Sláinte!"

"Sláinte!" the table responded and clinked their glasses together.

Conversation didn't stop through the whole meal and by the end, Audra's head was buzzing. She saw Liam glance at his phone and blush slightly.

So, maybe he *did* have someone.

He glanced up, meeting her eyes, and grinned as he raised a black eyebrow.

"Ma, I'm off, now," he said and kissed his mother on the cheek as he was heading out. She went to stop him but he was already at the door. He turned to Audra and gave her a quick wink. Her new brother was up to something.

After dinner, the children were getting tired and cranky as they were corralled by their parents. Patrick came over, giving Audra a hug and a peck on the cheek.

"Welcome to the madhouse, Audra," he said as he reached down and snagged a child attempting to run past him out the door.

"Thank you, Patrick."

Cara was a bit more standoffish at first, but Audra figured it was because she'd been raised with all boys. Eventually, she made her way over and smiled. "Nice to meet you, Audra. You take care of our Lucas. He's somethin' special."

That was it, then. She was worried for Luke. Audra hugged her, then tipped her head. "I want you to know, he's everything to me."

Cara nodded, her eyes reading Audra's face. "I can see that, yeah? It'll be nice to not be so outnumbered by all of these lads. I've never had a sister."

"Me either," Audra responded. She imagined having a sister would be nice.

Cara leaned in and kissed her on the cheek, accepting Audra into the family She gathered her three children and husband, then took their leave. This left just Luke, his parents, and Audra, the house suddenly seeming much larger. Much quieter. Luke's father made tea and they moved to the living room.

Luke rested his hand on Audra's leg between sips of tea. He leaned back in his seat, eyeing his mother as she responded in kind. Audra watched the wordless messages pass between them with fascination. Luke took a sip of his tea, then set the cup gingerly down. He straightened his back, clearing his throat.

"Right, Ma. Let the interrogation begin."

Chapter Twenty-Four

The thing Audra didn't know, was that Luke hadn't told his parents anything other than he and Audra were engaged. Not about the crash, not about the plutonium, not about the terrorist group... nothing. Just that he'd met a nice girl and they were getting married. So, when Luke's mother started asking questions, Audra had to keep her mouth from falling open as Luke answered. Luke's mother set down her cup, then sighed.

"Stop the lights, Lucas. No need to be dramatic. So, how did you two meet?"

"Funny story," Luke began. "We were both on the same flight."

"I don't see how that's funny," his mother replied, her eyes saying she knew more was coming.

"Not funny in that way, like. Odd, I mean. The plane crashed, actually. We were the only survivors. I lost me friend Adam, Ma. He died in the crash."

Luke's father set his tea down and stared at the two of them. "Let me get this straight. You both were on a plane that went down and you walked away from it? That's how you met?"

"More or less," Luke confirmed.

The room feel silent as Luke's parents tried to wrap their brains around what they were being told. A myriad of expressions crossed their faces. Audra sat tensely, her hands breaking out in a sweat. Finally, Luke's mother glanced from Audra to Luke.

"Lucas, I'm truly sorry about Adam, his parents must be devastated," she said softly. "I know your heart must be breakin'. This is horrific to hear. Why... how did the plane crash?"

"From what we understand, the cargo shifted and threw the plane off balance, so. The pilot was already off course, flyin' too low, too close to the mountains. The wing hit the trees and got ripped off, then we were spun into the side of the mountain. The only reason I'm alive is because Audra's seat belt wasn't buckled correctly. I unbuckled to help. We both got sucked out of the plane through the hole by the missing wing."

Audra could hear the ticking of the clock on the wall as Luke's parents absorbed what Luke said. Audra sat still, horrified they didn't know, and met Luke's eyes sternly. He shrugged in apology and kissed her quickly.

"Alright, so you got sucked out of the plane, then what?" Luke's father asked.

"I came to later and checked the plane, but everyone else was dead. I thought I was the only survivor and left to try and get me bearin's where I was, yeah? Until I heard Audra yell and came back to find her standin' by the plane with a wound on her leg."

"Were you injured, Lucas?" his mother asked.

"Surprisingly, just banged up with a gash on me head. I'm thinkin' we were close enough to the ground when we were pulled through the hole that we didn't fall far. Everyone else died from the impact of hittin' the mountain, I suppose."

"Luke stitched the wound on my leg closed," Audra offered.

His mother stared from her to Luke and shook her head. "So, he found you and sewed your wound up? Jaysus. Then, pray tell, what happened?"

"We found a cave to stay in while we healed. We needed food and a way out, so we checked the passengers for phones and the cargo for food. We found some food but the phones didn't have service," Luke interjected. "We also found somethin' else, like."

"For the love of God. What?" his mother inquired, exasperated.

"Plutonium in the cargo hold. It's what shifted and threw the plane off balance."

"Why would there be plutonium on a passenger plane?" Luke's father asked softly.

"The pilot must've been paid to transport it. A terrorist group was plannin' to set off a bomb or somethin' of that nature, we think."

"Why do you think that?"

"The police told us along those lines. Or the FBI. They said it was a homegrown terrorist group wantin' to make a statement," Luke answered, meeting his parents' eyes.

"Jesus, Mary, and Joseph," his mother muttered and took a sip of her tea.

"There's more," Luke said.

"Of course, there is," his mother replied.

"The terrorist group got to the plane before we were rescued and started trackin' us, knowin' we'd seen the cargo, like. A man accosted Audra while she was alone. When I came to help her, he drew a gun on us."

Luke's mother's eyes got wide and her mouth dropped open. "Well, you're still here, so go on, then."

"Audra tackled him and I shot him in the head."

"With what?" she inquired.

"I found a gun in the pilot's stuff and kept it in case."

"In case of what?"

"I didn't think because of terrorists, but in case of wild animals, so," Luke responded as if that was totally normal.

"And did you see any wild animals?" his mother asked incredulously.

"Actually, we did, yeah? I went to get water and heard Audra scream. I ran back and she was face to face with a mountain lion."

"You shot it?"

"No, she was yellin' at it and it was already ready to leave, so I fired the gun in the air to finish scarin' it off, like."

"Did it?" his mother questioned, not needing to hear the answer.

"It did, but only because Audra had already set it right."

Audra's father turned to Audra and cocked his head. "You survived a plane crash, tackled a man with a gun, and scared off a mountain lion, lass?"

"Not in that order, but yes," Audra replied.

"And stood up to an abusive husband," Luke added without thinking. Audra glared at him.

"You're married?" Luke's mother asked.

"I was. I'm not anymore," Audra answered, sensing the next question.

"How long ago was this?"

"Ma, to be blunt, it's none of your concern, is it?" Luke said firmly. "It's in her past and we're engaged, so. Anythin' else is Audra's business."

Luke's mother stared at Luke, back at Audra, then nodded. "This is true, but don't get too big on yourself, Lucas. I'm still your mother."

"Sorry, Ma. Audra's been through a lot and while I can take you givin' me the rundown, she doesn't deserve it, yeah? I love her, that's what matters."

"Fair. Apologies, Audra. Lucas here is me son and I can't help but want to protect him. Sounds like you're pretty good at that as well, aren't you?"

Audra didn't know how to reply and just bobbed her head. Her head was spinning and she needed to step away. She stood up, excusing herself, then practically bolted out the door. She breathed in the night air and tried to come back to reality. Luke stepped out to check on her and found her leaning against the wall, taking deep breaths.

"I'm sorry about me mam. She's very forward," he said and rubbed her back.

"It's not just your mother. How could you not have told them anything?" Audra replied in a harsh whisper.

Luke sighed, shaking his head. "Can you imagine bein' an ocean away, hearin' your child was in a plane crash, and part of a terrorist organization plot to be murdered? It would've sent Ma over the edge, like. I wanted to let them know once I was home safe."

"I guess that's fair. It was just weird to be there while you told them the play-by-play. I wasn't ready for it."

"Sorry, Audra. That wasn't the best of me. I kind of needed you there with me to do it, though. To have the courage, so."

Audra sat back and stared at Luke. She was his rock. They stayed outside in the crisp air for a bit, then headed back in. The house was dark except for light in the bedrooms. Luke knocked on his parents' door. He cracked the door open a bit.

"We're goin' to turn in. I see the bed was made in me old room? Liam still livin' here, too, is he?"

"Yeah, that lad will never leave, I think," Luke's mother replied and chuckled. "He'll likely be out til the mornin'. You and Audra take your old room. I love you, Lucas. I'm glad you're home safe, son."

"Me too, Ma."

They went to Luke's childhood room, which had posters of rock climbers and bands on the wall. The bed was what they call a double, smaller than a full but bigger than a twin, and climbed under the covers. Audra took off her pants but left on her t-shirt and underwear. Luke stripped down to his boxer briefs and eased up next to her. She could feel his desire but laughed, shaking her head.

"No way in your childhood bedroom in your parents' house, with them sleeping a room away," she chided.

He chuckled and wound his arm around her. "It'll go away on its own. For now, you'll need to feel me pressed up against you."

Audra slid her hand down and felt his hardness. She slipped her hand under his waistband and grasped him firmly. She kissed him deeply, moving her hand back and forth slowly until she felt him groan and release.

"That should do you," she whispered with a hint of humor in her voice.

"Indeed," he replied and grabbed a towel from the nightstand to clean himself up. "That's the first time anyone has gotten me off in here, except me."

"Now, I'm picturing teenage Luke getting himself off in here."

Luke laughed. "Teenage Luke loved that the most next to rock climbin'. Or maybe more, some days, yeah?"

"Ugh, Luke," Audra laughed and pulled him to her. "Kiss me, boy."

Luke met her mouth and drew her to him with his arm. She wanted him badly, but there was no way in hell she was going to do it with his parents next door.

She pushed back. "Wait, so you *never* had a girl in here? Not even for a kiss?"

Luke blushed. "No, the other thing about teenage Luke, is he had no confidence with girls. Not havin' two arms mattered a lot more then. Girls were nice but treated me like I was a kicked puppy. I didn't have me first girlfriend until I was an adult, so."

"Oh. I'm sorry, Luke. Now, I want to go back and let younger you know those girls were idiots."

216

Luke rested on his back and Audra put her head on his chest as he stroked her hair.

"Maybe it was better, though. It pushed me into rock climbin' full force and on to compete. That brought me to the United States where I found who I was."

"Did you date a lot of American girls?"

"Date? Yes. Seriously? No."

"So, no long-term girlfriends?" Audra pressed.

"Nope. Rock climbin' came first, like. Not to mention, it seemed like they thought I should be so grateful for their attention, I'd give up rock climbin'. That wasn't happenin'. Also, I felt like they liked an image of me they created, not who I was really. I'm not the rugged, Irish, rock climber they were wantin'. Or the sensitive, disabled lad to inspire them. I'm just me."

Audra knew the feeling. James had tried to make her into what his image of her was and didn't appreciate who she truly was. Luke was a lot like her. He said what he thought and didn't pretend to be something he wasn't. It's why it was so easy between them. They weren't trying to impress anyone or fit into a set mold.

She slid her hand up and wrapped his curls in her fingers, liking the way they naturally wound around them. She glanced up at Luke, watching him. He was off in a memory, giving her the chance to appreciate him. His eyelashes were long and framed his eyes in a way that was almost pretty. He had freckles across his face but so faint they almost disappeared when he got sun. She ran her finger along his jawline and his eyes shifted to meet hers. They looked greener in the lighting and he smiled.

"What is it, Audra?"

"I was just admiring how well-made you are. You're so beautiful," Audra replied without shame.

Luke watched her silently for a moment. He put his fingers on her chin and nodded. "When I was a lad and would sit in this room, not feelin' like everyone else, I resigned meself to bein' in a world where I was me own person. I wouldn't need anyone, so I couldn't be hurt. But, damnit, Audra, meetin' you tore that all down and I need you more than you could ever know."

"That's where you are wrong, Luke. I know. My walls may have been for different reasons. But I know."

Chapter Twenty-Five

A nightmare woke Audra and she was disoriented. The room seemed unfamiliar, so she reached out for Luke. He was there, breathing softly. She was in his parents' house, in his childhood bedroom. That's right. The nightmare had been more abstract, alleyways and darkness, but no specifics. She just knew she was being chased. She settled her breathing and thought better of waking Luke up. He needed to sleep. Slipping out of bed, she searched the floor for her pants and shoes. Once she found them, she dressed quietly and left the room, closing the door gently behind her. The clock on the wall told her it was three in the morning. She needed some fresh air to clear her mind.

Outside, the air was crisp and she breathed in deeply, letting it fill her lungs. She held it for a few seconds before releasing it. The nightmares had gotten better, so the stress of meeting Luke's family must have triggered it. They were a lovely family, however, Luke not having told them about what happened had been a surprise and put her on edge. She understood his reasoning but wished he'd told her they didn't know. She rubbed her arms in the chilly air and headed back toward the door when she saw a car slowly make its way down the street. She ducked into the shadows out of habit and watched its approach.

The car came to a stop outside the house and she saw Liam in the passenger seat. She almost stepped out to wave at him when she saw him lean over and kiss the other man in the car fully on the mouth. She pressed against the wall, hoping she hadn't been seen and waited. She heard the door open, then close, followed by footsteps on the path as the car drove away. The footsteps stopped and she thought maybe he'd gone in when she heard a soft voice.

"Hey, Audra. You can come out, like."

Audra stepped out, blushing. "I wasn't spying. I came out for air when you pulled up."

Liam eyed her with his steel-gray eyes, then chuckled. "I saw you. I know every shadow of this house. I suppose you saw, yeah?"

Audra nodded. She wasn't one to lie to glaze over a situation. "I won't say anything. It's none of my business."

"That's true, but I'm not hidin' it, necessarily. Just figurin' out the details, to be honest."

"Oh. Does anyone in your family know?"

"Nah. It hasn't come up, so. If I get serious about someone, I'll cross that bridge," Liam answered bluntly.

"That guy? The one in the car when you drove up. Is it not serious?" Audra asked, regretting her nosiness immediately.

Liam ran his hand through his thick, black hair and shrugged. "No idea. I like him, and all, but still havin' some good craic. Not quite ready to settle down."

"That's fair. You're still young. I think I'm just figuring out what I want, now," Audra replied, true to her thoughts.

"How old are you?" Liam asked.

"Thirty-two. I was married before but it was a huge mistake. I got married young."

"No rushin' that. I don't even know who I am, much less who I want to be with someone else, yeah?" Liam said.

"That's smart. I wish I'd had your foresight. It would've saved me a lot of pain."

Liam headed toward the door. "I'm knackered. You comin' in?"

"Yeah, it's cold. I won't say anything, Liam. I promise." Audra followed him to the door and he paused and smiled at her.

"Our," he said.

"Our?"

"You said *me* family, it's *our* family, yeah, since you're marryin' our Lucas."

Audra felt a warmth wash over her. "Thanks, Liam. You all have been incredibly welcoming. I don't know what I was scared of."

Liam held the door for her as they stepped back into the house. It was dark and quiet.

"Goodnight, Audra. Or I suppose good mornin', now." Liam whispered as he disappeared down the hall to his room. He lifted his hand in a wave, grinning at her as he ducked in.

Audra liked Liam. Like Luke, he was so open and true to himself. She was surprised he was gay but really didn't know him in the first place. She didn't know if Irish culture was different when it came to being open about homosexuality, however, she saw Catholic references in their home and mannerisms. Either way, it was Liam's story to share and she'd stay silent on it. He'd tell his family when, or if, he was ready.

She went back into the bedroom and saw Luke had turned on his side, so she crawled behind him and rested her hand on his chest. He shifted, placing his hand over hers. She kissed his back and yawned.

"I love you, Luke."

"I love you, *mo anáil*," he replied, still mostly asleep.

Audra felt an indescribable sense of gratitude and pressed against him as tightly as she could. She wasn't alone anymore.

When she woke up again, the house was in full swing and she was by herself in the bed. She could hear Luke joking and laughing in another room and stayed in bed, enjoying hearing the sounds of him with his family. They were so lively and happy. Finally, she needed to use the bathroom and climbed out of bed. She dug out fresh clothes and ran a comb through her hair before leaving the room. She brushed her teeth and splashed her face with cold water after using the bathroom, then dug up the nerves to go out where everyone was. She walked quietly down the hall, pausing outside the door of the living room where the family was gathered. Liam caught her eye and grinned. That helped.

Luke came over and took her hand, kissing her openly. His mother offered her tea or coffee and showed her where there were pastries if she was hungry. Audra waited until Luke's mother was back to talking and drew Luke aside.

"What do I call your parents? Mr. and Mrs. Riordan?"

Luke laughed, shaking his head. "Me sister and brother's spouses call me parents Ma and Da like we do, so."

Audra felt uncomfortable and shrugged. "What are their names?"

"Michael and Siobhan."

"Like the children?"

"We're big on namin' children after family."

"Oh." Thinking about calling them by their names was even more awkward than calling them Ma and Da. As a child, she'd always called her friends' parents Mr. and Mrs., as she had with James's parents.

"Audra, you're family, yeah?"

"Well, not officially, yet."

"So, let's make it happen. We could get married as soon as three months from today if you want."

Audra met his eyes and smiled, feeling her ears turn red. "Okay."

"Alright? Let's go to the registrar today, then," Luke said, his eyes twinkling.

As if it was the plan all along, Luke stepped into the center of the room and cleared his throat. "Audra and I are gettin' married in three months. We're goin' to the registrar today and as soon as the three months notification passes, we'll have the ceremony."

Everyone congratulated and hugged them. Luke's mother turned, tipping her head toward them.

"Church weddin'?"

"No, Ma. Audra isn't Catholic and I hardly am, like. I was thinkin' maybe out at Grandma and Grandda's house since we'll be livin' there. Audra, does that sound fair?"

Audra nodded, noting his mother's disappointment. They didn't seem like an overly religious family, but they were still steeped in tradition. It didn't really matter to her since she'd had the big traditional wedding with James and that turned out to be shit. She just wanted to be with Luke. She'd marry him today if they were able just to move forward with their lives. However, there was a three-month waiting period in Ireland once they submitted their notification.

Luke's mother sighed and resigned herself. "A spring weddin', that'll be lovely. I can help with the plannin' if you'd like, Audra."

"Thank you, um..." Audra froze, not knowing how to address her.

"You can call me Ma or Siobhan. Whatever you're comfortable with. Siobhan may get confusin' when the wee one is around, though. I guess you could call me Bonnie. That was me nickname when I was a lass."

Bonnie worked for Audra for now. Luke's father was Michael since little Michael was Mikey. Liam was leaning back in his chair with his feet kicked up, smirking at the names.

"Can I call you Bonnie and Michael, too?" he joked at his parents.

His mother spun around with fire in her eyes. "No, you may not, William."

"Ouch, fair enough, Ma. William was Grandda. I'm grand with Liam."

"Then don't get saucy, boy," Bonnie replied.

Liam knew he was riling his mother and smirked, satisfied. Luke eyed him and shook his head, chuckling. They were the two youngest and Audra could only imagine what hellions they'd been. Liam excused himself to get ready for work and Luke's father, Michael, left for his day. Bonnie was off work and was tidying up the house.

"Ma, do you mind if we use the car to go to the registrar and run some errands? I need to get some supplies to fix up Grandma and Grandda's place."

"Sure, you'll be back for dinner?"

"You know I will." Luke kissed Bonnie's cheek, the dutiful son.

Audra could see in Bonnie's eyes how much she loved and worried for Luke. She reached up and patted his cheek.

"It's grand to have you home."

Luke went to change and Audra sat down, sipping her coffee, not sure how to make conversation.

"You're good for him, you know?" Bonnie said as she wiped down the table. "Lucas has always been pushin' and searchin'. We were glad when he took up rock climbin' because it seemed to make him happy. But it was never enough, like. He had to be the best, go the farthest. I was afraid he'd fall and die. Though, he laughs it off when I say anythin'. He seems to have shifted focus some with meetin' you, doesn't he? Do you rock climb?"

"Very amateurly. I hadn't until I met Luke and he's taught me some."

Bonnie nodded and cocked her head back toward the bedroom. "Maybe now, since he has you, he'll be more careful, yeah?"

Audra doubted it. Luke was driven by something deep within him. She didn't think she made any difference in that. Luke came out and glanced between them.

"Talkin' about me, are you?"

"Of course. I was tellin' Audra, I hoped havin' her in your life would make you aware more of your mortality," Bonnie replied flatly.

"Were you, then?" Luke raised his eyebrows and looked at Audra. "What did you say?"

"Nothing, really. I sincerely doubt my being around changes your focus on what your life goal is."

Luke flinched and he gestured to the door. "You ready to go? You'll need your passport and anythin' else that shows who you are."

Audra bobbed her head and followed him out the door. They got in the car and drove for a bit when Luke pulled over on a side street. He turned off the car and faced her.

"I'd give up rock climbin' if it meant I could have you and keep you safe for the rest of me life. Every single thing I do now, you're in the forefront of me mind. I absolutely have changed me focus since fallin' in love with you. For fuck's sake, Audra, you have to know that. You are me primary life goal. Me family, like. I love rock climbin' and hope we can do it together with our children one day, but if havin' that meant losin' you, or you losin' me, I'd give it up today. Tell me you understand that."

Audra met his eyes and nodded. His eyes were intently focused on her and he grabbed her in a tight hug. Audra believed him and had to allow herself to trust his love for her. She needed to conquer her fear of not being worthy. He'd laid it all out for her and she was the only one preventing them from being totally vulnerable with each other.

She sighed, then kissed him. "Believe, trust, conquer. Right?"

Luke smiled and leaned back, watching her. She'd finally met him halfway.

"Right."

Chapter Twenty-Six

*T*he drive out to their new home, Luke's grandparents' house, was beautiful and Audra felt she should pinch herself to make sure it was real. They'd bought a car the day before with the money they were given from the FBI to disappear and for the truck. Luke still had money saved from competing, but they were trying to not touch it, so they could start building the rock climbing center.

It was about an hour out from his parents' home and Luke drove with the familiarity of someone who'd made the trek hundreds of times. The whole drive he had a slight smile on his face, excited to be home and beginning the next chapter of their lives. When they pulled into the long driveway, Audra caught her breath. The road led to a two-story, stone house surrounded by multiple outbuildings, including a large barn and stables.

They went down the driveway slowly, the road having been washed out from rain and not maintained well since his grandparents passed. Audra was in awe and turned to Luke, grinning.

"The only thing it's missing is a dog," she joked.

"That can be arranged, yeah?" Luke said.

The door stuck when Luke unlocked it and he needed to put his shoulder into it to get it open. They left the door open as they went in to allow air to move through the space. It was dark and musty. Luke cut on lights and went around opening windows. It was chilly but the air was stagnant and stale. Luke began to drag covers off the furniture and Audra jumped in to help. Once they were done, Audra peered around, feeling like she'd stepped onto the set of a movie filmed in Ireland. There was a large stone fireplace at one end of the living room, surrounded by two dark thick armchairs. Built-in bookcases flanked either side of the fireplace and were full to the ceiling. Another seating area was on the other side of the room with large merlot and gold couches around a hefty, carved wooden table. It almost felt like a small castle.

Next, they moved to the dining room and wiped the dust off the table and chairs. Luke ran the water through the pipes to clear them and they scrubbed the kitchen down. It was afternoon by the time they made it to the second floor and stripped the bedding to wash it all. There were four bedrooms, one master, and three others. One had been used as an office and the other two contained multiple twin beds. Audra thought with a pang how nice it would be to have a reason to use them. At least they could have Luke's nephews and nieces visit. *Their.* Their nieces and nephews.

By dinner time, the house was scrubbed clean and smelled fresh. Luke built a fire in the stone fireplace and closed the windows. Within minutes, the downstairs was toasty and they set to making dinner. Luke was comfortable in the space, having grown up helping his grandma cook, and dug out pots and pans. Audra observed him with fascination, picturing Luke as a young boy helping his grandma chop at the butcher block island. She thought about her own family and how they never really had a home base.

"My family moved a lot and since my parents were older when they had me, my grandparents were already living in a retirement village by the time I was old enough to remember. Well, my father's parents. My mother's father had passed and her mother was in New York, so the only time we saw her was when she flew out to see us. She wasn't the grandmother type, really," Audra said, thinking out loud.

Luke paused, watching her. "The grandparents in the retirement village. What were they like?"

"My grandfather was funny. Always cracking jokes and pulling coins out from behind my ear type of stuff. My grandmother was quiet, she read a lot. She was nice but kind of in the background. I like visiting them because they had a bowl of candy, which was always full. It was fun, but we pretty much sat in their living room and hung out. They passed within months of each other. Couldn't live without one another, I suppose. I thought that's what marriage was. It's how my parents are."

"It's supposed to be how marriage is, yeah?" Luke replied gently.

Maybe that's why she gave James too many chances. She'd been raised by people who loved and respected each other. Her parents were still affectionate and thoughtful of one another. James had taken advantage of her open heart and trust. She fought back tears, which surprised her. She'd worked through it or thought she already had. She bit her lip hard to push them down. Luke noticed and came over and tipped her face up to meet his eyes.

"It's how our marriage will be. I promise. I'm not James."

Audra nodded. "No, you're not. I know that. I just feel stupid for letting him treat me that way. For staying for so long."

"It's your big heart, Audra. You're willin' to sacrifice yourself to save others. Even those who can't be saved, or don't deserve to be, so."

"You have that same big heart," Audra countered.

Luke smiled and cocked his head, his eyes locked on hers. "Maybe so. I guess it's good we found each other, isn't it, then?"

Audra knew had she not stayed with James so long and boarded that plane almost a decade later, she'd never have met Luke. Her prison sentence led to her freedom in a warped way. She leaned up and kissed Luke. "Let's cook."

They made dinner in their new home and ate in front of the fireplace. One day, they'd have a table full of family, Audra told herself. After dinner, they took a walk down the long driveway, holding hands. Audra had never even considered visiting Ireland, much less living there. Her parents were supportive when she told them she was in Ireland the day before and promised to visit. She'd told them everything and that her location had to be kept a secret, not that the terrorist group would even try to follow them. Her parents begged her to be safe and told her how much they loved her. She cried when she hung up and wished there was a way for them to all be together.

By bedtime, the upstairs of the house was warm enough and they retired to Luke's grandparents' room. There was a picture of his grandparents on the dresser from when they were younger and Audra paused to look at it. She could see the family resemblance. His grandfather had Luke's eyes and his grandmother his face shape. So, his father's parents.

"I gather this was your father's parents. Tell me about your mother's parents," Audra said as she climbed into bed next to him.

Luke rested his head back against his arm and thought. "They lived in Dublin. Me parents met at college there. Me grandfather, Lucas, was a musician and I get me hair from him, like me mam. He was very outspoken and angry, me mam says. He hated the way Ireland was divided and wrote a lot of songs about it. Me grandmother, Cara, was an artist. Some of the paintings you see here and in me parents' house were hers. She had some notoriety and made a decent livin' at it. Mostly portraits for the money, but she preferred abstract art. She taught me some when I was very young."

"When did they pass?"

"Me mam's parents when I was just a lad. Me dad's father when I was seventeen. His mother, I guess about six years ago."

Audra put her arm over Luke's waist and kissed his shoulder. "So, neither of us has surviving grandparents."

"I suppose not. Time passes quickly, yeah? Have to appreciate it while you can."

Audra thought about that. She was already in her thirties and had nothing to show for it. Well, not entirely. She had Luke and a home now. Maybe they could get a dog. Eventually, they could adopt children since they hadn't been using birth control and she still hadn't gotten pregnant. It *had* been her all along. She shook off the thought. She needed to cherish what she had.

"I appreciate you, Luke."

"I know you do. If you're serious about gettin' a dog, I think it would be a nice addition to the house, like. To the land."

"I am."

"Tomorrow?"

"Sure."

They were too beat to do anything more than hold each other and dozed off with Audra resting against Luke's shoulder.

The next morning, they headed to the CSPCA to look at dogs. They filled out the questionnaire and were brought back to the available dogs. A litter of puppies had recently been brought in which were Irish Wolfhound, Beagle mixes. They were odd little dogs and the lady told Luke and Audra they were sure to be big once fully grown. They were stout and gangly at the same time with crazy hair and big, soulful brown eyes. They went into the pen with the pups and sat down, immediately being swarmed with wagging tails and wet tongues.

Audra was drawn to a male puppy, who came and clambered right into her lap, plopping down. Luke was being accosted by a female pup, who kept waving her paw at him like she was trying to shake hands. Their eyes met and they were in a predicament. They'd come for one dog but were connected to two. Luke put two fingers up and raised his eyebrows. Audra shrugged, there was no way around it. They stepped out and went to the front.

"We think we've decided," Luke told the lady.

She peered up from her desk and smiled. "Sure! Which one?"

"Two, actually," Luke replied.

"Oh! Wonderful, they'll have a playmate. Show me."

They went to the back and Luke and Audra pointed out their two. Trying to get them was another story. It took the three of them to catch the puppies and not the others who were scrambling toward them. Finally, out of breath and laughing, they separated them from the group and shut the pen door.

"Good news is they've already been spayed and neutered. Do you have names?"

They didn't. The lady waved it off and wrote down Ir.Wlfhnd/Bgl mix male and Ir.Wlfhnd/Bgl mix female on the paperwork.

"No problem, it takes a while to pick just the right name, doesn't it?"

They showed their identification and finished the paperwork. Before they knew it, were heading home with two rather large, exuberant puppies. They tried keeping them in the backseat but by the time they were halfway home, Luke had the male puppy lying on his lap and Audra had the female puppy on her lap with her head halfway out the window. They checked the leashes before they got out at home, then let the pups out to sniff around. The female pup was so excited, she kept tripping over her own feet and managed to slip the leash that Audra was holding.

"Oh, come here, you loosey goose!" Audra yelled at her, repeating the words her grandfather said all of the time to her when she was little.

The pup ran up to her when she knelt and knocked Audra on her behind. The pup immediately covered Audra in slobber.

Luke was laughing. "That's a grand name for her, isn't it, though?"

"What is?"

"Loosey."

Audra nodded, snickering as she climbed to her feet. She brushed off her clothes and snagged Loosey. "Spelled like that, too."

The boy pup was like a little old man just sniffing and plopped down at Luke's feet.

"I think he needs an old man's name," Audra said thoughtfully. "Like Morty or Monty."

"I like Monty," Luke agreed as he rubbed the dog's head. "Monty, you like that, boy?"

The dog looked up and yawned.

"So, Loosey and Monty. That fits." Audra laughed.

They took them inside and Luke set up a makeshift gate to keep them in the kitchen until they were housetrained since it had a door outside right off of the space. The dogs started playing together while Luke and Audra made lunch. For the first time, she wasn't feeling such heavy pangs to have children. One day she still wanted to, but right now having the joy and goofiness of Monty and Loosey was filling that void. They were going to be so spoiled. If one day she and Luke did have children, they'd get to grow up with some pretty awesome dogs.

Luke came up behind Audra and wrapped his arm around her as they watched the dogs lying on the floor, mouthing each other.

"Who would've thought that when I got on that plane last summer, I'd be standin' in me grandparents' kitchen, holdin' me soon-to-be wife, watchin' our dogs play, four months later?"

Audra shook her head and squeezed Luke's hand. "Too unreal, but absolutely perfect."

Chapter Twenty-Seven

T he holidays in Ireland weren't so different from the holidays back home, except for the sheer amount of food and drink. Audra thought she'd explode. Luke's family went to Midnight Mass on Christmas Eve and Audra went along, solely because she'd always been drawn to the Catholic church aesthetic. It didn't disappoint. The ancient church was decorated with greenery, candles, and red and gold bows. With the already impressive stained-glass windows, dark wood arches, and ornate decor, it was almost too much to look at. Audra didn't know where to rest her eyes.

Audra tried to follow along with all of the hand motions, kneeling, standing, shaking hands, and songs, but found herself laughing as she clumsily lost track and felt like the last-minute, unprepared stand-in for the Rockettes. Luke winked at her, then shrugged. He was doing this for tradition, not out of any commitment to the church. It was as much cultural as religious, if not more so.

After Mass, the family headed back to Bonnie and Michael's home. The farmhouse was an hour away and since they'd be coming back in the morning, Luke and Audra agreed to sleep in his old bedroom for the night. Some of the family stayed up to drink after church, the little ones tucked into bed in one of the other rooms. However, Audra was tired and excused herself.

Luke came a few minutes later, shaking his head and laughing. "Will be interestin' to see who gets the most pissed tonight by the hangovers in the mornin'."

By pissed he meant drunk, and they were well on their way. For Audra, it was strange to go straight from church to drinking, but she'd never been much of a drinker, anyhow. Luke didn't seem all that committed, either. They climbed into bed and giggled at the drunken carols coming through the walls. Audra hoped all this ruckus meant they'd be able to sleep in the next morning.

What she didn't take into account... children don't care what time their parents went to bed the night before on Christmas morning. They were up begging to open presents at the crack of dawn. It was just Cara's kids as Patrick stayed with his wife's family the night before and was due for Christmas dinner later. There was a family trade-off on the holiday, trying to spend time with both sides.

Audra longed for her parents and planned to call them later. They'd sent housewarming and Christmas gifts a few days prior. Since Audra told them the house was fully stocked they sent engraved candle holders, a photo frame, and a basket of regional delicacies, reminding Audra of the gift basket she and Luke ravaged after the plane crash. Her parents had already booked flights for the wedding and planned a week-long stay to check out Ireland, then.

The children were beautiful, their faces shining as they opened their presents. Audra was caught up in the magic of it all when Luke sat down next to her and took her hand.

"I have somethin' for you... well, for us, like. Hold on." Luke went over to the bookcase and pulled down a small wrapped box. He made his way over to Audra, handing her the box.

Inside were two corded bracelets. Each had two hearts made of different stones. Audra pulled them out and looked at Luke inquisitively.

"I had these made, so. Each one has a Wyoming agate heart and a heart made from fossil limestone from here in Cork. Where you entered this world, and where I entered this world. One for you and one for me."

Audra ran her fingers over the stones and was speechless. James always just bought her what he thought a guy was supposed to buy his wife. Perfume, robes, stupid shit. If she got jewelry, it was because he went to the counter and let them pick it out. Luke was watching her, trying to get a read off her face.

"Damn, Luke. You're so sentimental... thoughtful. Can you help me put it on?"

She stuck her wrist out and Luke fastened the bracelet on her wrist, kissing her upturned palm gently. She slid his bracelet on his wrist, made sure it was secure, and squeezed his hand.

"I have something for you, too. It's in the room, I'll be right back."

She dug under the bed for the package she'd hidden there the night before and sat on the bed for a moment. Now, she felt silly about it. She'd researched the family crest for Riordan and had something special made up. Luke came in and stood by the door.

"Everythin' alright?"

"Yeah, I just suddenly thought this might be stupid."

"We won't know now, will we, unless I open it?" Luke joked.

Audra slid the package across the bed and Luke came over to it, opening the wrapping paper. He exposed the item and stared at it, his face unreadable. Audra held her breath, waiting for a response and Luke met her eyes. Audra fumbled to explain.

"I was wanting to make a sign for our home, you know, to make it ours. I looked up the crest for the name Riordan and a lot of them showed two male lions. I always thought you kind of looked like a lion with your hair. Once you told me I looked like a lioness because of my eyes." Audra knew she was speed-talking and starting to turn red. "So, I sent this idea to a metal sign maker and he was able to create it. I'm sorry if it's offensive or wrong or dumb."

Luke started to laugh and shook his head. He lifted the sign, which had the crest cut out through the metal. It was the Riordan crest, but rather than two male lions, it had a male lion on one side and a female lion on the other side. Instead of them looking like they were growling at each other, their paws met across the top of the crest. Riordan was at the top and below was an inscription.

Believe, Trust, Conquer.

"This is fantastic. It's us, yeah? The new Riordans. Audra, I can't wait to get home and hang it outside our door. Can I show me family?"

Audra let out the nervous breath she'd been holding in, then nodded. "Okay. They won't be mad I changed it?"

"What? The crest? No. I'm not sure I've ever seen anyone in me family use it, and it has a few interpretations. I like yours best."

He carried the sign out and Audra followed behind, still unsure she hadn't crossed any boundaries. The family clapped and hollered when he held it up. Audra blushed and Bonnie met her eyes, grinning. The women in this family were strong. Luke turned and winked, she'd done well. Audra accepted a small glass of whiskey she was handed to make a toast. She was not used to drinking in the morning but it seemed more customary than imbibing. Everyone lifted their glass and Luke's father made a toast in Irish.

"Nollaig shona dhuit! Go mbeire muid beo ar an am seo arís! Sláinte!"

Audra looked to Luke for translation. He leaned in and whispered.

"Happy Christmas! May we be alive this time next year! To health!"

Audra chuckled at the both happy and somewhat somber toast. She repeated, "sláinte" with everyone else and they all took a sip. Whiskey wasn't her cup of tea in the morning and she winced, drawing laughter from Liam who downed his. She handed him her glass and he downed that, as well. Cup of tea. Now, that sounded lovely. She followed Bonnie to the kitchen.

"Could I bother you for a cup of tea? Or could you show me where the cups and tea are?"

"Oh, dear, I'll get it. I was about to make meself some. Too much of the drink last night. You were smart to go to bed."

Audra sat at the kitchen table and watched Bonnie go through the steps of making the tea. She came over with two cups and sat down with Audra.

"You must be missin' your family today?" Bonnie asked kindly.

Audra bobbed her head. "I do. I mean, I hadn't spent the holidays with them for the last few years, but it's hard knowing they're so far away."

"Why hadn't you spent holidays with them?"

Audra knew this would bring up James but she wanted to be honest with her new family. "My ex-husband James was very controlling. He drove a wedge between my family and me. Not directly, but he always had negative things to say about them. When I'd talk to them, he'd usually end up picking fights after. Before long, I simply avoided reaching out to them. I would sometimes at work, so they'd know I was okay... but never at home."

Bonnie watched Audra, her eyes boring into Audra's soul. "You can't let a fella do you that way, like. They aren't worthy of you unless they honor that. You weren't alright, though, were you?"

Audra shook her head. "No, I guess not. I thought he'd change, that I'd matter enough to him to turn things around. I knew the signs and I know it sounds dumb, but I thought this was different."

"Everyone does, so. We don't want to believe we let ourselves be fooled. That love is enough to turn the tide, however, some people are warped. You can't change their hearts."

Audra took a sip of her tea, then sighed. "I want you to know I love Luke and he has been a friend, a confidant, to me."

"I know. Be careful, though. You don't want to take all that pain and sufferin' and hope for a knight in shinin' armor. They don't exist. We're all mere mortals and can't carry another's weight, plus our own. Love is about sharin' the load and eventually bein' able to put some of it down. Lucas needs you as much as you need him, yeah?"

Audra knew Bonnie didn't mean it any certain way, yet she felt admonished. She'd been there for Luke, too. Right? She scanned back to their conversations and found while she had, he'd been carrying more of the emotional load for the two of them. She needed to change that before they got married, so he didn't assume that was his role. She met Bonnie's eyes and nodded. "Thank you."

"Of course. We're family now and family is honest, like. Would you like to help in the kitchen today? It's pretty much all hands on deck."

Audra agreed and went to find Luke before the house broke into chaos. He was in the yard tossing horseshoes with Liam, who appeared to be at least one sheet to the wind, working on two. Audra wandered over, smirking at Liam's boisterous game-taunting. Luke kissed her, tasting of whiskey.

"Nope," Audra said and wiped her mouth. The taste made bile rise in her throat and she stepped away. "If you want to do that, you need to brush your teeth."

Luke laughed and ran inside to do just that. Liam semi-eyed her, his eyes not really settling anywhere.

"I've never seen me brother so happy. Luke was always a pretty positive lad, but now he exudes happiness."

Audra wasn't sure if it was the whiskey talking or Liam was feeling sentimental. "Okay? Thanks?"

"Cheers!" Liam practically shouted. It was the whiskey. Or maybe both. Audra chuckled and went in to find Luke. He was just finishing brushing his teeth and kissed her again. Better, but not great. She put her finger to his lip, shaking her head.

"Maybe it's me. I can still taste whiskey on your breath something fierce."

Luke wrapped his arm around her, pulling her close. "*Mo anáil*, do you not want me?"

"Oh, I want you. Just not after you drank whiskey," Audra replied.

"Then I won't."

Audra eyed him. That would be a challenge around this crew. He crossed his heart and she laughed. Suddenly, a waft of cooking meat came from the kitchen and she pushed past him to vomit in the toilet. She wretched up what felt like everything she'd eaten over the last few days and then some.

So, it wasn't just the whiskey.

It wasn't just the whiskey! She did a quick mental calculation of the last couple of months and sat on the edge of the tub in shock.

Luke came over and sat next to her. "What's goin' on, Audra? Nerves, or have you come down with somethin'?"

"I'm late, Luke."

244

Chapter Twenty-Eight

*L*uke stared at her with his head cocked. "Late? As in you haven't had your period?"

"I think. I don't track it religiously because why bother? But I'm pretty sure I haven't had one since the apartment, so maybe seven or eight weeks ago. With everything going on here, I haven't even thought about it until I vomited."

"Oh. I should see about gettin' a test, yeah?"

"Is anything even open on Christmas day?"

Luke leaned forward on his elbows, then shook his head. "Not much of anythin'. Tomorrow, either, so. I could ask Cara, she might know."

"No! I don't want to be that girl you brought home unmarried and knocked up," Audra hissed.

"Don't you, though? I mean, does it matter how we do it? I love you, we want children. Who fuckin' cares in what order we do things? Honestly, I would rather have you be now, than maybe never. Isn't that what you want?"

Audra did. Part of her was also afraid to bring anyone else in and it be another disappointment. However, she also didn't think she could wait two more days for an answer. She met Luke's eyes and nodded, giving him permission to talk to Cara. They stepped out and went to the living room. Luke made his way across and whispered in Cara's ear. She looked surprised, then stared him dead in the eyes. She tipped her head and said something back to him. Luke came back across the room.

"Cara keeps a stock of pregnancy tests at her house. Seein' as she is rather motherly, like." He said motherly in the way that meant she was fertile. "She said she can run home and grab one if you want."

If she wanted? Luke was grinning, as Cara was already out the door. Audra slapped him on the arm. At least he had a sense of humor about these things. Cara was gone for a while and just about the time she returned, Bonnie came out to find Audra.

"Audra, I'd love it if you'd come help me in the kitchen?"

Audra looked helplessly at Luke. She wanted to assist Bonnie but didn't want to get stranded in the kitchen for hours before she could take the test.

"One second, Ma, Audra was helpin' me put this sign away right quick."

They grabbed the sign and took it to the bedroom with Cara closely behind. Cara handed Audra the test. Shit, it took five minutes for the results. Audra ran to the bathroom and peed on the stick. She covered it and brought it to the room, stashing it under the bed.

"Two lines yes, one line no," she whispered to Luke as she headed to the kitchen, not wanting Bonnie to come searching for her.

She set to chopping walnuts and watched the door anxiously. Five minutes seemed like hours. She focused on not slicing her hand when she heard Luke clear his throat. She glanced up and met his eyes. He put up two fingers, nodding. She gasped and sliced the tip of the knife across the end of her finger.

Blood started to drip on the walnuts and Bonnie rushed over. "For heaven's sake! You nicked yourself good, lass! Lucas, get her to the bathroom and put pressure on that."

Luke guided Audra to the bathroom, shutting the door behind them. He wrapped a washcloth around her finger, then drew out the pregnancy test from his pocket. Two lines. Audra stared in disbelief and began to bawl. Luke grabbed her, holding her tightly against his chest. Her finger was starting to throb in rhythm with his heartbeat.

She imagined another heartbeat joining in sync. It couldn't be real, could it? "Promise you won't tell anyone," she whispered.

"I won't, but Cara is goin' to have some idea, yeah?"

"Swear her to secrecy."

"I will, however, Audra, this is a grand thing, like. What we were hopin' for."

"It is, but I'm afraid to get my hopes up. In case."

"There is no *in case*. It'll be alright. Any child of ours is comin' into this world fightin'." Luke laughed softly.

Audra smiled and kissed Luke. "Still, let's hold this in our hearts for a bit. Just to protect us."

"Of course. But me heart is beamin'."

Audra was still afraid to let her heart accept it. Yet. A soft knock came at the door. Luke opened it and Cara was standing outside with her eyebrows raised.

"Well?"

Luke nodded and grinned. Cara put her hand to her chest and drew in her breath, smiling. She hugged Audra tightly.

"Oh, so excitin'! I won't say anythin' to let your two decide how and when to make the announcement."

She kissed Luke on the cheek. "Our Lucas is goin' to be a da. I'll take over with Ma in the kitchen, so she doesn't come to see how you are. We need a fresh batch of walnuts since you bled all over them."

"Sorry," Audra replied sheepishly.

Cara waved it off and slipped out. Luke unwrapped Audra's finger and fresh blood started to pool. The wound wasn't big but it was deep.

"You're just findin' ways for me to pull out me needle and thread, aren't you?"

Audra yanked her hand away. "No!"

"Just jokin'. I think a bandage will suffice, yeah?" Luke dug in the cabinets and found some gauze and medical tape. "Lucky for us, Liam likes to get himself into fights."

Audra rinsed the wound, sending pain through her hand, then stuck it out to Luke. He dried it and wrapped it with gauze and tape firmly. Audra peered at it, wiggling her finger. It would hold and get her out of anything to do with a knife the rest of the day, which was fine since the smell of the cooking ham was making her queasy. They headed out and went to let Bonnie know she'd survive. Cara was chopping fresh walnuts and grinned at them.

"Hey, why don't you take me three wild ones out back to play?" she suggested.

Luke rounded up the children and led them outside for a game of tag. Audra followed and considered calling her parents to wish them a Merry Christmas. Checking the clock, she realized it was still too early in Oregon and joined in the game of tag. For the first time, playing with the children didn't bring up feelings of sadness and she placed her hand on her womb.

"Please just hang in there," she begged.

She took a seat and watched Luke chase after the children. Somehow, with just one arm, he managed to scoop up two squiggling, screaming children. After longer than seemed possible, Luke tired and came and sat with Audra. He was out of breath, chuckling.

"They never get worn out. Truly."

The children continued the game until it was time to eat and Luke corralled them in to wash up. Audra's stomach had settled, thankfully, and she sat as far away from the ham as possible. The family gathered and toast after toast was given, followed by grace. Audra pretended to sip the whiskey with each toast, putting it near her lips but not going past. No one seemed to notice, happily refilling between each toast. By the time all was said and done, everyone was hungry and a little buzzed if they hadn't been before.

Luke leaned over to Audra, letting his lips brush her ear. "We don't always drink like this. I promise. Most times no one really drinks at all. Except for Liam."

Audra noticed Luke hadn't touched his whiskey, either, in solidarity with her. Besides, he wanted to be able to kiss her. As the food platters were handed around, Audra quickly discovered what she would and wouldn't be able to eat simply by the smell. Potatoes, yes. Anything with cheese, no. Green beans and salad, yes. Meat, no. She loaded up her plate with anything her stomach didn't revolt at and picked at it.

Unlike American meals, the family was in no rush to hurry through and talked, eating slowly. Over an hour passed, yet the family showed no signs of wrapping up. Audra liked this pacing and rested her hand on Luke's thigh. He reached over and placed his hand on hers. It was the three of them, now. By the time hour two came, Audra was full even though she'd been picking at her food. A wave of sleepiness came over her and met Luke's eyes.

"I need to lie down."

"I'll come lay with you, yeah?" he offered.

"No, be with your family. I'm just beat. It was late last night and my body feels exhausted."

Luke nodded, understanding. "They'll move to the livin' room soon and Da will be asleep in his chair within minutes. I'll come then, like. You rest. I love you, Audra."

"I love you." Audra kissed him and slid her chair back.

Luke saw his mother watching and laughed. "The likes of you all are wearin' Audra out. She's not used to the up all night and up at the crack of dawn shite."

"Watch your mouth, Lucas," his mother admonished.

He'd successfully drawn the attention away from Audra. Audra stepped into the cool room and yawned. It was still early and she could call her parents after a nap. She lay down and slipped her feet under the comforter. Within minutes, her eyes were too heavy and she dozed off. A while later, she felt Luke slide in next to her and place his hand on her belly.

"*Mo anáil*," he whispered and rested his head next to hers.

She knew he meant both of them and felt butterflies in her stomach as she let sleep take her back under. When she woke up, the sky was getting dim and Luke was gone. She'd slept for hours. She stretched and decided to call her parents from the room since it sounded like the chatter in the house was picking back up. Cara had left to see her inlaws, but Patrick's children were running, screaming through the house. The phone rang and her mother picked up.

"Mom! Merry Christmas!"

"Audra, it's so good to hear from you. Merry Christmas. We miss you."

"I miss you, too. I can't wait to see you in March."

"Us, either. We're already making plans on what to see and do. We may extend a week."

"That would be great. The longer the better. Maybe I can convince you to stay."

Her mother laughed delightfully, making Audra wish she could tell her about the baby. However, she wanted to wait, to make sure. At that moment, she felt like a little girl again and wanted nothing more than to wrap her arms around her mother's neck.

"Audra, we'll visit often. We can't wait! It gives your father an excuse to finally retire and travel. Let me get him on the line real quick."

Audra heard soft talking and her father came on the line. "There's my girl! I was just remembering when you were little and after you opened presents, you wanted to keep the wrapping paper because you thought it was so pretty. You'd cry if we took it away, so we made you that wrapping paper photo book. Do you remember?"

Audra did. They cut squares of the decorative paper and put them into a photo album for her. She let tears roll down her cheeks. How did she let James separate her from her parents? They were her connection to who she was. "I do, Dad. I love you."

"I love you too, Audra. We can't wait to come over there in a few months."

"Me too, Dad. It can't come soon enough. I'm sorry."

"For what?"

"For not being a better daughter when I was married to James."

Her father fell silent. "Now... knowing what he did to you, I'm sorry we didn't know and couldn't help. I want to kill him. For hurting my little girl."

"I know. I wish I'd just told you and come home. He had my head so messed up. At least he's out of my life."

"About that, Audra. He called here last night, asking about you. He was drunk and was very adamant about finding out where you are. I reminded him that you have a restraining order against him and I was calling the police."

Audra felt her stomach drop. "Did you tell him anything?"

"Of course not. But, Audra, he knew a lot of things. Like Luke's full name. That he was from Ireland and that you might be there. I don't know what he's after, but he was being strange. Talking about you needing to be held accountable. Just be careful. I did notify the police but there wasn't much they could do. Maybe talk to your contacts in law enforcement. See if there is anything they can do to intercede. He could've been drunk talking, however, I don't trust him."

They finished the call and hung up. Audra sat on the edge of the bed and thought about what her father said. She didn't trust James, either. He was up to something. But what?

Whatever it was, Audra knew it wasn't over and she needed to let Luke know.

Chapter Twenty-Nine

uke and Audra decided to make the drive home that evening to spend some time alone with their secret. Besides, Luke was afraid he'd slip up and say something if they stayed. They wanted the next week through New Year's alone to plan out their wedding, and now impending child. If Audra figured out her last period correctly, she was due sometime in the summer. However, she was getting ahead of herself. No sense in making plans for something which wasn't guaranteed to happen. Luke, on the other hand, couldn't contain his excitement over the upcoming changes in their lives, openly talking about them.

"We can clean up one of the rooms near ours to make a nursery, like. We can have the babe in our room, first," he thought out loud.

Audra didn't want to squash his joy but was afraid to say too much. She nodded and smiled, pushing down the fear inside her. To change the subject, she thought about what

Bonnie said to her in the kitchen. About Audra and Luke balancing each other out.

"Luke? Can I ask you something?"

"Sure, anythin'."

"How are you doing with Adam's death?"

Luke glanced at her, then back at the road. He swallowed hard and shook his head. "Alright, I suppose."

"Can you talk to me about it?" she pressed.

Luke drove in silence for a bit and Audra allowed it to sit between them, instead of trying to fill the space in with platitudes. Finally, he took a deep breath and chewed his lip.

"It's unfair that the same event which brought me the greatest joys in me life, took away any chance of him ever havin' these same things, yeah? I feel selfish and small for bein' happy sometimes. He boarded that plane just like me, except he died and I didn't. I feel guilty for livin'. On the other hand, had I not, or had you not, we wouldn't have this child comin' to us, so. This child deserves life, too. Honestly? I'm conflicted, Audra."

Audra listened and put her hand on his leg. She could see tears rolling down his cheeks and resisted the urge to say something to make it better. It was her place to just be there and let him work through it. That was the balance. He cleared his throat roughly and went on.

"Through the tragedy which took him away from me, from his family, from himself, I was given the most sacred gift of me own. I miss him every day. I ache to hear his voice and see him laughin' about some ridiculous joke I told. To look down and see him below me on the rock, urgin' me onward. It's not like he's just gone, is it? He's missin', like. I go to turn and tell him somethin' random, but he isn't there. It fuckin' breaks me heart. Because some asshole wanted to make a pound and other assholes wanted to destroy other people's lives on some fucked up backward stance, I lost me best friend."

His tears were falling harder now and he pulled off to the side of the road. He leaned his head on the steering wheel and let go. Audra slid close to him and rubbed his back, murmuring she was there for him, that he wasn't alone. He didn't register her and talked with his face pressed to the steering wheel.

"They crushed his head. I don't know if you saw, but it was caved in on the side. When I took off his necklace, I saw and vomited right there beside him. There was bone and it was dented in, compressed into his brain. It was like somethin' out of a horror movie. Except it was me friend, me companion for years. The only person I saw consistently day after day. I fuckin' hate them and what they did. I fuckin' hate it all."

"I know, Luke. I'm sorry. It's not fair and you have every right to hurt, to be angry. You've been there for me all of this time and while I'm grateful, it wasn't fair to you. I'm here for you."

Luke didn't turn or respond. He pushed the car door open and stumbled into a nearby field. She watched him as he stood staring off into the night. She could tell he was weeping by his shoulders shaking. He knelt on the ground with his hand around Adam's necklace.

Audra knew in a way, her own issues had prevented him from truly feeling his grief and was aware she needed to be the strong one, now. He needed a safe space to grieve. She opened her door and walked slowly toward him. He'd stopped crying by the time she got there and she knelt beside him in the dirt. He rubbed his nose and sighed, defeated. Audra wiped the tears off his cheeks and put her arm around his waist. Luke's voice was raspy when he spoke.

"I'm grateful for you and the babe. I just wish we could've met without it killin' Adam."

"Luke, we didn't kill Adam. Whether or not we'd met, he would've died. If I had died, he would've died. If you had died, he would've died. Our walking away from that crash didn't change that. He died because of a greedy pilot and hateful people. Don't blame yourself, blame them. Good people die because of other people's actions. It's not fair and they deserve to pay. The pilot paid for his stupidity. Hopefully, the other people will pay for their actions."

Luke listened, staring blankly at the ground. He nodded slightly, then stood up. Audra rose next to him and they watched the sky. It was clear and the stars were brighter than she'd ever seen.

"What can we do at our home for Adam's memory?" she asked quietly.

Luke turned and smiled weakly, his eyes filled with pain. "I hadn't thought about that, yeah? We can build a rock wall in his name and start teachin' people."

Audra nodded. "That would be nice."

They walked back to the car and Luke paused before getting in. He turned to Audra.

"Cheers, Audra. I've been needin' to talk about Adam, so. It has been buildin' up inside of me for some time and I didn't know how to let it out. You're me best friend, too, you know that, right?"

"I know, Luke. I wish I'd gotten to know Adam, but maybe you can share more stories about him with me and eventually our children?"

Luke cocked his head. "I'd like that."

The rest of the ride home was quiet and Audra fell asleep against Luke's shoulder. He woke her up at home. They'd boarded the pups, knowing they'd be too much to handle with the children at his parents. The house felt empty without them. Audra thought to herself how she wanted every room full eventually.

They could start with the one.

They climbed into bed and fell asleep immediately. The next morning, they were groggy and made coffee before going to pick up the dogs. Luke's hair was bushy like a mane around his head, making Audra chuckle. She got her hands wet and ran them through his hair in the kitchen, reforming the frizz into curls.

"My lion," she joked.

He put his hand in her hair, now almost shoulder length, and kissed her. "Me lioness."

They were anxious to get the dogs and showed up twenty minutes before the kennel opened. Audra thought about what her father told her about James and sighed. For their safety, she needed to tell Luke.

"I talked to my parents last night. They're doing well and told me to wish you a Merry Christmas. They're so excited to come visit."

Luke met her eyes and nodded, reading there was more in the tone of her voice. "That's nice, yeah? I can't wait to meet them."

"Or them you. So... uh, James called them," Audra stammered out.

"What? Why?"

"He was drunk and was asking where I was. They told him they were calling the police, however, he went on and said your full name, that he knew you were from Ireland. That he thought I was in Ireland, too."

"Fuckin' hell. What do you think he means to do?" Luke ran his hand roughly across his face.

"I don't know. I can't see his cheap ass buying a ticket and trying to find us here, but he's definitely up to something. My father said we should contact the agent we've been working with to let him know, either way."

Luke nodded, frustrated. "Why do fuckers like him get to live and good people like Adam die?"

"I'm sorry, Luke. I had to tell you. I need to call the agent today and let him know, see if James is up to anything."

"I'm not mad at you, like. I'm mad at James and want him the hell out of our lives once and for all. I'll kill him if he comes near you or the babe."

"*I'll* kill him if comes near me or the baby."

Luke chuckled, taking Audra's hand. "Of that, I have no doubt."

The kennel manager arrived and waved cheerily at them. They climbed out and followed her to their puppies' pen. Monty and Loosey were beside themselves with joy, clambering over each other to get to them first. Luke knelt, scratching their heads, and rubbed them vigorously. They leashed them up and paid for the boarding, anxious to get the pups back home. The ride home was adventurous and Audra was covered with slobber by the time they arrived. They released the dogs off their leads and let them explore the yard again. The dogs knew home and weren't going anywhere.

Audra called the FBI agent that evening and left a message with what her father told her, making sure to leave James's full name and location. After that, she and Luke played with the dogs and forgot about any of it. The next day, she had a message from the agent, saying he'd look into it and get back to her. They played phone tag for a few days until she finally reached him.

"This is Audra Banner," she said when he answered.

"Audra, yes. I was just about to call you. We put some tabs on your ex-husband and found out some information."

Audra waited and could hear papers shuffling in the background. She heard a child's voice asking for juice and the agent saying, "In a minute." It was strange to think he had a family and the everyday woes of anyone else. The child whined and she didn't hear it again, hearing another voice guide the child away. The agent came back on and cleared his throat.

"Okay, so James Letsky of Spokane, Washington. Age thirty-four?"

"That sounds like him."

"It is. We were able to run his social to your marriage license and old address," the agent confirmed.

"Did you find anything out about why he's asking where I am?"

"More than we thought. I don't know if you remember, we have an informant on the inside of the group behind the plutonium case?"

"Yes?" Audra was thoroughly confused.

"Well, in searching up Mr. Letsky, we found he'd recently sought that group out. Do you know if he had any radical beliefs or ties which may have connected him to the organization?" the agent asked.

James? Radical? He was a dick but the only thing he believed in was capitalism. Audra's head was spinning. "No? James doesn't believe in anything."

"From what we researched, that's what we thought, as well. No history of crime, no ties to organizations. All in all, a regular American citizen."

"Who likes to beat his wife," Audra responded dryly.

"Sadly, no record of it, so we can't use that. But we did find he'd connected with them and began attending meetings. The informant approached him and in the course of the conversation, James did mention his ex-wife and her new boyfriend. How he wanted to get back at them. The informant pushed for more information. Mr. Letsky said he could find out where you were and give the organization your location."

"I don't understand. How did he find that group or get all of this info on us?"

"In this day and age, it isn't that hard. The news did blips on the crash and the plutonium. He probably found out about the group through legal filings and your names were on the news. Mr. Riordan was a well enough known rock climber to be searchable. Being from Ireland and one-armed, set him apart from the crowd. A little information can go a long way, using technology. Who knows exactly, but it isn't hard."

Audra felt dizzy, bracing against the wall. She and Luke had registered to get married... their names and exact location. "Are we in danger?"

The line was quiet. "Honestly, I can't say. Do they care enough to listen to some ex-husband with a vendetta? Probably not. However, that doesn't mean no. They're in the news enough with the case and aren't looking to travel halfway around the world to kill a couple of pointless witnesses. The plutonium was found and their plot was uncovered. They have bigger fish to fry. But lay low. I'll dig around some more and call you with any updates."

Audra hung up the phone and crumpled to the floor. James was so egotistical and sadistic, he was willing to join a terrorist organization to track her down and have them killed?

What fresh hell had she brought onto her new family?

Chapter Thirty

Luke found Audra sitting on the floor with the phone in her hand. He knew immediately the news wasn't good and sat down beside her. Audra explained everything the agent told her, attempting to keep emotion out of her voice but she cracked a couple of times. Luke listened with a stone face. It was one thing to face off with James, it was a whole different issue if they were marked by a group. They didn't know who they were supposed to be looking for or how far the organization's presence reached. Once Audra was finished, neither spoke, silenced by the weight of the situation. They were helpless, outside of keeping an eye out. The agent said it wasn't likely anyone would come to Ireland, but who knew what trouble James was stirring up.

It was New Year's Eve and Audra didn't want to go anywhere with this news. Just to stay home with the dogs and each other. Luke agreed and got up to start making dinner. Audra watched him with his back to her, pulling items out of the cabinets. His shoulders moved fluidly and Audra caught her breath at his strength. Physically and emotionally. She got up and wrapped her arms around him.

"Eventually this all has to end. This running. We'll be okay, Luke. This is our home and our family. No one has the right to take it away from us," Audra reasoned.

Luke stood silently for a moment and then slammed his hand down on the counter. "Fuck it all to hell!"

Audra flinched and stepped back. Luke took a deep breath and walked out the door. She watched him head down the driveway with the dogs trailing behind. He held his head low and moved at a fast pace. The dogs thought it was a game and chased each other around his feet. He gave them a quick pat on the heads but kept moving. She watched as he reached the end of the road and swung the large gate closed over the driveway. He leaned on it for a few minutes, staring out. Audra understood. They hadn't done anything wrong but kept getting knocked down. He began the trek back home and she wandered out to meet him. He put his hand out and she took it as they made their way back to the house. He paused at the door and peered down at her.

"I'll admit, I'm about at me breakin' point, so. Tomorrow I want to take you somewhere, to get away from all of this if you're up to it. It'll be a hike and climb."

"I think so. Let me just get through the morning nausea, then we can go."

Luke watched her, his eyes softening as he placed his hand over her lower stomach. He pushed the door open and they went back to making dinner, letting the conversation about James drop. Audra built a fire and they ate by it. The dogs played for a bit, then crashed at their feet. They barely made it to midnight, gave each other a kiss, and went to bed.

The next morning after her routine morning vomit, Audra went to the kitchen to find Luke had made her tea and toast. He held her in the middle of the kitchen and looked down at her.

"The start of a new year. I'm glad you're here with me, Audra."

"Me too, Luke. I'm excited and nervous about today. Where are we going?"

"When I was a lad, we'd go hikin' at Coumshingaun Lough. It's a lake with steep cliffs, like. I loved goin' because it made me feel the world was much bigger than I could ever understand. I thought we could hike and have lunch, yeah? Maybe do a small climb."

"Sure, as long as you don't mind I'm moving slower than usual."

"That's understandable. It's no rush. We aren't bein' chased," he replied with attempted levity.

"Haha, very funny. Let me drink this tea and eat, then I'll get ready."

She nibbled the toast while Luke buzzed around, loading the car with what they needed. By the time she was done, all she needed to do was get dressed and they were ready to go. It was chilly but surprisingly sunny for January. She slipped on workout pants, a t-shirt, and a hoodie. She paused at the mirror, trying to comprehend there was another life inside her. Staring back at her was her regular, messy self.

Luke was excited on the drive, which took about an hour. He hadn't been there in almost a decade and he was thrilled about climbing again. He told her about the area, how they thought it'd been formed by moving glaciers. By the time they arrived, Audra was pretty well versed, but nothing could have prepared her for what she saw. A deep, dark lake was surrounded on three sides by cliffs jutting up out of the ground. There were trails along the lake and up the cliffs. It was nothing like she'd pictured; nothing like how Ireland was presented on American television. It was majestic.

Luke was grinning and squeezed her thigh. "You ready?"

"Now, I'm not so sure. This seems challenging."

"It is but you have this, yeah? We can do the hike, then eat. This will let you get used to the terrain. There is a loop and some small trails off of that," Luke assured her.

"I trust you. Remember, I'm walking for two," Audra joked.

"How could I ever forget? Don't worry, it's scarier from far away."

They began their hike and Luke was right, it was big but rocky, so they were able to scramble over the rocks. Audra enjoyed the pull on her muscles and was glad they stepped away to hike. By lunchtime, she almost didn't want to stop, however, her stomach did. They found a smooth place to sit and took sandwiches and a thermos of tea out of the bag. It wasn't busy, they only saw one other couple pass them. Audra let her eyes drift around, taking in the large rock walls.

"We're going to climb this?"

"I know of a spot we can scale that isn't too high, like. I need this, Audra. I don't expect you to climb if you don't want to. No pressure."

"Is that a challenge?"

Luke laughed deeply, pushing the curls out of his face. "If it gets you to climb with me, it is."

"Challenge accepted. But if I fall, you have to carry me back to the car."

"Deal."

He led them to the wall and while it was daunting, Audra had no doubt she could climb it. Luke went first, setting the course and Audra followed quickly, finding finger pockets and moving along with him. All of the worries fell away and nothing mattered, except the rock and their dance with it. Audra paused to take in Luke's incredible skill. He hit a place where he couldn't find a finger hold and he peered around. His eyes landed on a place to grip but it was out of reach.

Audra watched in amazement as he launched himself over and up, using the strength of his legs, and deftly caught the rock as if it was nothing. Audra gasped and clung tighter to the rock. Her mouth was still open when Luke grinned mischievously down at her.

"Don't worry. I know what I'm doin'."

She shook her head and slowly inched her way over to him. He crept up and kept laying out the path for her. When they made it to the top, she almost wished there was more to climb. She sat down and gazed out over the landscape.

"I can't wait to show our child all this," she whispered in awe.

"You know, you're talkin' more openly about the babe," Luke replied.

Audra nodded. It was true. Even though she was afraid about losing the baby, she also wanted to recognize it because regardless, it was there. Even if she did lose it, it didn't mean it didn't exist. It was still their child. "I guess I'm manifesting it."

Luke smiled and stared out. It'd been a good day. They collected their things and headed back down. By the time they got to the car, the sun was starting to set. Audra was ready for dinner and an early bedtime. She was exhausted but satisfied. She turned to Luke.

"We should start getting the climbing center going. Begin building the walls?"

"Sure, that would be grand! I can show you me plans when we get home. The barn is the first project. Rock walls all the way up to the ceilings, like."

Audra fell asleep on the ride home and woke up a little way out. She had her head against the glass and shifted so she could watch Luke. He was intent on the road and didn't notice her watching him. His window was opened a bit. Luke was so beautiful, his dark golden curls gently blowing around his face in the wind. She wondered what he was thinking. About the baby? Adam? The rock climbing center? She leaned on him.

"Hey," she said.

"Hey," he replied.

"How far are we from home?"

"About fifteen minutes."

Audra peered at the road and the dust being kicked up in front of the headlights. How could two people in the middle of nowhere in Ireland matter to anyone? She yawned and sat up. They were ants in the grand scope of things. This made her feel better. They were inconsequential.

Luke glanced at her and raised his eyebrows. "You alright?"

"Yeah, I was just thinking how there are billions of people on this planet and we're just specks. Why does one speck care about another speck, half a world away?"

"Because that speck doesn't believe they're a speck, yeah? They think they're a god and other specks should recognize them as such, so. It's all ego and insecurity," Luke answered.

"It's better to believe you're a speck, I think. Keeps you humble and in awe of the world around us."

"True. It's good to feel small sometimes."

"Small... but like vulnerable small, not bad small," Audra agreed.

"Like a child on your da's lap with your feet danglin' off," Luke murmured, caught in the memory.

"Exactly."

Audra smiled to herself. She could have these abstract conversations with Luke and they made total sense. They were approaching home and she was relieved to see the gate was still closed as they left it. The dogs would be excited to see them. Soon they could go hiking, too. Luke unclipped the gate and drove through, securing it back behind them. Anyone coming from the road would be seen a long way off. Someone trying to come from elsewhere would be called out by the dogs. They drove down the drive and saw two furry heads appear in the window from the living room couch. They'd clearly escaped the kitchen.

The dogs greeted them at the door, all wags and wiggles, having demolished a living room pillow and wooden footstool. Luke started to gather the tufts of fluff while Audra ran the dogs out. The dogs sniffed around and did their business quickly. Audra let them in after Luke reset the living room and petted the dogs on the head. No sense in getting angry over something they didn't know was wrong. They got the fire going and ate leftovers.

For the next couple of weeks, they stayed home, ate, and played with the dogs. At the end of the second week, Audra had a midwife appointment which confirmed she was three months along. The midwife put the Doppler on Audra's belly and moved it around until a steady rhythm filled the room. Audra and Luke locked eyes in amazement. It was real. Their baby had a heartbeat.

Luke teared up and Audra held her breath. They made their next appointment and headed home, reveling in the knowledge. They could tell people if they wanted but agreed to get a little past the three-month mark to keep it their secret a bit longer.

When they got home, Audra noticed her phone blinking with a message. She checked the calls and saw the agent's name. The message asked her to call as soon as she could. She closed the phone and let out a heavy breath. She wanted to just revel in hearing her baby's heartbeat and not think about the world outside of that.

Luke was playing with the dogs in the yard as she watched from the window. The dogs seemed to have doubled in size already and were working together to outsmart Luke, who was laughing with his head back. God, he was stunning. He caught her eyes and touched his heart. She waved back and stepped away. She needed to get it over with. She dialed the agent and after a few rings, sighed with relief that he wasn't picking up.

Until he did.

"Audra? I'm glad you called back. There's been a development with your ex-husband. Do you have time to talk?"

"Yes, what's going on?" Audra replied, fearing the worst.

"Okay, I don't know how you're going to take this. James had been attending meetings with the Brotherhood and was upset that they didn't seem interested in finding you. Our informant said he started getting belligerent with them. They quickly caught on he wasn't there for the cause but rather to get revenge on you. They tried to have him removed and he began threatening them. Vowing to expose things he'd found out about the organization."

The agent paused and Audra waited. The agent cleared his throat uncomfortably. "Audra, they found his body dumped at an undisclosed site outside of town. He'd been shot in the head."

"I'm sorry. What?"

"James Letsky is dead. He crossed the wrong people."

Audra was stunned. But worse, she couldn't figure out why she felt the urge to laugh.

Chapter Thirty-One

*T*hat was it, then. James was dead and the Brotherhood had no interest in coming after Audra or Luke, the agent told her. The organization didn't want to draw any more attention to themselves or the case. What'd been haunting and chasing Audra and Luke for months was over. The agent said the case against the Brotherhood was solid and their leadership started to crumble, turning on one another. Infighting had taken over and one by one, members were coming forward to confess, in hopes of saving their own skin.

A court date was announced and it broke in the news. James' death was tied to the group and rather than him being a victim, he was listed as a disgruntled member, which forever tarnished the image he'd worked so hard to portray. The court date was close to Audra's due date, so they were permitted to do their testimony over video. A question still lingered in Audra's mind and when she asked the agent, she wasn't prepared for the answer.

"How did they get the money for the plutonium?"

"Drugs and sex trafficking, it appears," the agent responded.

"Wait, so a group claiming to want a more conservative and family values America, raises their money through drugs and trafficking?" Audra replied, astonished.

"The thing about these groups is that it ultimately all comes down to hate. They use rhetoric to justify their true meaning, but as I've seen over my years in the FBI, it's about supremacy. They don't actually have ethics. They have beliefs, and if committing crimes to further those beliefs brings them money for their cause, they see no issue in committing them."

"Are they done? Like, will this dismantle the group?"

"Sadly, no. It may dismantle the existing leadership and the name, however, these beliefs run deep. They'll crop up somewhere else with new branding, but they'll still be there. I'll always have a job."

Audra sighed. Before all this occurred, she'd never understood the scope of it. She'd lived her suburban life, going from work to the grocery store to home. She was fighting her own demons but had no idea there were people and groups around her so hellbent on their beliefs, they were willing to bomb a city and kill innocent people. She watched the news but anytime something happened, it was always presented as some radical individual and not an underworld of organized hatred. Odd that the two worlds coming together, hers with James and theirs, eventually freed her. In his attempts to manipulate their hatred, he spun it on himself.

"I don't know how you do it, seeing all this and going on with your life," she told the agent.

"Oh, it gets to me sometimes, but every time we win against them, I know I'm doing my job. I stopped someone from being hurt. It's not easy, but it is satisfying. Thank you, Audra, and to Luke, as well. I know all this took a toll on you both, however, your being willing to come forward and testify does make a difference. Every little cut adds up to bring the body down."

"May I ask your first name?" Audra asked, feeling weird to have talked to this person for so long and not really know who they were.

"Jack," the agent replied.

"Thank you, Jack. For watching out for us and not treating us like we didn't matter."

"You're welcome, Audra."

They wrapped up and Audra put the kettle on for tea. She started to laugh, first out of stress, then out of relief. When Luke came in, he found her leaning against the counter, laughing hysterically. He glanced around the kitchen, confused, then stared at her with his eyebrows furrowed.

"Have you cracked, then? Gone mad, like?"

Audra nodded and wiped tears of laughter from her eyes. "Maybe a little."

The kettle began to whistle, which for some odd reason set off a new round of giggling as she took it off the burner. She made two cups of tea and motioned for Luke to sit at the table. He slowly sat, not taking his eyes off her, and shook his head.

"What's goin' on, Audra?"

She brought cups over and hiccuped from the laughter. "James is dead."

Luke's eyes widened and he waited for her to elaborate. When she didn't, he sighed. "You have to give me more than that, yeah? What do you mean James is dead? How?"

"He threatened the Brotherhood and they shot him in the head." Audra felt laughter bubble up again and tried to push it down, which resulted in it coming out as a snort.

Luke shook his head and took a sip of tea. "You're so strange. I take it you talked to the agent?"

"I did. It's over. They'll need us to testify in a few months, but we can do it by video from a location here. The organization is turning on each other. When James tried to get them to come after us and they wouldn't, he threatened to go to the police with what he knew. The police found his body dumped with a bullet in his head."

Audra wiped her eyes and looked at Luke. He was silent, taking it all in. James was dead. The Brotherhood wasn't coming after them. The baby was healthy. There was no other shoe to drop. He grabbed Audra's hand and grinned. This made Audra start to giggle again and this time Luke joined in. The dogs hearing them, ran in, trying to jump in their laps. Audra stepped away to call her parents and the relief in their voices made her happy she called. No one seemed crushed about James's death. Audra was sure his parents would be and that did make her sad. They never knew their son wasn't who he pretended to be. It wasn't their fault he chose to be cruel. Before she hung up with her parents, she broke the other news.

"Luke and I are expecting a baby."

The line was quiet when she heard her mother sniffle. "Really? When?"

"In late July."

"Audra, that's wonderful. We're so excited!" her father exclaimed.

"I'm going to be a grandma?" her mother asked.

"Yep!" Audra knew they'd seen her struggle with not being a mother over the years with James. "It means you have to come back to Ireland in the summer."

"You aren't twisting our arms. We were already trying to figure out a way to come every few months. We miss you terribly," her mother replied.

They said their goodbyes and ended the call. Audra turned to Luke. "Let's have a party out here and invite your family, tell them the news."

"Which news?"

"The baby news. I don't think they need to know about my dead ex-husband."

"I think they do," Luke said, then winked.

He rang his parents and told them to spread the word to come out in a couple of days. They promised to bring food and drink, as well. He hung up and finished his tea. He eyed Audra, taking her by the hand to the bedroom. He kissed her deeply, sending a shiver through her and they made their way to the bed, removing their clothes. She ran her finger across his chest and then across his lips. He placed his hand along the side of her face, meeting her eyes.

"You were always mine, so. I just needed to find you."

Audra pulled him to her mouth and slid her hand down to feel him. She opened her legs and drew him inside. He moved gently, aware of the baby, and his slow, intentional rhythm brought Audra to climax quickly. Everything was more heightened for her being pregnant and sensations more electric. He leaned down to her and shuddered, being careful to keep his weight braced on his arm. He gently rolled off and placed his hand on her breast as he lay next to her. His hand was warm on her tender skin. She ran her fingers over his knuckles and peered at him. His greenish-brown, forest-floor eyes were fixed on her face and he smiled slightly.

"Yours are the most beautiful eyes," he said. "I didn't know humans had that eye color. The deepest gold."

"You're one to talk. You have these eyes that are emerald and umber. I feel like I'm in the most remote part of the woods when I look at you. I could stare at you all day."

"No one is stoppin' you," Luke teased.

"How would I get anything done?"

"Mmm, true. Speakin' of. Do you want to help me with the walls tomorrow? I got the metal braces in to shore up the walls but need to get the panels in place. I was goin' to see if Liam wanted to stay overnight after the party to help get the hand and footholds attached, too. With the three of us, it should make quick work, like."

"Sure. I can hold the panels in place if you want to get up there and screw them in."

The following morning, they dressed and grabbed a bite to eat before heading to the barn. It was still in good shape and sturdy. Luke swung the big doors open and the dogs bolted in, tripping over each other in their excitement to explore a new space. The walls were two stories high and ran along either side to a loft at the end.

"So, I was thinkin' about both sides bein' tall climbin' walls and a smaller one at the end for kids, so they could climb up into the loft. In the middle, I was goin' to have ropes for strength buildin' and maybe some other shaped rock walls for adaptive climbin'. I want to make sure anyone who wants to climb can."

Audra gazed around and could picture it. Luke had been saving his winnings for years to make this dream come true. It was at their fingertips, now. She stared up at the tall walls, imagining climbers all the way at the top.

"What about safety?"

"People will have to sign waivers, yeah, but I've been workin' with a guy in New York City who owns a rock climbin' facility there. He's been walkin' me through the design and how to make sure it's solid. He was goin' to fly out after the weddin' to check it out and help me go over licensin' and insurance requirements."

Audra beamed at how well-organized Luke was. This wasn't just an idea, this was a plan laid out to the final detail. Luke began gathering panels and leaning them against walls. He collected his tools and they started at the far end. Once a panel was in place Audra would hold it and Luke would use his power drill to screw into the metal studs. The panels had to be able to hold their own weight plus the weight of the holds, people, and equipment. It was hard work and moved at a terribly slow pace. By the time dinner rolled around, they'd only completed the bottom row across one wall.

Audra leaned against the wall and rubbed her back. "I can make us sandwiches and we can keep working," she offered.

"Let's take a break, I don't want you overexertin' yourself," Luke said. "We have time. Besides, I can put Liam to work. That lad needs some focus."

They ate a light dinner and returned to the barn, committed to at least getting the next row up. This row was higher and Luke refused to have Audra get on the ladder.

"I go rock climbing with you," she pouted.

"That's safer than this, yeah? I trust a rock with anchors more than a rickety ladder. Let's just lift them into place and if you help brace from the bottom, I can use me body to hold it in place long enough to place a few anchor screws. Then it will hold itself while I do the rest."

"You're the boss."

Luke laughed and muttered, "Hardly."

They lifted the panel and set it on top of the other. Luke quickly drove in a few screws on the bottom and climbed the ladder while Audra braced her arms against the panel to keep it from falling on them. Luke pressed his body weight against the panel and put screws in each corner. Audra's arms were already shaking from the weight of the panel. He motioned for her to let go. She gingerly removed her hands and winced, expecting it to fall. It held. Luke gave her a thumbs-up and drove countless screws into the studs. He climbed down and grinned.

"Only eleven more, so. On this side. Liam can help me with the top ones. We're goin' to need to build some scaffoldin' and pulley system first for those."

They grabbed the next panel and Audra groaned, knowing her arms were going to be water by the time they finished this row. They plugged along until almost midnight when they got the next row done. Audra was beat and hungry again. Luke promised her a midnight snack and they woke the sleeping dogs to go inside. The dogs yawned and stretched, following them calmly in, not even bothering to play in the yard. They went straight to the fireplace and back to sleep. Audra built a small fire while Luke cooked. He brought out some fried potatoes with onions and peppers, one of her favorites.

After eating, Audra could hardly keep her eyes open and leaned her head back against the chair. She heard Luke get up to take the dishes to the kitchen and come back in. She could feel him standing above her and opened an eye to peer at him.

"Come on, let's get you to bed, love," he said, guiding her up.

She wearily followed him and crashed into bed fully clothed, not caring about anything but rest. Luke pulled off her shoes and chuckled. She rolled over and felt him climb in next to her and slide his arm around her. She laced her sore fingers through his and promptly fell asleep.

Chapter Thirty-Two

*T*he whole family descended on the farmhouse a couple of days later, excited to see what they'd done with the place and to celebrate. It was initially put out as a housewarming, so Luke and Audra could relax and tell the family when they were ready. Audra and Luke hadn't done much different, other than clean and clear out one of the bedrooms for the nursery. They hadn't added anything, waiting until they spilled the beans. Luke hung the family crest sign outside the door, however, everything else was pretty much as his grandparents left it.

A little early, cars started coming down the drive and Audra took a deep breath. They'd be happy but maybe a bit put off by the timing. Family poured out of the cars, carrying food and gifts. Children, ecstatic to be in the country, began chasing each other around, exciting the dogs who forced their way through the outer door to see the children. Before long, children were screaming and laughing as the dogs licked them incessantly. The adults came in to make sure the food made it safely to the table.

"I grew up here, did you know that?" Luke's father asked Audra.

She shook her head. It was logical but she'd never pictured him as a small boy living there.

"We had cows and chickens. Dogs, too, and cats, which kept rats down in the barn. A couple of horses and out in that field we grew our food. I had five siblings, I was the youngest," he explained.

Audra smiled, picturing the farm full of animals and children. It's what she wanted. "That's lovely. I hope we're honoring your memories."

"You are," he said softly and kissed her on the cheek. "It's grand to see the place bein' lived in and not just sittin' here empty. Me parents wanted Luke to have it because they were old-fashioned and were afraid he wouldn't have many chances in life because of his arm. They left it to him in their will. Little did they know, he'd prove everyone wrong, like. That lad, he's a fighter. I've no doubt he can conquer the world."

Audra nodded, glancing at Luke, who was explaining how they were converting the barn into a rock climbing facility to his brother-in-law. His eyes were lit up and he was gesturing wildly as he talked. He caught her eye and grinned. It had been his dream, now it was both theirs. He led anyone interested out to the barn and showed where they were putting the walls and how they were focusing on people, including children, with different abilities. Audra stayed in and helped uncover the dishes of food that were now completely covering the table.

Her stomach grumbled loudly. Now that she was past the morning sickness, she was always ravenous.

Bonnie came in with spoons and started plopping them in each dish. "It's good to see the place again. Our children would beg to come out here and stay. Gave Michael and me much-needed alone time, so. Since his mother passed, we haven't been out much more than to check on things."

"You're welcome out anytime. I like having a house full," Audra replied honestly. She loved her time with Luke but enjoyed hearing laughter and chatter through the walls.

Liam came to the door, motioning for her to come outside. She followed him and they walked up the driveway a bit before he turned with a devilish smile. "I met someone, yeah?"

"Hadn't you before?"

"I don't know. This time it's different, like. I think I might love him." His eyes twinkled as he spoke.

"Liam! Growing up, are we?"

"Only slightly. It's been about a month, but I can't go a day without talkin' to him... thinkin' about him."

"Tell me more. What's he like?"

"He's smart and quiet. Very focused. We met at the market of all places. He caught me eye but I didn't know his persuasion, so I kind of followed him around. Finally, on one of the aisles, he spun on me and asked me name. We started talkin' then and I was smitten. He has these big, dark brown eyes and cocoa skin. I mean, he's black ethnically, so. Sorry, I didn't grow up around many black people, not sure if I'm properly sayin' that."

"I think you're good. Is he Irish?"

"Not from birth, but his parents moved here when he was in his teens, so his mother could teach at the university. Originally from England. Now I have to tell me parents I'm in love with a gay, English, black man. They should take that fine, right?"

Audra laughed, feeling his pain. "Are you telling them?"

"Not just yet. I need time to see if this is the real deal."

"You could bring him to the wedding," Audra joked.

Liam's eyes sparkled evilly. "I just may because you said I could."

Audra thought about it, everyone *would* be on their best behavior at the wedding. Maybe not at the reception with alcohol, but at the wedding, they'd withhold their comments. She looped her arm through Liam's as they wandered back toward the house. Luke came out of the barn and seeing them arm in arm, cocked his head. Audra waved at him and smiled. Still, not her secret to share.

"Well, you do have a plus-one invite and the offer stands. What's his name?"

"Sean."

"There you go, at least he has an Irish name," Audra teased.

Liam busted out laughing and gave her a little shove. "Grand. I'm sure that'll be enough to cancel out the rest, yeah?"

They got to the house just as Luke did and he peered at them. "What are you two on about?"

"I'll tell you later," Liam replied. "I wanted to ask you a favor, anyway."

"I've one to ask you, as well. You think you could stay out here for a few days and help me get panels up in the barn?" Luke asked.

"I'll do you one better. Do you think I could stay out here for a while, maybe until the weddin'? I love Ma and Da but I need some space from them. I need to work some things out, like. I've some money saved from work and could chip in and help around here," Liam explained.

Luke looked at Audra and she shrugged. They certainly had the room.

"I think we could work it out. As long as you aren't eyein' me fiancé, boy," Luke joked.

Liam glanced between them, then grinned. "I don't think that'll be an issue, so. She's a grand girl, but not me type."

Audra almost laughed but bit her lip and turned away. Luke didn't notice and patted Liam on the back.

"It's settled then, yeah? You'll take the old parlor off the front door. We aren't usin' it and will give you easy access for your late nights," Luke offered.

They went in and joined the rest of the family, who were already digging into the food. The dogs followed the children around, happy to eat the bits of food they invariably dropped along the way. Once everyone had a drink and a plate, Luke made his way to the front of the fireplace and stood up on the hearth.

"Cheers all for comin' out to help us warm our home and make it what it was always meant to be, full of family. The sounds of children playin' has truly brought it back to its original intent."

Everyone raised their glasses. Luke grinned at Audra mischievously and for the first time, she saw the family resemblance between him and Liam. He raised his glass again, waiting for the room to settle.

"Me lovely bride-to-be, please come join me up here."

Audra blushed furiously and gave him the evil eye. Still, he waited. She made her way through the children to the fireplace, climbing up next to Luke. Luke met her eyes and gave a small nod before he spoke.

"As you well know, Audra and I are gettin' married in less than two months. However, I've never been one to do things traditionally, so we want to announce the upcomin' birth of our first child in July."

The room fell to a hush and Bonnie's mouth hung open. Cara met Audra's eyes and winked. Liam jumped up, raising his glass.

"Grand, isn't it? Congratulations!"

That broke the silence and the family responded in kind. Audra glanced at Bonnie for approval. Bonnie tipped her glass to Audra and bobbed her head. Luke was right, they may have done things out of order, but it was how it was meant to be. Luke leaned down, kissing her on the cheek, and whispered in her ear.

"It's about what they'd expect from me, like. I think they're just happy I love somethin' more than rocks. That I came back home to Ireland, so."

Audra chuckled. It was true. Luke got away with more because he dealt with more challenges, Liam because he was the youngest. One by one, the adults came over and congratulated them. Bonnie and Michael came together.

"First, we get another daughter, and now another grandchild? It's double blessin's. Do your parents know?" Bonnie asked.

"I just told them, too. We wanted to make sure I was at least three months along to make sure everything was okay with the baby."

"Is it, then?"

"It is. We heard the heartbeat and in the next month, we go for an ultrasound. So far, so good," Audra replied.

Bonnie hugged her tightly and murmured, "Sláinte chugat."

Bonnie made her way back to the table as Luke took Audra's hand and led her away, sensing she was getting overwhelmed.

"You alright? You're startin' to look like a deer in headlights."

"I am. It's just a lot. What did your mother say to me?" Audra asked.

"Oh, it's Gaeilge for wishin' someone good health."

Audra placed her hand on the tiny bump below her belly and repeated the words silently. Sláinte chugat. She wrapped her arms around Luke and rested her head on his chest. He rubbed her back as they enjoyed the peace and quiet for a moment before the children ran past, bumping into their legs. Luke caught one of the boys and told him to be careful. The boy stared up at Luke with big, blue eyes and ran off.

Liam came around the corner and cleared his throat. "Hey, Lucas, may I talk to you for a moment?"

Luke turned to him, then furrowed his brows. "Sure. You aren't in any trouble, are you, boy?"

From the look on Liam's face, it appeared he could be, but Audra knew better. Liam was going to tell Luke he was gay. His eyes flitted to hers and back to Luke's. He put on an impressive bravado, however, Luke was his big brother and he was nervous about letting him know.

"Nothin' like that, so. Can we take a walk?"

"Yeah. Audra, you alright?" Luke asked.

"Of course. You go for a walk. I think I'm ready for more food." She winked at Liam, then made a beeline for the dining room.

Luke and Liam headed out, strolling through a field. Audra took her plate of food and observed from a window as she ate. They paused as Liam looked down and dug at the dirt with his foot. Luke watched him, placing his hand on Liam's shoulder. Liam peered up at Luke and began to speak. Audra couldn't hear them, but she didn't need to.

Liam was no longer the brash young guy, mocking the world. He was vulnerable, laying himself on the line. He stopped talking and eyed Luke, who was staring at him intently. Luke pulled Liam close in a hug and ruffled his hair. When they came apart, Liam wiped tears off his face and grinned at his big brother. They headed back to the house side by side, not saying a word.

When they came back in, Liam darted to the bathroom to wash up, so no one knew he'd been crying and Luke came over to Audra.

"You're grand at keepin' secrets, aren't you?" he said.

"He told you I knew?"

"He did. Thank you for protectin' him like that."

Audra nodded. "I accidentally saw him one night with a man and promised to keep it secret as it wasn't mine to tell."

"You know, he considers you a sister, yeah? Like blood. Liam usually doesn't let people in like that."

"I kind of forced my way in," Audra replied, laughing.

Luke met her eyes and tipped his head. "You are a force to be reckoned with."

Chapter Thirty-Three

*O*ver the next month, Luke and Liam finished getting the panels up around the barn. Audra was more than happy to not help with those but chipped in on the easier tasks. She was definitely starting to show but could still hide it if needed under looser clothing. The midwives scheduled an ultrasound once she was past four months along and both she and Luke were anxious to see their child on the screen. To get further confirmation everything was moving along fine. The morning of the ultrasound, Luke was up early, keeping himself busy around the farm until it was time to leave. He always seemed confident about the pregnancy and baby, however, Audra saw he was as nervous as she was. They loaded up in time to get to town a little early in case of contingencies. Liam hung back to keep an eye on the farm.

They arrived at the hospital a bit early and walked the grounds. The midwife was to meet them for the appointment and she had yet to arrive. They'd discussed having the baby at home, but ultimately Audra's nerves got the better of her and they agreed to have the baby at the hospital. It was a drive from the house, however, the midwife said first babies usually took their time. They saw the midwife pull up and walked over to meet her. She smiled and waved.

"Grand, you made it early! We can go in and get the paperwork filled out. I bet you're anxious to see your wee one. Just so I know beforehand, are you wantin' to know the gender if it's discernible?"

Luke glanced at Audra and she smiled. She didn't need the mystery. He nodded.

"If we can," he answered, grasping Audra's hand tightly.

They'd discussed the possibilities, though neither cared. Any child of theirs would be lavished upon. Audra also knew this wouldn't be their only child. Even if she wasn't able to bear any more children, they'd agreed to adopt because both wanted multiple children. A farm full.

Audra was taken back first to get prepped and the technician to set up. Once they were ready to begin, the midwife brought Luke in and they flanked Audra on either side, the midwife closest to the screen and Luke across, so he had a clear view. The technician squeezed cool gel on Audra's belly and placed the wand in it, moving it around. At first, the images on the screen made no sense to Audra, but the midwife began pointing out aspects so they understood.

"Look at that heartbeat! Nice and strong," she said, pointing to a steady flutter in the middle of the screen. Her finger moved along the image. "Over here is the top of the head and along here the spine."

Luke and Audra peered at the screen, not able to contain their grins. They met each other's eyes and clasped hands. Their child. The technician and the midwife were silent, taking notes which made Audra nervous.

"Is everything okay?" she asked.

"Yes, we're just recordin' measurements and other things to make sure everythin' is progressin' as it should. Part of the ultrasound, but nothin' to worry about. If you look here, you can see the babe's kidneys which look healthy. One is laggin', but that's pretty common. The organs are still growin' and developin'. Look, there are the feet, appears like the babe has them crossed over each other. The elbows and hands, if you look closely, it seems the babe may be suckin' its fingers."

The baby shifted on the screen and Audra could see its eye sockets. She was mesmerized this was going on inside of her body right at that moment. The baby seemed to turn toward them and the ultrasound technician glanced at the midwife. The midwife nodded and leaned in. She smiled, then looked at Audra and Luke like she had a secret.

"We can tell the gender if you'd like to know. Now, I should say we can't say it a hundred percent because of legalities, but I'm pretty much a hundred percent."

Audra bit her lip and squeezed Luke's hand. He met her eyes and winked. They nodded at the midwife.

"It's a boy!"

A boy. A son. A little Luke running around. Audra teared up and locked eyes with Luke. Their son. He wiped tears from his eyes and bent down to kiss her. She wiped a tear from his face and said one word.

"Adam."

Luke lost it at that moment and had to excuse himself. He went out for a few minutes, then came back in with tissues. His eyes were red and his nose slightly swollen from being rubbed. He walked over to Audra and hugged her, being careful not to bump the wand.

"I fuckin' love you," he whispered hoarsely.

Audra buried her face in his soft curly hair, which she hoped the baby was fortunate enough to inherit. He stood up and rubbed his nose again, his eyes fixated on the screen. He smiled to himself and repeated her.

"Adam."

They knew they were having a son and he had a name. It was no longer this abstract concept of just *baby*. The midwife and technician were continuing to move the wand around, making notes when the wand was removed and the screen went blank. The technician wiped the gel off and adjusted Audra's pants back over her belly. The midwife smiled at them.

"We'll have a video and pictures printed off for you in a few minutes. Everythin' looks grand! Babe's right where he should be and the due date appears to be about the same, end of July. We'll keep an eye on that kidney but, honestly, I'm not worried about it. Congratulations on your son. If you want to go out to the waitin' room, I'll be right out with those pictures. I can email you the video."

Luke helped Audra off the table and they went to the waiting room, too energized to sit. The midwife came out and handed them pictures from the ultrasound. She'd picked really clear images and Audra teared up. One had a full image of the baby from the side with his knees pulled close to his body, one of his hands floating almost in a wave. She couldn't wait to show her parents.

"Two worlds apart, a plane crash, and now a baby," she murmured.

Luke grinned, squeezing her hand. "We don't do things in the normal way, do we?"

"No, we certainly don't," Audra agreed and chuckled.

They left to grab lunch and run a few errands in the downtown area. Audra wanted to find a gift shop to get something for Luke's birthday, which was just a couple of days away. They were going to his parents to celebrate and were going to let them know the gender then.

They ate lunch at a small cafe and strolled through the streets, window-shopping. Audra saw a baby outfit in a window and decided they could now officially purchase clothes. It was a tiny set with cargo shorts and a t-shirt with a man hiking up a mountain. She pointed it out to Luke and he smiled. They went in and bought it plus a few other baby accoutrements. Holding the bag felt like holding gold. Audra needed to figure out a way to shake Luke for a few minutes to get his birthday present. She asked if he could go into a store to buy some things they needed for the house, feigning exhaustion as she collapsed on a bench. He obliged and went into a variety store.

As soon as he was out of sight, she backtracked to a store they'd passed with outdoor gear and ducked in. She bought him a new insulated water bottle, a hiking baby carrier, and a set of quickdraws, as she'd noticed his were getting pretty worn. She asked for it to be double-bagged and was back at the bench before he came out with their supplies. She took a few bags from him and placed her bag between them, hoping he wouldn't notice. He was weighed down with the rest of the bags, so they made haste back to the car. When he wasn't looking, she put her bag in the back seat and threw a sweatshirt left back there over it.

Once they were home, Liam came out to help unload and Audra waited until they carried a load into the house to grab the bag and take it upstairs to hide under the bed. While she was up there, she noticed the crib and bassinet were put together. The bassinet was beside her side of the bed and the crib was in the nursery. The nursery had been cleaned and organized, now looking more like a room than a storage space.

"I hope you don't mind. I got bored, so," Liam said from behind her.

"Mind? This is awesome. Thank you, Liam."

"For sure, can't have me niece or nephew without a place to sleep," he teased.

"Nephew. We're calling him Adam. Don't tell anyone yet, though. We're going to let them know at Luke's birthday party."

"Your secret is safe with me, yeah?"

She knew it was. They headed downstairs and helped Luke unload the bags. Once they were done, Liam glanced at the time, a small smile tugging at the corners of his mouth.

"I'm gettin' picked up shortly by me fella. We're goin' on a hike, you want to join us?"

"I'm up for it if you are, Luke? I have some pent-up energy to work out," Audra replied.

"Yeah, we'll follow you out. It's about time we got the dogs used to hikin'. Let me pack up some things," Luke said.

By the time Liam's ride arrived, they were ready to go. A young, black man pulled down the drive. Liam waved him in to let him know he was at the right place. Liam slid into the passenger seat and they headed out. Luke whistled to the dogs, who came barreling from a field and jumped right into the car. They followed the car Liam was in, to a trail about twenty minutes away. Audra was relieved to see it wasn't too strenuous and climbed out of the car. They walked over to meet Liam and his boyfriend. Liam blushed and introduced everyone.

"Sean, this is me brother, Lucas, and his soon-to-be wife, Audra. Lucas and Audra, this is me boyfriend, Sean."

Luke reached out and shook Sean's hand. "Nice to finally meet you, Sean. Liam has told us all about you."

Audra smiled and shook Sean's hand, which was cool to the touch. He met her eyes and smiled sheepishly.

"Nice to meet you, too." His voice was low and soft.

Liam and Sean led the way up the hill and Luke took Audra's hand as they walked slower. The dogs were on long leashes but seemed to understand to stay close, so the leashes were slack as the dogs trailed quietly behind them.

"It's grand to see this side of Liam. To see him happy," Luke said. "Whether it's from Sean or time, he's finally started to calm down and find himself."

Audra agreed. Even a couple of months ago, Liam was getting into fights and staying out all night. Now, he was content to help Luke on the farm and turn in by midnight. He was still going out but only about once a week. Those nights he must've been staying with Sean, as he wouldn't come back until the next day. He was still mischievous and rowdy but didn't seem like he was trying to prove so much anymore.

They made it to the top of the hill to find Sean and Liam embracing. If it made Luke uncomfortable, he didn't show it. Luke typically wasn't bothered by things and he was genuinely happy for his baby brother. The four stood together and gazed out over the miles stretched below them. Liam had his arm around Sean with his thumb hooked on Sean's belt loop. They made a striking couple, as if they had stepped out of a magazine ad for some trendy new cologne.

Audra's stomach rumbled with hunger and she was hit with a wave of exhaustion. The hike was nice but had taken any energy left in her out. She was ready to head home and put her feet up by the fire. Getting Luke's attention, she motioned she was ready to leave. He nodded, then cleared his throat.

"Hey Liam, lad, we're goin' to head back down. I think Audra's done for the day."

"Sound's grand. I'm goin' to stay over with Sean until your party. I'll meet up with you there? I can ride back out to the farm with you after if that's alright."

"Of course. We'll see you then," Luke replied. He walked over and grabbed Liam in a hug. "I love you. You make me proud, boy."

Liam blushed and for a moment Audra could see him as a little kid, trailing behind Luke. He glanced at her and she smiled, tipping her head. He was so much her little brother now, too. He grinned and put his head down.

"I love you too, Lucas," he muttered.

"I'm sorry Liam, I couldn't hear you, like. What was that?" Luke lied through his teeth.

Liam shook his head and set his mouth in a twisted smile. "I love you too, Lucas!"

Luke reached out and ran his hand through Liam's hair. "I know you do."

Audra was in awe at the connection between them. She could see how much Liam missed Luke for the years he was in America. Maybe part of Liam settling down was having Luke back in his life. Having not grown up with siblings, she didn't know what that was like, however, Liam was quickly filling that void in her. Cara, too, but more slowly. Luke came over and took her hand as they headed back down.

Once back home, Audra texted her parents a picture of the baby and his gender. Lastly, she typed Adam Charles Riordan, his full name. Charles after her father. A text shot back. "Now, you are making us cry!"

Luke insisted she go and put her feet up while he made dinner. She got the fire going and dragged a stool over in front of the fire, sitting in the chair with her feet on the stool. It was nice having Liam around, but it was also nice to be alone with Luke. They didn't always feel the need to talk and she liked when they sat watching the fire in silence. He brought her a cup of tea and kissed her on the top of the head. Then he leaned down and kissed the curve of her belly.

"Hey, Adam," he whispered, placing his hand on her belly.

It was heavy and warm. Audra felt a sensation inside of her she hadn't felt before. Like the beating of butterfly wings under her skin. Almost like someone had taken a feather and lightly dragged it across the inside of her lower abdominal wall. She gasped.

"I think I felt the baby move!"

"Did you, then? What did it feel like?"

"Like a cross between a touch and a tickle. Very light. Almost not there, but there. It was when you put your hand on my belly," Audra explained.

"That's amazin', yeah? Well, let's get you two fed, so he can get stronger. Our lad."

Luke returned to the kitchen and Audra placed her hand where she felt the sensation. She didn't feel it again but marveled at how real it was all becoming. She sipped her tea and gazed at the flames dancing in the fireplace. She wasn't meant to be a mother before this because James wasn't meant to be a father. Almost anyone could have a child, however, not everyone deserved to be a parent. What James put her through, he likely would've put a child through, and at no point would he have understood the miracle of a child.

Luke was all in. He was honored to become a father, to become a husband. He treasured Audra and their baby. He was the father a child should have.

Every child deserved.

Chapter Thirty-Four

*B*y the time the wedding date arrived, all the walls with foot and handholds were installed. Luke and Liam were still working on building the free-standing center for the middle of the barn but had the pieces in the stable, so they could use the barn for the wedding ceremony and reception in case of rain. It was the end of March and the weather in Ireland could be unpredictable.

Cara and Bonnie had been an invaluable source of planning for the wedding as Audra found her increasing pregnancy taking its toll on her energy and memory. The ceremony was to be simple with traditional vows. The real focus was the party after. Bonnie and Cara hung lights, using the colorful holds for placement, and set up chairs on either side, leaving an aisle down the middle. They strung flowers and ribbons along the walls with flowers at the end of each row.

Liam and Luke built a wooden arch for Audra and Luke to say their vows under and clean sawdust was scattered along the center aisle to cover the worn floorboards. It was elegant, yet basic.

Audra's dress was floor length and cream with an empire waist to leave room for her growing stomach. She'd decided against any head adornments. Luke picked cream slacks and a matching blazer with a button-down shirt.

Audra's parents flew in a few days before and outside of marrying Luke, this made Audra the happiest she'd been since finding out about the baby. She hadn't seen her parents in a few years and as soon as they came off the plane, she burst into tears and hugged them, not wanting to let go. She didn't know how she'd ever say goodbye again.

Luke was thrilled to finally meet her parents and towered over them in the airport. Her mother was just over five feet tall and her father somewhere around five foot seven. Audra was just under her father's height, but Luke was six feet tall, so he seemed like a giant next to them. As her parents went to get their baggage, Luke and Audra hung back.

"You look like your father but have your mother's hair, like. Do you know what your ancestry is?" Luke asked.

"My father's side is Scottish and maybe French. My mother's is a mishmash. I think there's Italian and Spanish in there. German maybe? As far as I know, we're our own little melting pot."

Luke nodded. "Well, I think you got all of the best ingredients, so."

By the day of the wedding, both sides of the family were well acquainted and Audra's mother had gone shopping with Bonnie and Cara for some last-minute items. Her father had whiskey with Luke's father and let him take him on a tour of Cork. They came back a little buzzed, talking about the things fathers do, like history and politics. Her parents began to bounce around ideas about having a small apartment in Ireland, so they could stay for extended stays. Audra crossed her fingers and considered ways to make it happen.

The morning of the wedding was chaotic and as soon as their feet hit the floor, Luke and Audra were whisked off to separate areas to get ready. By this point, Audra's hair was at her shoulders and Cara brought up the front off her face, fastening it in the back with a crystal broach. Audra slipped on her dress and laughed at how it certainly didn't hide her stomach. The wedding was just about making it official, she and Luke had already been a family for some time.

Her father walked her down the aisle and Luke looked dashing in his outfit with his curls falling around his shoulders. He clasped Audra's hand in his own and smiled down at her. Audra peered around the barn and noticed Liam had Sean with him. No one seemed to notice they were there as a couple and Audra grinned at him with a twinkle in her eye. He'd kept his word to her. Whether, or not, he'd let on Sean was his boyfriend, remained to be seen.

The vows were short and sweet, neither Luke nor Audra wanting to make a big deal of them, then end up bawling in front of everyone. Even so, they each shed a couple of tears. They exchanged rings and were pronounced husband and wife. Cheers went up when they kissed and by the time they made it down the aisle, chairs were already being moved and tables set up for the reception. Luke pulled Audra outside and kissed her for real.

"God, you're beautiful," he whispered.

"You are, too. That's it. I'm Audra Riordan, now."

Luke beamed. "On paper, like, you've been mine for a while."

"Luke, I'm so grateful I met you. Not the circumstances, but had those not happened, we may never have met."

"I'd like to believe we would've, yeah? Somehow, somewhere."

Audra drew in close to Luke and slid her hand up under his shirt to feel the skin on his back. Luke pressed her to him and quickly they realized they might be going down a path they didn't have time for. They pulled apart, laughing.

"Alright, let's go in and do the party," Luke said, taking her hand.

"If you say so," Audra replied, making eyes at him.

Luke glanced at the house, considering, when Bonnie appeared, calling to them. He shook his head and led Audra back to the barn. Immediately, they were swarmed with well-wishers, and her brother-in-law, Patrick, set up with a couple of extended family at the far end to play music. Food was spread out on the tables and alcohol appeared in copious amounts. Luke and Audra grabbed plates of food, then sat at the head table with both sets of their parents on either side. After an hour, everyone was stuffed and most were feeling the booze. Luke and Audra had their first dance and from that point forward, the barn seemed to almost vibrate with everyone dancing, talking, singing, and drinking.

Audra observed Liam take Sean over to his parents and sit with them. She couldn't hear the conversation but could tell he was telling them everything. That he was gay, that Sean was his boyfriend. They listened and eyed Sean. Bonnie put her hand over Liam's, then kissed him on the cheek. She smiled at Sean. Michael watched them and nodded. It was obvious they were surprised and not familiar with the situation, however, weren't going to disown Liam over it.

After Liam and Sean went to the dance floor, Michael and Bonnie whispered to each other. Audra could tell they were struggling with the new information about their son but were trying to work through it. Liam and Sean danced together to a slow song, bringing some stares and confusion from other guests, but Cara made sure to hug Liam as they left the dance floor as a show of solidarity. Audra and Luke went over, embracing them both, and chatted for a few minutes. Liam thanked them, appearing relieved his family was at least attempting to wrap their brains around who he was.

By midnight, it was clear the party wasn't ending anytime soon and Luke and Audra headed to their bedroom. They'd decided against a formal honeymoon but planned to go stay in the Comeragh Mountains for a few days after her parents left. She didn't want to lose a minute with them while they were there.

Luke shut the bedroom door and they sat in the silence for a few minutes, their ears ringing from hours of noise. Luke moved over and began rubbing Audra's shoulders as she sighed, allowing the tension to release. She nestled back against him, feeling supported. Luke kissed her neck and wrapped his arm around her.

"I know you must be exhausted with the babe and all, so. Let me just give you a massage, and we can pick up later when you've rested."

Audra turned to him and laughed. "And not consummate this? Are you already trying to get out of our marriage?"

Luke kissed her fingers, shaking his head. "Never."

Audra rose and removed her dress, standing naked before him. "Take off your clothes, Mr. Riordan."

Luke did as he was told and Audra pushed him back on the bed. There was no doubt either of them was ready. Audra placed her legs over his hips and felt him slide inside her. She leaned down and kissed him as she slowly started to move her hips. Luke grasped her buttocks and matched her every motion. Audra moaned, leaning back as she felt herself let go and let Luke take over. He sat up and slipped his arm around her waist, as he buried his face in her breasts, groaning as he climaxed. They held each other like this for a moment, breathing heavily. Audra sat back to meet Luke's eyes. He reached up and put his hand around the back of her neck.

"Welcome officially to the family, Mrs. Riordan."

Audra kissed him gently and eased down beside him. "Now, I'm beat and ready to put this day to bed."

She rested next to him and put her arm around his waist. A year ago, she was lying next to a different husband... a shell of a person. Defeated and unloved. Luke didn't save her, she knew that. She saved herself. She discovered within her a strength she'd never known and escaped the prison only she held the key out of.

By boarding that plane, she'd unlocked the door not only to her freedom but to the dark recesses inside herself she was hiding in. By surviving the crash, she'd taught herself she wasn't as fragile as she'd believed. By standing up to the mountain lion, she'd learned she was powerful. By taking down the man with the gun, she'd accessed the anger she'd been forced to bury. By free-climbing the rock wall to escape, she'd accepted she was brave. By standing up to James, she'd determined she'd no longer take anyone's shit.

With these lessons, she found the girl buried beneath the surface and in setting her free, was able to allow someone else into that freedom. Luke didn't save her, but he reminded her she was worth saving. He never doubted her ability to conquer what was thrown at her. While he wanted to protect her, he knew she was more than capable of protecting herself. That was why he was the one she chose. He was aware of his strength but knew she needed to find her own.

Luke loved her because he loved her. Because they were equals and came together with their histories, baggage, and struggles. They allowed each other to work through those in their own time and in their own way, acting as spotters, like in rock climbing. There to catch and redirect each other when they slipped. She didn't doubt he'd be there if she needed him, but he wasn't going to push himself onto her. Luke was one in a million. His life taught him to depend on himself and let others in. It was a delicate balance so few people ever figured out. Audra was well on her way to this understanding.

The next morning, they joined her parents in the kitchen for coffee and tea. Her mother looked like she had a secret. Audra narrowed her eyes, cocking her head.

"What are you up to, Mom?"

Her mother broke out in a grin and looked at Audra's father. "We talked last night and I think we're moving to Ireland!"

"What? Really?"

"Well, you're our only child, all of our parents are gone. While we have extended family in America, it makes more sense to live here and visit them, than to live there and visit you. We want our grandson to know us. We want to see you on holidays. We have a big retirement fund and it's more important to tap into that now than to wait until we're old and miss out on your lives."

Audra was beside herself with delight. They'd have to go back to wrap things up but would be back by the time the baby was born. They wanted to get an apartment in Cork so they could still do the things they enjoyed in a town and not be far from Luke and Audra. Plus, they'd hit it off with Luke's parents. The families were able to come together more than Audra even thought possible. Adam was going to be one lucky little boy.

Liam came down followed by Sean, and gratefully grabbed some coffee, looking worse for wear. Sean stood back uncomfortably and Audra introduced him to her parents. Her mother never met a stranger and started asking him about what it was like to be black in Ireland. Audra was mortified, however, Sean seemed happy to talk about it. Soon they were knee-deep in conversation. Liam made his way over to her, leaning next to her on the counter.

"Here you are, me sister for real, like."

"From day one, Liam. You know you and Sean are always welcome here. Not just because of a party. He's welcome over any time. My mother will talk his ear off."

Liam chuckled watching her mother and Sean, trying to decide if he needed to save Sean. It was apparent he didn't.

Sean's eyes were lit up and he was laughing, telling Audra's mom some story about tourists and how they assumed he was American and wouldn't believe otherwise.

Audra sat down to join the conversation and Liam excused himself to shower. Sean didn't seem to notice. Before long, they were all chatting and Sean was just another member of the extended family. Liam joined back in and wrapped his arms around Sean from behind. Sean rested his hand on Liam's and Audra smiled. They were so natural together. Luke caught Audra's eye and motioned to the door.

"Take a walk?" he asked.

She nodded and they slipped out to wander the fields. It was perfect out, cool but sunny. The dogs saw them and joined in to traverse the bumpy soil. They walked out a distance and turned back to look at their home, full of their family.

Luke sighed, sliding his arm around Audra's waist. "I'd board a thousand planes for the chance to meet you again."

Audra smiled up at him and felt the baby shifting around. She placed Luke's hand on her belly, observing his face. As Adam moved his little body inside her, Luke stood in awe. Audra put her hand over his, feeling the movement through his hand.

"Just one plane. But two countries and three of us. At least."

Chapter Thirty-Five

*T*he way birth is portrayed in movies is often not accurate, sped up for the sake of entertainment. After contractions for weeks and being four days overdue, Audra started to believe it might never happen. The midwife assured her the baby would come when he was ready. When Audra woke in the middle of the night with the sheets soaking wet and contractions coming every ten to twelve minutes at slightly under a week overdue, she guessed Adam decided he was ready. She shook Luke awake.

"Luke, I think my water broke."

Luke stared at her and lifted the covers to peer under. "I'd say so. Or one of us wet the bed."

"Haha. I'm going to call the hospital. Can you strip the sheets and throw them in the laundry?"

Luke nodded and climbed out of bed. He grabbed the corners of the sheets and dragged them off in a heap. Audra discovered that breaking her water wasn't one fell swoop but a continuing trickle. She changed her clothes and stuck a washcloth in her underwear to stop it from running down her legs. Luke threw the sheets in the washer and rinsed in the shower before changing, while Audra spoke with the hospital. By the time she was off the phone, he was ready and waiting at the door. They let Liam know, so he wouldn't wonder when he woke, asking him to let the dogs out in the morning.

The contractions picked up on the car ride and by the time they got to the hospital, were four to six minutes apart. The midwife was already there, and the doula was on her way. Audra was led back to a room with a bed, couch, table, and television. It was more like a hotel room than a hospital room. There was a large ball and different massage tools to help ease Audra's pain, but she was nervously pacing. Luke hung back while the midwife checked her and she was already three centimeters dilated. Audra was progressing nicely. A check of the baby's heartbeat showed it was strong and steady.

The doula arrived and immediately made herself indispensable to Audra, showing Luke good pressure points to massage during contractions. As the contractions picked up their pace, Audra sat on the ball and leaned her head against the edge of the bed while the doula and Luke took turns rubbing her back and encouraging her. The pain was like nothing she'd experienced. However, being used to pain, she hid inside herself, which seemed to make it worse. The doula nodded at Luke, who came to her side and gave her focal points when the contractions hit their peak.

"Remember swimmin' in the cold river in Idaho, floatin' on our backs? How we felt so light and free?" he asked.

Audra nodded. "The sky was so blue."

"You were so beautiful and I couldn't stop watchin' you, like."

Audra remembered... it was the first time she'd seen Luke naked and how badly she wanted him. How comfortable he was in his own skin. How the lines of his body came together perfectly like the mountains around them. As she thought back, she felt the contraction ease and let her breath out to rest. As another contraction came just a couple of minutes later. Luke brought up another memory of getting the puppies and how they romped in the field, exploring when they were first let out of the car.

With each contraction, he reminded her of their life and how they built it together. The doula took over, massaging Audra's back and giving her ice chips as the contractions came to full force. The midwife checked her again. Audra was fully dilated and ready to push.

Audra moved to the bed and Luke came up next to her head. He registered when she could no longer hear him and held her hand in his own, murmuring gentle words of encouragement as her body took over. As each contraction crested, she pushed with all of her might and collapsed as it subsided. Contraction after contraction came and she pushed, feeling like she wasn't making any headway. The midwife reminded her that her body knew what it was doing. She checked again and told Audra she could feel the baby's head making its way down.

On the next push, Audra tapped into her body and followed its lead, pushing when her body felt the urge. The midwife said the baby had moved down substantially. One or two more pushes and his head would crown. She let Audra know doing it this way was allowing her body to naturally stretch to let the baby's head come through without much tearing, if any. Audra felt the contraction coming on and an urge to push like no other. She bore down and could feel the burning as the baby's head made its way out of her body. The midwife told her to relax as she cleared his nasal passages. On the next contraction, the rest of his body slid out easily. There was no crying like in the movies and Audra was worried.

"Is he okay?"

"He is perfect," the midwife replied, placing him on Audra's chest.

She helped Audra unbutton her shirt, so the baby could lie on her skin. He blinked and rested against her breast. Luke put his hand over Adam's tiny head and leaned in to kiss him as he squawked.

"Welcome to the world, me lad."

Audra rested her hands on her son's wrinkled body and smiled down at him. "You have no idea how long I've waited for you. I just had to find this guy, first."

She met Luke's eyes and he kissed her gently on the lips. "I'm in awe of you, yeah? Of your strength," he murmured in appreciation.

Right now, she didn't feel powerful and her body started to shake uncontrollably. The doula laid warm blankets over her, letting her know her body had put in a lot of energy and the shaking was normal. The midwife waited for the placenta to be delivered and the cord to stop pulsing before asking Luke if he wanted to cut the cord. He cut the cord and climbed in next to Audra and the baby. The midwife told them to rest for a bit and she'd be back to check on them. Luke put

his arm over Audra. Adam rested quietly on her chest, continuing to stare at them. She wasn't sure what Adam was seeing but felt humbled he was looking at her like that.

Luke rubbed his son's head, seeing the tiny curls as they dried. His eyes were still the dark gray babies' eyes could be at birth, but it appeared he would have his father's curls. "Hey, Adam. Grand to finally meet you, boy."

Audra leaned her head against Luke's, his own curls tickling her nose. "I wanted him to have your curls."

She wasn't sure when she fell asleep or for how long, however, when she awoke Adam was still on her chest and now sleeping, too. Luke was awake with his hand over Adam, watching him sleep. Audra smiled down at her tiny son and put her hand over Luke's. Luke brushed his lips against her cheek.

"I was here, watchin' both of you sleep. Me mind was blown I was granted such an amazin' gift. I feel like Adam, me friend Adam, is present in all of this, like. I don't know how to put it into words, but I feel he is in our Adam, yeah?" Luke explained.

"I know. I feel it, as well. Maybe we gave him another chance. Maybe he wasn't done with you," Audra whispered.

The following morning, the midwife came in to check on the baby and Audra. "Everythin' looks grand. You can head home whenever you're ready. I'll come out once you're settled and see how you're doin'."

Audra's eyes widened. "Is it safe to leave?"

"Of course. Women have been doin' this for eons, at home, in fields, wherever. You and the babe look healthy and home is the best place for you. Go get some rest and I'll call you in a few hours to set up a time to come out for a follow-up. You're in very good care with this one," she replied, motioning to Luke. "Not all fathers are so in tune with their baby's mother, so."

Audra grinned, squeezing Luke's hand. "He's my best friend." She thought about how bad it would've been with James and shuddered.

Luke blushed and shook his head. "Go on now, you two. You're embarrassin' me."

The midwife laughed and got up to leave. "Go home. Enjoy that beautiful son of yours. No rush, of course. I'll be here for a while workin' on things, so take all the time you need."

She left and Luke helped Audra sit up. Adam grunted and made a face of discontentment, being moved off his mother's breast. They diapered and dressed him, learning to wriggle his clothes over his small but wily arms and legs. Audra sighed as she slipped on her clothes. She was sore. She put the pad the midwife gave her in her underwear to catch any blood and put on a skirt. When she stood completely up, her legs shook and she stretched her back. She was ready to go home and recover in her bed with her own things. Luke put Adam in the car seat and grabbed their bag. Audra made her way carefully to the car and sat gingerly in the passenger seat. Luke buckled the car seat in, then loaded the bag. He sat next to her and glanced over.

"You ready?"

Audra bobbed her head. She wanted to be home with her son and husband. The sun was up and the drive home was beautiful. They rolled the windows down for fresh air but not so much it would blast Adam out. Audra considered how everything was new to him. She peered back at the most amazing person she'd ever met and smiled.

"You know his birth sign is Leo?" she asked Luke. "The lion."

Luke raised his eyebrows and did a quick peek at his son. "Is it, now? What were the chances of that?"

"I guess it was meant to be."

"That goes without sayin', so. We're comin' up on a year since we met, as well."

They were, it was the end of August when she boarded that plane, running for her life. It was August third, now, and she was living the life she was meant to have.

"Wow, just a year? I feel like I've known you forever," Audra said thoughtfully.

"You have, like. This is only one lifetime, we've been together before and will be together again, Audra. You're me eternity."

"Fucking romantic," Audra replied and leaned in to kiss Luke.

He grinned at her, shifting his eyes back onto the road. A smile played at the corner of his mouth the rest of the drive home.

Adam slept the whole way home and only briefly stirred when he was taken out of his car seat. The dogs were out in the driveway playing when they got out and ran over, sniffing incessantly. Luke held Adam in his arm and the dogs circled him with uncontained excitement. When Audra came out they smelled her, understanding her story and what recently occurred. She patted each of them, then followed Luke into the house. Liam met them at the door and grinned at his nephew.

"Ah, he's goin' to be a wild child like Luke, you can tell from the hair, yeah?" he murmured, rubbing Adam on the head. "You hungry? I can make breakfast."

"God, yes," Audra replied.

Liam laughed and headed for the kitchen. Luke brought Adam to their room, laying him on the bed. He curled up next to him. "While he's sleepin', why don't you grab a shower and I'll keep an eye on him?"

"That sounds absolutely glorious. I feel like I was in an accident," Audra said truthfully. Her whole body ached.

"Like a plane crash?"

Audra chuckled. "Yeah, like a plane crash."

Their eyes met and for a moment they went back to that day. How they'd survived but were bruised and battered from it. How they met and leaned on each other to make it through. How through it all, they were there at that moment and had Adam. They lost Adam and found Adam. He was the beginning after the end. Audra thought about what Luke said, about being his eternity. Adam, his friend, and Adam, their son, were part of that eternity. Luke peered down at the baby and leaned in to kiss his tiny, golden, lion cub head. Audra watched them from the door and hoped it was true they'd be together for many lifetimes.

For now, she was just happy to have caught them on earth for this one.

Epilogue

She stood in the doorway, watching him sleep. He had a ratty fabric bear tucked under his arm and his thumb firmly planted in his mouth. She came over and sat down on his bed, brushing the chaotic, golden-brown curls out of his face as he slept. They'd never cut his hair. It was hard to believe over three years had passed since they first laid eyes on his tiny head. He stirred and opened his eyes, still caught in dreams. He turned to face her, his large, golden eyes watching hers.

"Mama, is it today?"

Audra nodded. "It is. We are going to pick up your brother and sister in America. Are you excited?"

Adam bobbed his head and sat up. "Are they goin' to sleep in me bed? Like Monty and Loosey?"

Audra laughed, shaking her head. "No, they'll have their own. Henry is just a baby, so he'll be in a crib in our room and Daisy is going to share a room with you. That's her bed over there. Uncle Liam is going to be with you because we have to fly to get them. He and Uncle Sean are going to stay with you for a couple of days. Okay?"

Adam nodded and pushed a curl out of his eyes with a chubby hand. They walked downstairs to the kitchen where Liam and Sean were making breakfast. Liam scooped Adam up and gave him a kiss. Adam giggled and kissed Liam back. Audra couldn't wait to have more children running around.

It hadn't been an easy road. Adoption in Ireland was pretty much non-existent and they had to pursue it in America. Even so, Ireland didn't make it easy to get there. Audra didn't get pregnant again and was required to try IVF, which also failed. By the time Adam was two, they'd given up any hope of having any more birth children and didn't want to wait too long because they wanted Adam to have siblings he could grow up with. With her American citizenship, they were able to put in for adoption in the US, stating they were specifically looking for siblings and open to special needs.

They focused on the climbing center which brought people from all over the country and beyond. They turned the stables into rooms and offered bed and breakfast for those traveling long distances. Because of the focus on working with disabilities and Luke's own, they made international news. While they still went and climbed regularly, Luke paused competing to be home with his family and to run the center.

They still longed for more children, though, and were ecstatic when they received a call about a pair of siblings, a three-year-old and a six-month-old who were in need of a home. The six-month-old had his lower left leg amputated because of a tumor. The children were turned over to child services as the parents split around that time and neither wanted the children.

Neither wanted the children.

Luke and Audra asked about the medical history and status of the six-month-old. They were told while he had the leg amputated, the tumor had not been malignant. He was no more at risk than any other child for cancer. However, he required special care and prosthetics. Because of Luke's history and their willingness to take in special needs and siblings, they were contacted immediately. They booked flights to finalize the adoption, having done the initial paperwork from Ireland.

The flight there was long and they missed Adam terribly. Once they landed, they rented a car and headed for the lawyer's office. The social worker met them there and they went before a judge. Considering the severity of the children's situation, the process was expedited and went smoothly. The children were in temporary care and the baby needed more attention than could be provided long-term. Once the paperwork was finalized, Luke and Audra headed to meet the children, having only seen them through pictures and video. They met at a park with the social worker, who was in contact with the foster parent.

As they approached, Audra spied Daisy sitting near the foster parent, seeming detached. She had her little hand on Henry's arm, who was being held by the foster parent. Daisy would still remember her parents and probably wondered where they were. Henry was sucking on his fingers and grinning. His leg, amputated right above the knee, was now healed and covered with a sleeve much like Luke's. The children both had dark brown hair like Audra's and gray eyes.

Luke scooped Henry up in his arm. Henry stuck his wet fingers in Luke's mouth immediately. Audra sat down by Daisy.

"Hi, there. You must be Daisy."

Daisy nodded. "Are you my new mommy?" Her voice was tiny and afraid. She peered up at Audra too seriously for a child.

"I'd like to be. We have a little boy your age, named Adam. He'd love to play with you. I know you're sad and that's okay. We can just get to know each other if that is alright."

"Is Henry coming? He lost his leg."

"He is. We want to bring both of you to our home to meet Adam. We have to take a plane. Have you been on a plane before?"

Daisy shook her head and looked up at the sky. "Will it be okay?"

"It will. We'll be there to hold your hand," Audra said, gesturing to Luke.

Luke knelt down to Daisy. "We can't wait to show you your new room, like. You'll be sharin' with Adam. Would you like that?"

"Yes," Daisy whispered, sounding somewhat defeated. She'd already changed too many hands, seen too much.

"Daisy, we're not leavin' you, yeah? You're comin' home with us, to live. To be our little girl," Luke promised.

"On the plane?"

"On the plane."

They got the children's passports and headed to the airport. It was a fast turnaround, however, they were anxious to get back home. They traded off holding Daisy and Henry on the flights while they slept, and entertaining them while they were awake. By the time the plane touched down in Ireland, the children trusted them. The family all gathered at the airport to greet their new family members and Daisy held tightly to Luke's hand. Henry was happily passed from person to person, but Daisy hid behind Luke's legs. Until she saw Adam.

Adam ran up to hug Audra and glanced at Daisy. He had a new, matching teddy bear he put out toward her. She smiled and took a small step forward. Audra and Luke kneeled behind them.

"This is Adam. He's your new brother," Luke explained to Daisy.

"Adam, this is your sister Daisy," Audra whispered in his ear.

The children took another step toward each other and Daisy took the bear, her eyes locked on Adam. Adam was excited and took her hand.

"Let me show you." He led her over to the big window where the planes were taking off, and they climbed on the seats backed up to the window.

They stood at the window in awe as a plane taxied down the runway and took flight. Adam clapped with delight. Daisy mimicked him, giggling. Henry made his way back to Luke's arm and snuggled into his neck, falling promptly asleep. Audra and Luke watched their other two children bond over the same thing which brought them together in the beginning.

In all the chaos and running, everything had finally fallen into place. As long as they stayed together, they survived. It all made sense now.

The circle was complete.

Acknowledgments

Thank you to Joshua Woroniecki for the use of your original photograph for the cover. To see Joshua's original work visit https://www.etsy.com/shop/JoshuaWoroniecki

Thank you to my Aunt Lenora, Uncle Jim, Grandma Juliette, and my other family on my mother's side for always sharing our Irish heritage and history through stories and photos. It gave me a strong sense of self, a great sense of humor, and stories of my own to pass on.

As always, thank you to my children for being so supportive and letting me bounce ideas and chapters off them. It's a never-ending chore, ha.

Thank you, Leigh Kenny and Isla for your reading, edits, and cultural feedback.

To my readers and supporters, thank you for taking a chance on me! Do we all now have ABBA stuck in our heads? Take a chance, take a chance, take a chance on me...

About the author

Available Books:

Do Over (Contemporary Fiction)

We Don't Matter (LGBTQ+ Contemporary Fiction)

Prick of the Needle (Contemporary Fiction)

Through the Surface (Horror)

Trigger Point (Contemporary Fiction)

Carrying the Dead (Visionary Fiction)

Catch the Earth (Contemporary Fiction)

In Dreams, We Fly (Nostalgic Sci-Fi)

Please visit my website for upcoming books, events, and news:

authorjulietrose.com

www.ingramcontent.com/pod-product-compliance
Lightning Source LLC
Chambersburg PA
CBHW021535250626
47154CB00006BA/2128